It's that line between what is right under the eyes of God and what is rightfully your—perhaps—one and only chance for something more. . . . [Joy is] one of the bright flames of this next generation of southern noir novelists." —*Smoky Mountain News*

"Appalachia provides the evocative setting for this tale of a brutal world filled with violence and drugs. . . . Lyrical prose, realistic dialogue, and a story that illuminates the humanity of each character make this a standout." —*Publishers Weekly* (starred review)

"Joy neither condescends to his characters nor excuses them but simply depicts them amid the crushing poverty and natural beauty of their environment. With prose as lyrical as it is hard-edged, he captures men still pining for childhood and stunned to find themselves as grownups with blood on their hands. Joy is one to watch—and read." —*Booklist*

"Readers of Southern grit lit will enjoy Joy's excellent sophomore outing, which is both dark and violent. Ron Rash aficionados will appreciate Joy's strong sense of place in his vivid depiction of rural Appalachia." —*Library Journal* (starred review)

"Not a single word is wasted in *The Weight of This World*, a dark and violent literary page-turner that burns with a white hot intensity rarely found in fiction today. A perfectly executed novel, this is a book that will endure."

—Donald Ray Pollock, author of *The Heavenly Table*

"David Joy's *The Weight of This World* is a tale of exquisite grit. A fearless writer, Joy is willing to go to all the dark places, but his voice and his heart serve as such strong beacons that we'll follow him and take our chances. Those chances pay off in a story that is as tense and harrowing as it is achingly tender. Don't miss this book."

—Megan Abbott, author of *You Will Know Me*

Praise for
WHERE ALL LIGHT TENDS TO GO

"[A] remarkable first novel . . . This isn't your ordinary coming-of-age novel, but with his bone-cutting insights into these men and the region that bred them, Joy makes it an extraordinarily intimate experience."
—Marilyn Stasio, *The New York Times Book Review*

"A savagely moving novel that will likely become an important addition to the great body of Southern literature."
—*Huffington Post*

"[An] accomplished debut . . . In Appalachia, a young outlaw, Jacob McNeely, struggles to escape what Faulkner called that 'old fierce pull of blood,' a violent meth-dealing father, the dark legacies of an unforgiving place and the terrible miseries it breeds. [A] beautiful, brutal book."
—Minneapolis *Star Tribune*

"Bound to draw comparisons to Daniel Woodrell's *Winter's Bone* . . . [Joy's] moments of poetic cognizance are the stuff of fine fiction, lyrical sweets that will keep readers turning pages. . . . *Where All Light Tends to Go* is a book that discloses itself gradually, like a sunrise peeking over a distant mountain range. . . . If [Joy's next] novel is anything like his first, it'll be worth the wait."
—*Atlanta Journal-Constitution*

"This beautiful brutal book begins with despair but ends in defiance."
—Milwaukee *Journal Sentinel* (Best of 2015)

"Joy's grim but satisfying story of the McNeely family faithfully echoes the language and atmosphere of this largely lawless mountain culture. . . . A story skillfully written."
—*Shelf Awareness* (starred review)

TITLES BY DAVID JOY

Fiction

The Weight of This World
Where All Light Tends to Go

Nonfiction

Growing Gills: A Fly Fisherman's Journey

THE WEIGHT
OF THIS WORLD

DAVID JOY

G. P. PUTNAM'S SONS

NEW YORK

PUTNAM

G. P. PUTNAM'S SONS
Publishers Since 1838
An imprint of Penguin Random House LLC
375 Hudson Street
New York, New York 10014

The Library of Congress has catalogued the G. P. Putnam's Sons hardcover edition as follows:

Names: Joy, David, 1983- author.
Title: The weight of this world / David Joy.
Description: New York : G.P. Putnam's Sons, 2017.
Identifiers: LCCN 2016033604 | ISBN 9780399173110 (hardback)
Subjects: LCSH: Veterans—Fiction. | Mothers and sons—Fiction. | Triangles
(Interpersonal relations)—Fiction. | Afghan War, 2001—Fiction. |
Psychic trauma—Fiction. | North Carolina—Fiction. | Appalachian Mountains—
Fiction. | Psychological fiction. | BISAC: FICTION / Literary. | FICTION / Crime.
Classification: LCC PS3610.O947 W45 2017 | DDC 813/.6—dc23
LC record available at https://lccn.loc.gov/2016033604

First G. P. Putnam's Sons hardcover edition / March 2017
First G. P. Putnam's Sons international edition / March 2017
First G. P. Putnam's Sons trade paperback edition / June 2018
G. P. Putnam's Sons trade paperback ISBN: 9780399574245

Printed in the United States of America
1 3 5 7 9 10 8 6 4 2

Book design by Meighan Cavanaugh

For Paco

[T]he dead remain dead, the maimed are forever maimed, and there is no way to deny one's responsibility or culpability, for those mistakes are written, forever and as if in fire, in others' flesh.

— PETER MARIN

PROLOGUE

AIDEN McCALL WAS TWELVE YEARS OLD THE ONE TIME he heard "I love you." Even then he didn't so much hear the words as read them on his father's lips. His mother was folding a hamper of whites on the arm of the couch. He sat across from her in a recliner that was permanently locked flat and watched a fuzzy episode of *Ren & Stimpy* he'd seen a thousand times before. The satellite card was dead, and even before his father had quit paying the bill, the mountains blocked most channels from reaching Little Canada. Every afternoon when Aiden came home from school he watched that VHS tape of the same five episodes over and over. He knew the whole thing by heart.

Aiden was miming the words from the television when his father opened the screen door. The man stood bare-chested on the threshold with a short-nosed revolver clenched in his fist by his side. Aiden's mother turned to face her husband, rolled a pair of socks in on themselves, but didn't say a word. His father raised the pistol and blew the top of her head off when he pulled the trigger. There was a flash of light and blood, a short-lived smell of bourbon before the room reeked of burnt gunpowder like Black Cat firecrackers.

His father stared at him with a look in his eyes like he blamed him and him alone for the way life turned sour. Aiden had his fingers jammed in his ears, but it was too late to guard against the gun's report. His skull hummed. "I love you," the boy saw his father say just before he shoved that wheel gun into the back of his own throat until he gagged, the metal clanking against his teeth as he pulled his second shot.

Aiden lay in his mother's blood on the floor, piecing pictures in the popcorn ceiling together like connect-the-dots. The blood was sticky on his back. There was even a sound to it when the law finally came and the deputy peeled him off the floor. His father's eyes still held that same look and there was no chance it would ever change. He would blame his son for eternity, and Aiden would never forget.

He woke sweaty from the same dream every night those first few weeks in the group home. It was a dream that would haunt him the rest of his life. His eyes would pop open and he'd come up gasping for air, as if he were about to drown. He'd scan the room for anything familiar and find nothing at all.

The dream was a replaying of the earliest memory the boy knew of this world. He stood on wobbly legs in the kitchen doorway with food smeared sticky across his stomach. He might've been three years old, and he watched his father strangle his mother against the edge of the kitchen counter. Aiden remembered how her bare feet slipped and slid against crusty linoleum that rolled like birch bark at the edges, how her upper body flailed, then seized when her spine could bend no further. She gurgled for breath while his father screamed something about potatoes. He held Aiden's face to the red glow of the stove eye when the child wouldn't stop crying, and threw him where his mother lay sprawled on the floor when that didn't work. Mother and child kept still after that. But that memory wasn't what shook him from the dream.

What scared him was what he knew in that dream. He seemed to have some unquestionable understanding, something seemingly divine, that ensured in time he would become his father. There are things passed down that escape reflections in mirrors, traits that paint the inside. Those were the things that he understood, and those were the things that he feared. What he heard before he shuddered awake each night were the words of God Almighty, the Lord God saying, "In the end, blood always tells."

IN THE GROUP HOME, the children shared beds. Aiden shared his with a boy who mumbled facts about baseball in his sleep. The boy memorized career stats from the backs of mildewed trading cards, his collection rubber-banded together like a wad of money that he hid beneath his pillow each night. Whenever something went wrong, the kid would ramble random factoids, like how many RBIs Jose Canseco had with the Oakland A's in 1990, or what Andre Dawson's nickname was in the Chicago Cubs' clubhouse, an answer the kid would repeat over and over like some sort of crazed mantra: Awesome Dawson, Awesome Dawson, Awesome Dawson. But what Aiden hated most was that the kid wet the bed. Aiden couldn't even remember the boy's name, but every night he woke up sticky with the boy's piss, and he hated him for it.

He hadn't counted days, but he'd been there around a month when he stole another boy's clothes, a boy with the same lanky build but a bit older. Aiden would have packed his own had he not outgrown them. His joints ached and by summer he figured the growth spurt would stretch him to a spindly marionette. He stuffed his book bag with what he took, raided the kitchen for canned goods, and weighed the bag down with as much as he thought could be carried without drawing suspicion. When he rode the school bus that morning with the rest of the orphans, he was one of them. But when afternoon came and they loaded their bus, Aiden climbed aboard another, one he knew went into Caney Fork. Theirs was not a home to which he would return.

He rode to the last stop on Sugar Creek and climbed off with a brother and sister who gazed at him in silent confusion as he walked farther up the road. "Where you going, kid?" the boy hollered after him. Aiden stopped and stared at their scrunched faces. It was midspring, and the pollen and gnats floated in the yellow glow between them. He offered no answer. He just turned and headed on.

Farther, the pavement crumbled into packed gravel that cut a dusty logging road through the mountains along a stream that narrowed the higher it rose. The road was rough as a cob, with rivulets from spring rain having rutted it into a continual washboard that ran a crescent-shaped route seven miles south from Caney Fork back to Little Canada.

Aiden knew the road frontward and backward. He followed a small branch of water east from Sugar Creek to a hunting camp where bad fathers gathered during open season on deer and bear to drink their memories into extinction. They'd empty bottles, then turn the glass to target practice, slur their words as they bickered about who was the better shot, none of them ever killing a goddamn thing but brain cells. His father would drag him there. Then when the booze dried up and the old man couldn't stand, he'd ask his son to drive them home.

The camp was empty now. A crude shack slapdashed together

from barn wood and tin stood in a saddle of land, with another four just like it scattering a shantytown across the hillside. Aiden stood on a rusted iron pot to reach the place where the key was hidden along a shallow sill above the door.

Inside, sunlight diffused through smeared windows to make barely visible two cots against the back wall, a card table centering the room, and four mismatched chairs strewn in no particular order at all. Pots and pans hung on nails around a flattop woodstove. By the doorway, outside light shone onto a mischief of mummified field mice that lay gnarled with tiny, yellow-toothed smiles atop rotted food scraps and litter in the bottom of a dull silver trash can. The cabin smelled like wet paper, but more important it smelled like something familiar. He thought he could stay there awhile.

Those first few weeks, spring made it easy to scrounge meals from the mountains: ramps and wild potatoes, speckled trout and branch lettuce. He even found hickory chickens, wild mushrooms that had bloomed from the black soil along rotten logs overnight after a late-afternoon rain poured the valley full of fog. But soon spring was gone and the petals of trilliums wilted, melted back into the earth as if they'd never existed at all. Before long, the days grew hot and the mountains were swallowed in green.

Aiden was crouched in a small grove of black balsam that stood at Sugar Creek Gap, where the road peaked out as high as it climbed. Down the other side, switchbacks snaked down the mountain to Charleys Creek, and just a mile or two from there is where he'd grown up. The stand of balsam had always seemed unnatural where it grew. Folks in Little Canada had always told stories about that place, about the strange mounds of earth that swelled beneath gnarled roots. They said there were bodies buried there, and maybe there were. Aiden squatted with his elbows braced on his knees and drew patterns in the dirt with a stick. He never even saw Thad Broom walk up.

"You know, I kind of wondered if this is where you might've run off to."

Aiden looked up at the redheaded boy. He stood with no shirt on in the middle of the road, mud caked about his chest and face, a pair of jeans that were too big for him cinched into a wad around his waist with a length of nylon rope. Aiden didn't speak.

"There's a lot of folks looking for you."

Aiden looked up with squinted eyes to where the sun reflected white off the boy's pale body. "The law?" he asked.

"Hell." Thad huffed and shook his head. "The law, churches, everybody."

Aiden flicked his eyes to the ground beneath him where he'd scribbled his signature in shoddy cursive. He rubbed his name out with the toe of his boot and looked back to where Thad stood. "You going to tell them where I'm at?"

"Why, hell no. What do you think I am? Some goddamned rat?" Thad walked over and collapsed Indian style into the dirt.

He was the only friend Aiden McCall had ever had. They were the same age, and both lived on Charleys Creek, had always ridden the same school bus and been in the same class. While most kids their age shaded their eyes with snap-back Atlanta Braves caps, fielded grounders, and shagged fly balls, Aiden and Thad stole soft packs of Pall Malls from behind the counter of Ken's Grocery while the old man who owned the place slathered mayo on chuckwagons neither boy could pay for.

Thad leaned back and pulled a pack of smokes from his pocket. He slipped a coffin nail into his lips and struck a match from a book he kept fitted in the cellophane. He pinched the cigarette between his fingers, drew smoke into his mouth, and puffed his cheeks out before he inhaled. He tried to blow smoke rings but only little clouds sputtered out like ellipses. He took another quick drag and passed it.

Aiden hadn't had a cigarette in months and that first taste was as if he'd never had one at all. He held in his first drag until he was light-headed, then blew the smoke into the balsams above. "What you doing back in here anyhow?" Aiden asked.

"Been camping at Bee Rock. Trying to stay in touch with my heritage."

"Your heritage?"

"Why, hell yes. You know I'm half Cherokee, don't you? My daddy was full blooded. Hell, he was chief over there on the rez for a little while."

"You're full of shit."

"Like hell I am."

The boys sat there passing cigarettes back and forth, neither saying anything of great importance. It was the happiest Aiden had been in a long time. After a while, Thad asked where Aiden had been living, and Aiden told him about the camp.

"You know you could come live with me, don't you?" Thad asked with a cigarette jumping about his mouth as he spoke.

"I don't think your mom would go for that."

"I don't live with her anymore."

"What do you mean you don't live there?"

"I mean you know that trailer that was down there below the house, at the bottom of the drive?"

Aiden nodded.

"Well, that old cocksucker my mama's married to cleaned it out and moved me in down there. Said he didn't want to look at me no more and I told him I wouldn't piss down his throat if his guts was on fire."

"And your mom just let him?"

"She ain't say a word." Thad stared off to where Sugar Creek Gap opened a view to mountains shaded grayish blue by distance and haze. He lowered his brow as if he were thinking long and hard about something that he couldn't quite figure out. After a while his face relaxed. "It ain't that bad. Really it ain't." He glanced at Aiden with a slight grin. "I can do anything I want down there. I've got a whole shoe box of titty magazines."

Aiden shook his head and spit between his knees into the dirt.

"Hell, check this out." Thad leaned to one side and pulled his bill-fold from his back pocket. He tore the Velcro to get inside, picked a folded magazine page that looked to be the only thing the wallet held, and opened the crinkled centerfold on the ground between them. "You know what I'd say to her if I ever got the chance? You know what I'd say, Aid?"

"What's that?"

"I'd look her right square in them baby blues and I'd ask her if there was any tread left on them tires, or if it'd be like throwing a hot dog down a hallway. That's what I'd ask her."

Both of them snickered and ogled the dark-haired vixen who bit the tip of her finger, her back arched and breasts up, with her other hand disappearing to someplace between her legs that neither boy knew a thing about aside from lies and pictures. Thad said pussy tasted like cherry pie and Aiden told Thad that girls could get pregnant if they swallowed. That's how the conversation went for most of the afternoon, just boys being boys.

By the end of it, Aiden took Thad up on his offer, and as the heat followed the sun toward evening, he felt about as happy as he'd ever felt in his good-for-nothing life. There were lightning bugs playing Marco Polo back and forth across the field grass, and by the time the boys made it back to the hunting camp to gather Aiden's belongings, night was almost upon them. They slept on the ground, each with his hands interlocked under the crown of his head for a pillow. Through a scant opening in the canopy above them they watched stars move on to someplace else, and woke the next morning curled in the leaf litter and ferns like a pair of stray dogs. Their bodies shimmered with dew and they shivered to reclaim what warmth had escaped them. Thad gathered wood and Aiden built a fire. The world would never again seem so open.

$$(1)$$

AIDEN WAS DAMN NEAR STARVED TO DEATH WHEN HE inhaled the last half of his sausage biscuit in one gigantic bite. He balled up the Bojangles' wrapper and shot it through the open window of his '76 Ford Ranchero into the hospital parking lot. The front of his shirt was littered with crumbs and he picked one of the specks off his stomach, then brushed the rest into the floorboard. Shuffling in the seat, Aiden chewed that last morsel of food between his front teeth, a yellowed smile clacking on something too small to swallow.

If he'd had any money, he would've bought Thad something too. Of course, if he'd had more money, he would've bought a second biscuit himself. But aside from a few hundred dollars stashed away that he wouldn't touch, all Aiden had was ninety-four cents to his name. He'd counted it while the acne-faced kid wrapped his order up and pushed the bag across the counter. That first sausage biscuit cost $1.22 after taxes, so Aiden just asked for a few extra packs of grape jelly, shook his head, and cussed his way through the door when the teenager told him that would cost him another fifty cents.

Aiden had always believed that as time moved on the world would open up, that life would get easier rather than harder. But as he closed in on his twenty-fifth birthday, things had just never turned the corner. Hard led to harder. Life had a way of wearing a man down into nothing. No matter what he did, it seemed some higher power had it out for him, and that kind of certainty comes to leave a man numb after a while. He ticked his teeth together even after there was nothing left to chew, him just staring off through the windshield onto memories.

Those years when they were boys, there were nights so still that as they paddled across the sky's reflection on Balsam Lake, the borrowed canoe seemed to slice the moon in half. The world split in their silent wake and lapped back together in their passing.

The lake was just a ten-minute walk from Thad's trailer and the state kept an Old Town canoe hidden in the crawl space of the game warden's cabin. The warden was never there. He had his own house and family somewhere down in Cullowhee and only used the cabin at Balsam Lake as a last resort when nights drew long chasing bear poachers and folks shining deer. In spring and fall, the state stocked rainbow trout, brookies, and browns, and they advertised those dates on a bulletin board.

When the days came, Aiden and Thad would hide in the woods and watch as the truck pulled up to the lake and a man in coveralls scooped bucketfuls of trout in a giant net and catapulted the fish out over the water. Come nightfall, the boys would string a trotline from one end of the lake to the other and paddle that canoe around catching fish on corn niblets and red wrigglers. They'd smack those trout on the head with a Maglite, and by the end of the night the fishes' quivering bodies would fill the boat to the brim. Aiden and Thad would eat good for weeks.

The older Aiden got, the more complicated the world had become, and so he preferred to live in the past, to relive those moments in his mind as often as he could. He believed that, given the right set of circumstances, he could re-create what had been before. With enough money and a fresh start, Aiden and Thad could set things right, but, as he waited in the hospital parking lot, that was about as far away as a man could dream.

When the housing bubble burst and the jobs dried up, Aiden thought it might last through the summer, maybe drag out a year at most, but sooner or later it would have to get rolling again. He was wrong and he'd been out of work ever since. Thad wasn't around for the worst of it. He didn't get to see job sites go from dozens of crews with contractors raking up dollar bills one day to abandoned, stick-house skeletons without so much as a roof to stop the rain the very next. Thad was on deployment in Afghanistan when the construction business went to pot.

Those years Thad was gone, Aiden was jealous he was the one who got to leave. It was partly Thad's fault Aiden couldn't. When the school resource officer and a K-9 unit swept through the hallways and parking lot one morning at Smoky Mountain High and found two ounces of pot in Aiden's car, the truth was it was Thad's bag. But it was Aiden's ride and he kept his mouth shut. With a record filled with fistfights, him even stabbing a bus driver in the shoulder with a protractor once in middle school, Aiden fit the bill and administrators didn't bat an eye. He took the blame and the suspension and the felony and the community service and the drug class. The reality was that he and Thad were just two punk kids smoking pot, but the state determined severity, and anything over an ounce and a half was a felony's worth. That was the start of his adult rap sheet and that was the reason he couldn't join the Army. But, looking at how Thad came back, Aiden wasn't entirely sure who'd had it worse. They'd both had the rug yanked out from under them and now here they lay.

The Thad that ran off gung ho at eighteen years old ready to kill ragheads for flying planes into buildings wasn't the same Thad that hobbled back into the holler four years later with a ruptured disk at the base of his spine. The physical scars were trumped only by mental ones, by the way he never averted his eyes from the ridgeline, or how his dreams sent him into a sweaty panic. Thad left Jackson County just a dumb-to-the-world kid and came back malformed and hardened by bitterness and anger. That was the Thad who busted through the hospital door with a score to settle.

Aiden grabbed a pack of USA Gold Full Flavors from the vinyl bench seat. He lit a cigarette and watched as an older nurse, a pissy-looking woman in teal scrubs with gray hair curled into a bun, followed Thad out the door. Aiden could hear her yelling, "Mr. Broom! Mr. Broom!" but Thad wasn't paying her one bit of attention. Instead, Thad walked over to where a short wall of bricks, maybe a foot and a half high, held back a bed of monkey grass and pansies.

Thad bent over and settled his hands onto one of the loose bricks and rocked it back and forth until the mortar crumbled from the edges like ash. When he'd freed the brick from the wall, he held it over his shoulder and turned. The nurse crouched down with her hands over her face as Thad neared, as if he were going to kill her with it, but he didn't. He walked right past and she looked up in confusion as he took a few long-strided hops and smashed the glass door.

He stood there long enough to wrestle a pack of cigarettes from the pocket of his jeans and light a smoke. He was in no hurry as he strolled to the car with his jaw cocked out and puffs of cigarette smoke marking every two or three steps. Aiden already had the Ranchero running when Thad slammed the door. Thad situated himself in the seat, ashed his cigarette into the floorboard, and gave Aiden a look like, What the hell are you waiting for? The nurse stood dumbstruck as they passed, and Aiden found himself thinking that they were leaving that place no different than they'd found it, that most everything that came through the front door of the VA was broke all to shit.

The needle on the gas gauge teetered just left of half a tank and Aiden wasn't sure they had enough to make it home. There was an hour between Asheville and Jackson County, at least another forty-five minutes from the county line to wind their way from Sylva to Little Canada. The bottom of the tank always burned up faster than the top, and Aiden figured best case they'd coast in on fumes, but he didn't say anything. He steered down the ramp that led to I-40 and waited till Thad flicked that first cigarette into the wind before he spoke.

"What the hell happened back there?" Aiden asked.

"Same shit as always, Aid." Thad jostled against the passenger-side door and slid his billfold from his back pocket. "They give me an appointment to see a doctor, then that doctor tells me I need to see a specialist, and then that specialist takes six months to tell me he's going to need me to get an MRI and then I go to get an MRI and they tell me it's going to be another few months before the specialist can work me back in." Thad leafed through the few bills in his wallet slowly, then perused them a second and third time as if it might yield better results. "I told that bitch that the VA benefits and that VA hospital ain't worth a fuck. I'm on IRR for two more years and she tells me to calm down and I tell her that I ain't about to calm down, that it's been two goddamn years they've been dicking around and my back's still broke all to shit. That's when she ran me out of there and that's when I broke her fucking door. We'll just see if those benefits cover glass."

Aiden felt around on the bench seat for his pack of cigarettes and shook one into his lips once he'd found them. He slapped around the seat for his lighter, then traded hands on the steering wheel to pat his pants pockets, but came up empty.

"Here," Thad said, holding his own lighter across the cab. He leaned to put his wallet back into his pocket, winced for a second as the pain seemed to run up his spine like current. "Says an awful lot about a country that'd rather cut a man a disability check than fix him up so he can go find a job."

Aiden steered the Ranchero with his knee and cupped the fire from the wind. When the cigarette was lit he passed the lighter back to Thad and said, "There ain't no jobs anyway."

"Still don't make it right," Thad said.

They rode along and did not speak for some time, just the sound of the world blowing past through the open windows. A mile ahead I-26 joined 40. There was much more movement here on the outskirts of Asheville than where the boys were headed. Off the highway over a line of trees, a crane swung a crossbeam into place on a three-story steel skeleton where welding arcs burned white as stars in the daylight.

"One thing's for sure," Aiden said. "There's a lot more jobs to be had over here."

Thad glanced toward the construction and nodded.

"We could probably find something if we left."

"I ain't ever leaving the mountains," Thad said.

"I'm not talking about leaving the mountains. Hell, I don't want to leave the mountains, Thad. I'm talking about leaving Jackson County."

"And going where?"

"Here. Asheville. Maybe Hendersonville. Shit, they're putting up buildings every day. It'd be easy for a man to find a decent job, and we wouldn't even have to move that far to find it."

"I don't have no interest in moving to Asheville."

"Why the hell not? You said you want a job, and I'm telling you they're here. Right here. So why not move to Asheville?"

"I ain't moving to Asheville." Thad shifted irritably in his seat, his frustration evident in his voice. "I ain't leaving Little Canada."

"And why the fuck not?" Aiden looked over to Thad, who was rubbing his palms up and down his thighs nervously. He took a final drag from his cigarette and flicked the butt through the open window.

"Because there ain't but two places that'll ever make sense to me, and one of them is a place I can't ever go back to."

AT THE SYLVA ABC STORE, Aiden waited in the car while Thad went inside to buy whatever whiskey was cheapest. Aiden was starved and he hoped the job that night might ease things for a while, might get them enough cash to last a month.

When the market fell to pieces, Aiden turned to stripping the same houses he'd helped build. Thad was right about how the world seemed backward, how it was easier to eke out a living than to hold an honest-to-God job. A man could put in a half night's work for a full week's pay and never pay a dime in taxes. On top of that, the smart ones caught checks for unemployment or disability. So outlawing gets in a man's blood in such a way that even if there comes a day when he wants out, even if he gets tired of scraping by and wants to go honest, there isn't much of a demand.

In that way, this day was no different from any day that had come before, and that was part of what kept Aiden up at night: the cyclical nature of it all. For his entire life everything had been a continuous whirling of disappointment, the circle seeming to tighten and become just a little more certain with each passing year. Small arrest led to small arrest, and rap sheets became résumés. Three-day sentences turned to ten and ten days turned to thirty, and in a place like Jackson County, second chances were given but third and fourth chances never happened. Aiden's reputation preceded him and he was too broke to leave. Too broke to leave is what gets a man to do it again and again, and before he knows it he's right back where he started. That's just the way the world turns. Every place has a backside and that was all he'd ever known. In a county where 99 percent were hardworking, god-fearing people who'd do anything for one another, folks like Aiden and Thad were walking, talking prayer requests.

At this point, even if the market turned around and the jobs came back, Aiden was out of favors. The only thing he could hope for was to save up enough money to move away. For months, he'd been setting aside whatever little bit he could, nothing more than a few hundred dollars stashed in a hide at the house. He didn't want to leave the mountains. He would never leave the mountains. Flat land made him anxious, like the world was just too big. But he needed to get out of Jackson County, and a place like Asheville, where there were more people and more money and more jobs, made the most sense. That's where they needed to be.

Thad walked out with a bottleneck clenched in his fist, a fifth of Aristocrat Supreme 80 or Gold Crown or Travelers Club in a crinkled brown bag. He'd no more than stepped off the curb before he twisted the cap off and took a long slug with his head back and eyes closed. Before he capped the bottle, Thad swiped his fist across his mouth to catch the dribble and sucked at the back of his hand thereafter so as not to waste a drop. He hopped into the passenger side and turned the bottle up twice more before Aiden made it out of the parking lot. The old beater sputtered and Aiden knew there wasn't a chance in hell they were making it back to Little Canada.

"You got any money for gas?" Aiden asked.

Thad took another drink and fished a cigarette out of his pack, spoke with that cigarette clamped between his teeth. "Probably got enough for two or three gallons," he said.

Up the road, they coasted into the Sylva Dairy Queen, one of those half-restaurant, half–filling station deals designed to prey on traveling parents whose road-worn children won't shut the hell up without ice cream. Aiden pulled up to the pump and Thad hopped out to go inside to pay. When he returned, he stood with a lit cigarette dangling from his teeth while gasoline fumes waved a haze around him. The pump crawled when it hit the eight-dollar mark. Through the opened window, he reached into the cab and grabbed his bottle of whiskey. He took two sips while rattling the gas nozzle against the tank, nursing the bottle now to try and make it last through the night.

They drove through town and on into Cullowhee and past the university to East LaPorte, where the river came to run parallel with the road. The water was low and had been all summer, its current pocked with stones. Heat bugs cursed the sun from the same trees where their dried husks clung to bark, and a flight of swifts seemed to make a game out of dive-bombing the stream to trace the tips of their crescent wings across the water's surface. They passed harrow-turned fields in Tuckasegee and passed Ken's Grocery, where they used to steal cigarettes as kids, and then turned onto Highway 281 upward into the mountains toward home. Aiden watched the world, but his mind was someplace else. He wondered if there would ever come a time when Thad would be back to the way he was before. Aiden was thinking about the space between them, that two feet of space in the car that in reality stretched as wide as a universe. Things were different now. He and Thad were different. And no matter how much he wanted, he couldn't think of a single way to turn back.

(2)

THAT AUGUST WAS AS HOT AS THAD EVER REMEMBERED a summer in Jackson County. Most of the houses he and Aiden stripped for copper were bank owned, had been closed off and powerless for months, some even years, so that the only thing the homes seemed fit for anymore was to trap heat like ovens. Beads of sweat blistered Thad's forehead and washed over his face, dripped from his chin onto the plywood subfloor. Aiden sweated just the same, and it seemed to bog him down, his toil sluggish and halfhearted. But Thad worked through the heat and the pain with his mind someplace else entirely.

Thad thought about the first few months after he'd come home. The place where he'd grown up didn't seem real anymore. Everything from before was now a production in which he was an actor stumbling for lines that he simply couldn't remember. Even Aiden was unfamiliar. Things had changed, and rather than bear it, Thad loaded up his ALICE pack, laced his boots, and headed off into country that felt more like the one from which he'd just returned.

He went into the gorge where there was nothing more than rocks, trees, and sky. On a shallow ledge cut into the hillside, he hung a tarp on paracord stretched between trees to make camp. The river offered water and food, but even more so, its current seemed to fill some hole inside of him. At night, that place was so dark that he could lie on his back and see nothing but stars, a place so absent of light that even the blue-green nebulas clouding the heavens could be seen hanging like smoke left by fireworks. The place was quiet, and when Thad sat completely still he could decipher the subtleties in how the silence broke: the rustle of a sparrow in the leaf litter versus a chipmunk burrowing, the difference between a deer and a bear brushing through a copse of laurel, the sound of animals that moved on four legs from those who moved on two. And that last one was why he felt at ease there, because no matter how many sounds he heard, he almost never heard the footsteps of men.

It was winter when Thad finally came out of the woods dirtied and unshaven. Aiden looked at Thad as if he had lost his mind, but what Aiden couldn't understand was that the place from where Thad emerged felt more real than home. Combat had made him forget the before, and there was nothing that mattered afterward. There was only war. Going to the woods had rebuilt some sort of reality, and now that the division between those two places was constructed, Thad could start to separate war from home.

He focused on the work at hand and took a long pull from the bottle of whiskey that was now half-gone. They wore headlamps that Aiden had stolen from Walmart, the type hunters strap to their foreheads to follow blood trails after sundown. Thad grabbed a pair of channel locks from the plywood floor and moved the headlamp onto the top of his head so that he could wipe the sweat from his brow. His back was killing him, it was always killing him, but he said nothing of it. He just kept his head down and worked.

He watched Aiden uncoil a thick tangle of wires wadded in the outlet box. The house was new construction that had been abandoned. The drywall wasn't even up, so stripping the wire was a piece of cake. Aiden straightened the wires and yanked twice, and they pulled free. Thad plucked U-nails out of the framing, worked his way from top to bottom until each line was freed and the wires piled in the sawdust on the floor. A thought came to him that made him laugh.

"What's so funny?" Aiden asked.

Thad looked over at Aiden, saw how the years had stretched the rangy boy he'd grown up with into a man. "Nothing," he said. Then a few moments passed between them with both turning back to their work before Thad couldn't hold it in.

"What the hell's so funny?"

"I was thinking about that time when you and me broke into Mama's house and super-glued her old man's balls to the bed." Thad laughed. "You remember that?"

"I remember." Aiden stopped what he was doing and smiled.

"You remember when she tore ass down to the trailer screaming about how that son of a bitch got out of bed that morning and the sheets came with him and his feet got all tangled up and he damn near ripped his own balls off?"

"We almost castrated him."

They both broke into hysterics and the sound carried all around the empty house, the copper wire balled up like spaghetti at their feet. Thad's headlamp beamed into Aiden's eyes, his long, narrow face in spotlight. For a second or two, Thad forgot how hard life had become and the two of them just joked back and forth like children.

"I swear I thought that old man was going to kill us in our sleep," Aiden said.

"He couldn't have killed us if he'd tried." Thad took another sip of whiskey and passed the bottle to Aiden. Right about the time Aiden turned the bottle up to his lips, Thad added, "Son of a bitch ain't have the balls."

Bubbles gurgled deep into the bottle as Aiden busted so hard that the whiskey shot out of his nose and sprayed from his lips. He coughed and laughed, hollering, "Goddamn! Look what you've done," and Thad keeled over.

The two stripped the house and Thad went back to dreaming. They worked until there were bird nests of wire bunched along every wall, worked until their bodies were sticky and spent. Aiden had his hands inside his overalls and stood in the open doorway. Moonlight cast his lanky shadow across the plywood floor. He mashed a mess of wire flat as he could with his boots, picked up the pile, and hugged it to his chest. Thad gathered a load of his own, the snipped ends digging into his skin like briars. Five trips and they'd carried all the wire out of the house. They'd already pulled the main line and the coil from the air unit outside, and the house was plumbed with PEX, so there was no need to strip that. They were out of that place in a jiffy. Not even midnight yet. New houses were always a piece of cake.

THAD'S TRAILER SAT ON a ridgeline off Charleys Creek above Balsam Lake. When winter left the trees naked, he could make out the water in the valley if there wasn't any fog. But right now it was summer and he couldn't see the lake at all.

Up the hill, Thad's mother, April, lived alone. The property had belonged to George Trantham, a man twice her age, who drank heavily and used fists rather than words. When the old man finally kicked the bucket, Thad and Aiden were in high school, and April inherited six acres, a run-down house, and a single-wide with only a few bent scraps of aluminum still serving as a skirt.

Thad believed the cancer that killed George Trantham came from all the radio waves whizzing about the property. Trantham leased a half acre to the federal government way back when and they built a radio tower halfway to heaven that transmitted everything from airplane chatter to WGRC radio. On Wednesday evenings and Sunday mornings, Thad and Aiden could hear the fire-and-brimstone swindlings of Wesley Browne, a snake-oil-sermon evangelical from Richmond, Kentucky, more clearly from their front porch than from the front pew of the church. Whether or not they'd kill off from cancer in the long run was unknown, but what remained certain was April took in seven hundred fifty dollars per month on the lease like clockwork.

There wasn't a cloud in the sky. The moon spotlighted everything on the mountain. Whether it was stars or the moon or people in town, everything always seemed to look down on them. Thad sat in a ratty recliner that reeked of mildew long before he moved the chair onto the porch. Aiden was sitting on the edge of the top step. A small radio on the railing between them blared bluegrass being recorded live from some greasy spoon in Nashville.

"I ever tell you about that time me and a couple of boys at basic went to see Jason Isbell and the 400 play at some dive in Wilmington?" Thad hunched out from the recliner. He whittled with a dull pen blade at rubber insulation on gauge too thick for wire strippers. Long threads of black rubber rolled back along the blade until the knife slipped free and the coiled shavings fell onto the back of Loretta Lynn, a mangy Pekingese that always slept in Thad's lap. The dog's face was smashed flat and she scowled with an underbite and one half-rotten tooth protruding from her bottom jaw. She was too old to eat dry food anymore. He'd found her almost starved to death in a ditch not long after he came out of the woods, about a year before. Thad brushed the wire shavings from Loretta Lynn's back and she glanced up for a second. She batted her eyes, shook matted tufts of hair from the sides of her face, and licked her tongue a few dry laps across that rotten tooth before she fell back to sleep. "I ever told you that story?"

"I don't think so," Aiden said.

"Well, I don't know if they lied to us or if we wound up in the wrong place or what, but when we walked into that bar there wasn't a soul," Thad said. "One of the boys I was with was Todd Cunningham, and he got all riled up. But me and Charles—we called him Chaz—started pouring drinks down Cunningham's throat, and before you know it, all of us were shithoused. Every week we'd go out and get tanked, and it ain't matter a bit because we'd get back to base and one of the medics kept all these IVs stashed in his locker and he'd hook us up to one and we'd be good as new come morning."

Aiden stopped what he was doing and set the wire strippers onto the step. He opened and closed his hands to stretch the cramps out of his fingers, then stared toward April's house on the hill.

"We're all drunk and start jawing back and forth about how bad we need to get laid," Thad continued. "About that time this old gal stumbles in all by herself, and I'm telling you I was on top of her before the door shut. I couldn't tell you what she looked like in daylight, but I wound up going home with her."

Thad stopped his story and took a drink of whiskey. He checked the bottle against the porch light, closed one eye, and measured what sloshed in the bottom. "So when she'd passed out, I gathered up my clothes in my arms and tiptoed my way out of there. About halfway through the living room I got tripped up and fell flat on my face. I'm naked and I look down and this girl's mama is passed out in the floor.

"I'm standing there with my dick in my hand and that old woman leans up and starts rubbing at her eyes and looking at me all funny and I don't know what the hell I was thinking but I just held out my hand and introduced myself. You'd think she'd have come out of her skin to be woke up like that, but she was just as polite as could be and told me it was nice to meet me. Then she asked me what I was doing and I told her it wasn't a matter of what I was doing, but what I'd done." Thad smiled and looked up from the thick wire he was working. "You hear me, Aid? I told her it wasn't what I was doing, but what I'd done."

Aiden hadn't turned from April's house. All the lights were out except the one in her bedroom. Thad looked at him for a second, then turned his attention back to what he was doing. When Thad came home, Aiden was living in the house with his mother and the trailer held a musty smell from having been empty for some time. Thad knew that while he was gone something had happened between Aiden and April, and in his mind that was her way of taking one more thing out of his life. Thad didn't trust her at all. The past year or so April'd been trying to sell the property, and the way Thad figured, whatever was going on between her and Aid was just some sloppy payment for Aiden's work. Aiden did everything from weed-eating banks to renovations. He spent a whole week splitting locust rails to build a fence that separated the trailer from the house so that potential buyers would think the place Thad lived was some derelict eyesore unattached to the parcel above. Lately, she'd had Aiden painting the inside of the house, and when he finished, she had plans for a wraparound porch, a nice screened-in section around back. Thad ran the knife along the wire, whittled the insulation back to twisted copper strands.

"How much you think we'll get for all this, Aid?"

"What's that?" Aiden turned back from April's house.

"I said how much you think we'll get when it's all said and done?"

"Usually somewhere around two hundred fifty pounds in a house that size when there ain't no plumbing. We ought to get six hundred, I'd say."

"Aww, come on now, Aid. We'll get more than that. Surely."

"I doubt it."

"Well, either way I'm ready to get lit." Thad smiled. "We ain't been by to see Wayne Bryson in a month."

"Jesus, Thad," Aiden said. "Just as soon as we get any money at all, you're wanting to get fucked up. We can't keep blowing every dime we get just as quick as we get it."

"You're always right there beside me. So why you getting mad at me?"

"We ain't ever going to get ahead. We keep on doing the same thing and we ain't ever going to get out of here. Ten years from now, right here we'll be. Ten years from now, won't a damn thing be different."

"And what does it matter?" Thad said. "That's the difference between me and you, Aid. I don't have plans on going nowhere. I'd be just fine to sit right here from now till the day I die."

"There's going to come a time when you're going to regret every bit of it," Aiden said. "Whether it's ten years or fifteen years from now, there's going to come a time when you're not okay with just sitting around shoving dope up your nose. There's going to come a day when you wish you'd played your hand a little different."

"Fifteen years from now?" Thad huffed. "What the fuck do I care what happens fifteen years from now, Aid? I'm just trying to get through the day without blowing my fucking brains out." He regretted saying it just as soon as the words left his mouth.

"What the fuck are you talking about?"

"Nothing."

"You sitting here saying shit like that. That ain't nothing."

There were things that Thad could never explain, things like wanting to go back to the very place that had destroyed him because war made more sense than home, or feeling so confused and scared that dying seemed easier than living. But men didn't speak of such things. The conversations of men had always been muddy rivers, the surface's roiling a reflection of what's buried, but the bottom some mysterious thing that would always be hidden. The two of them sat there for a second or two, neither saying a word, both staring each other down and Thad wishing he could take back what he'd said.

"That's the difference between us." Aiden finally spoke. "I ain't all right with just getting by. I'm sick of it. I'm sick of busting ass for peanuts. I'm sick of staying in a place where there ain't no jobs. I'm sick of sitting in the same spot I've been sitting my whole goddamn life. I'm just sick of it." Aiden stood up from the steps and dusted the insulation from his lap. "I'll finish stripping this shit in the morning, or we can burn the insulation off for all I care, but right now I'm done."

Aiden headed across the yard and Thad watched him, but the trailer's porch light shined only so far and in a moment Aiden was gone. When Thad stood from the recliner, Loretta Lynn hopped from his lap and waddled down the stairs into the yard. He turned up the radio to some half-assed rendition of Bill Monroe's "My Last Days on Earth," grabbed what was left of his bottle of whiskey, and followed the dog into the moonlight. After she finished her business,

Loretta Lynn stood by Thad's feet. He knelt down and scratched behind her ears, and she leaned into his hand until she almost fell over.

Thad hadn't been to sleep in three days. When there was no money for dope, he'd pop Stackers and Yellow Jackets and any other kind of road dope to keep from sleeping. After a few days of caffeine pills, his hands would get to shaking and his stomach would hurt so bad that only the whiskey could level him out. He hated to close his eyes because it meant he couldn't stop his mind from turning to questions. Most of the time on deployment was just groundhog days, a bunch of goofy, sweaty eighteen-year-olds joking and wrestling like high school gym class. They'd walk patrols across the moondust, then play cards and smoke cartons of cigarettes and swap stories about home on their downtime, just dicking off. These were good memories and sometimes he thought of them, of the men he'd served with, men who'd become brothers by blood saved and blood shed, but it was the moments when he'd witnessed the world crumble that now turned to questions. In the two years he'd been home, he'd learned that memory could be a terrible thing. He was haunted by memory, by thoughts that felt more real than anything else around him.

On the morning that played again and again, he'd drawn the short straw and run point into a small village on the outskirts of Zawaka, a place in the middle of Paktika Province that really wasn't anything more than a rock outcrop with a name. The whole place was kinetic. Thad's squad had been engaged at least once a day for the past week, usually just a shot or two that cracked down from a hillside and kicked up sand, but the chance was always right there, death some ball and chain dragging behind each of them. They'd seen it happen before. And so even though the Afghani men sold themselves as shepherds, Thad wasn't buying. The men who leaned against the buildings and crouched against the walls were the same hajji mother-fuckers who'd fired on them just hours before. That he was sure of. So when the girl appeared from behind a dusty wall, Thad was already on edge.

Even from some distance, he could see that she was crying. He stopped, and the men behind him stopped and turned, readied their guns to the sides and rear as Thad took a knee and drew his sights just to the left of the girl's body. He screamed for her to stop, but she kept on. No more than nine or ten years old, the girl made her way toward them with a look of hesitancy and fear. Thad knew the enemy was not afraid to use children. He'd been trained to think that way. He'd heard stories of how they'd skin the parents alive, hold a knife to the child's throat, and tell her they'd do the same to her if she didn't keep moving forward. If that's what had happened, then he couldn't blame her. He'd seen the bodies of women and children flayed and beheaded. He knew it just as the girl did, that these were not idle threats.

The sun was in his eyes and she was no more than twenty yards away and he thought he saw something under her tunic, something that was not a part of her body pushing against fabric, and he panicked and he screamed for her to stop and she kept coming and he pulled the trigger and she fell to the ground like a dropped doll. His first thought was that he'd killed a child, but then all of that feeling escaped him as another infantryman, a man named Billy Thompson who wanted to teach kindergarten in Georgia, took off toward her only to disappear in a flash of smoke like a magic trick.

Thad saw only two Americans die while he was in Afghanistan, one of those being Billy Thompson, and it was his death and the death of that little Afghani girl that now drove him into a panic. Anyone could understand being haunted by something like that. But the deaths themselves weren't exactly what haunted him, and that was the problem with trying to explain it to anyone who wasn't there, or anyone at all. What haunted Thad was the realization that he lived in a place where both sides of good and evil saw that girl's death as an act of heroism. Evil men strapped explosives to a child's body in the name of God, and good men promoted Thad from private first class to specialist for pulling the trigger. In the end, she was just a girl and Billy Thompson was just a schoolteacher, and the two of them died together. Those were the only truths to be had. To think either side was moral was a goddamn lie, and that was the biggest problem of all because Thad needed there to be a morality to it. He needed some type of justification.

There were feelings and regrets that he couldn't even share with the men who'd been there, good men who'd lain beside him in the gravel when things went to shit. These were the greatest men he'd ever known and would ever know, and they'd promised to stay close forever. But after coming home, Thad quickly realized they hadn't all brought back the same burden and so he came to feel as disconnected from them as everything else. Maybe some men were stronger than he was. Maybe some men were just more cut out for compartmentalizing what they'd seen and done. Or maybe it was the fact that they came home to family and friends and he came back to nothing. But whatever the reason, it didn't matter because the end result was just the same.

When he thought of these things, the memories became questions that he could not answer, and it was that inability to answer that made him not want to go to sleep. So tomorrow he and Aiden would sell the copper and Thad would buy dope to stay awake for a few more days. At least that was something. But right then, all he could hope for was to polish off that bottle in one swallow and pray for forgiveness, pray that there was a God who could understand. Up the hill, the bedroom window was still lit, but aside from the faint yellow glows at the house and trailer, the rest of the world was painted blue by moonlight and sky. With his eyes set on those pinholes of light above, Thad took one great gulp and emptied the bottle, but he did not close his eyes.

(3)

IF IT HADN'T BEEN FOR THE EYES THEY SHARED, THOSE light green eyes that glowed bronze as scuppernongs in the right light, Aiden would have sworn April was not Thad's mother. But those eyes proved she had birthed him, or at least proved they were kin, and once blood gets that close, it really doesn't make a damn.

When Thad was little, he told everyone his father was Cherokee. Thad said his daddy's last name was Walkingstick, sometimes Pheasant, but usually he stuck with Walkingstick. He carried a big bowie knife with him all the time, twisted crow feathers in his hair, and smeared his chest with mud clods. The way he told it, he was going to be chief, and when that time came, Aiden would be one of the few white people he didn't have it out for. But Aiden had never seen a redheaded Indian.

In truth, Aiden had always believed, just as everyone else, that the most likely man was the church deacon, Samuel Mathis, the only other redhead ever to come out of Little Canada. All the kids bullied Thad and called him Sam, and more than once Aiden had bloodied a kid's nose or blacked his eye because of it. Though April could've gotten knocked up somewhere off the mountain, it didn't take a DNA test to see Samuel and Thad were spitting images of one another. Back when Aiden slipped into pews to pilfer the offering plate, there was more than once when he saw how Samuel stared at April the entire service, and how she seemed to notice but for some reason or another refused to meet his eyes. Either way, Thad's and Samuel's heads were both as red as ginseng berries. Sometimes the proof was in the pudding.

She was already asleep when Aiden walked into the house. The television was on in the living room, but muted, and flashed an unsteady blue about the walls. A tabby cat named Mittens was curled at one end of the couch. The walls were covered with knickknack shelves, different shapes and sizes, but all having the same square nooks. April collected Stone Critters, chalk animal figurines that fit in the palm of her hand. She bought them from flea markets and yard sales, and though Aiden thought it was silly, collecting those figurines made her happy.

There were things Aiden would never understand about her, like how she demanded the lights be on when they made love. Likewise, she always slept with the lights on, and on nights that Aiden lay beside her, he would get up and turn them off once she'd fallen asleep. Some nights she woke up panicked and would scream when she found someone in bed beside her, so most nights he left the lights on and slept by himself on the couch.

April was gorgeous. Aiden had always thought that. And every time they lay together, in that moment just before he came, he would stare into her eyes, those jade-green eyes, and it was enough to push him over. He loved her and always had, even when he and Thad were little. Sometimes he'd even tell her that he loved her, though she never said it back. She always responded with something like, "I know you do, sweet one." But she never said those words in return.

The rest of the house was dark as he walked to her bedroom and stood at the doorsill. She was on her side, facing him, the sheet pulled down to her waist and bunched around the curve of her hip. Her body was tan from sunbathing naked in the backyard when no one was around. There were freckles on her shoulders and chest, freckles he'd traced so often with his fingers that he could map them on paper. One arm was tucked under the pillow. The other hugged around her chest. Honey-blond hair streamed over her shoulder and ran into the place where her breasts pushed together.

Aiden turned off the light and climbed into bed beside her. When he drew close she turned over and he spooned in behind. He was wide awake as he pulled close to her, their bodies together in every place they could be. For a long time, he lay there and couldn't sleep. He'd been hungry so long that the pangs had gone and now returned. He thought about getting up to eat, he thought about a lot of things, but it felt so good beside her that he didn't want to move. When he shifted his legs to get even closer, she stirred against him.

"Will you turn the light back on, sweet one?"

"I will," he said. He stood and then did as she asked on his way out of the room. Down the hall, a light was on over the stove in the kitchen and he opened the refrigerator to look for something to eat. She'd made him a plate for supper: cube steak, mashed potatoes, green beans, and a slice of tomato covered in plastic wrap on a plate. He ate the food cold, and when he'd had his fill, patted the plastic wrap down and slid the leftovers back into the fridge.

In the living room, he shook one of her cigarettes from a pack on the coffee table in front of the couch. Mittens rose from where he'd been curled and sleeping and let his front paws down on the floor, his haunches still on the couch as he bowed. The cat lolled over to where Aiden stood by the window and ran its body against his bare legs. Aiden drew the curtain back and stared down the hill to where Thad sat. He finished his cigarette, watching him, glad that Thad was there simply because his being back meant that Aiden was no longer alone.

When Thad left for Fort Bragg, Aiden felt something he hadn't felt since he was a child. Those nights in the group home while he lay beside the boy who memorized baseball cards, Aiden was frozen with fear. He was alone and helpless, and that feeling was like the world was out of control, like his mind was trying to fathom the speed of light. His palms would get clammy and his ears would ring and his heart raced and he would forget to breathe and he would just lie there knowing for certain that he was about to die and there wasn't a soul on this planet could stop it.

There'd been so many years since he'd felt it that he'd forgotten. All that time, the feeling lay dormant inside him, buried and unnoticed, until that first morning he woke up alone, that first morning Thad wasn't there. Aiden couldn't understand why the feeling came back, he couldn't connect one time and another, but nevertheless there it was day in and day out.

He told himself that things would be different now. Those dark, racing thoughts were gone, and he'd come to believe that if he and Thad could get off this mountain and head to Asheville, they could get back to the way things were before. That hopeful feeling was as nice a thing as he could remember. So he closed his eyes, the same way he did every night, and tried to think of nothing else.

(4)

AIDEN HATED TO SPEND EVERY DIME THEY MADE FROM
the copper on dope, any kind of dope, but he especially hated to
blow it all on crystal. Even though he wanted to get high, methamphetamine had never been his drug. Back before Bennie Hazel got
gooney and smashed the old lady's head to a pulp with a T-ball bat,
Aiden used to buy pills from Gerty Brinkley. She may have just been
the unluckiest woman ever to be born of this earth.

The way the story was told, Gerty and her husband, Frank, had a
little girl named Pearl, and Pearl was the cutest thing God ever made.
Pearl wasn't more than five years old, chasing lightning bugs at the
edge of a honeysuckle thicket, when a black coyote poured off a hillside and took her without so much as a gasp. Gerty caught sight
from the kitchen window and Frank grabbed the gun, laid the lead
to that dog, but, when it was settled, that darling girl was mauled
something long past saving.

Folks said Frank never spoke another word. One morning he
woke up, took his shave like he always did, and ran that long razor

right straight across his neck like he was opening a sack of seed. They said he just stood there in front of the mirror and watched without a sound or expression until what washed over him left him too woozy to stand and he collapsed into the puddle he'd made. That's how Gerty found him. That was before the cancer ate her.

When Aiden came to know Gerty Brinkley she lived off Shook Cove, and doctors kept her prescriptions coming just as fast as pharmacists could fill them. She always had OxyContin and when he was lucky she had Dilaudid. Once she'd had morphine suckers, but the OxyContin was what Aiden fancied.

The old woman barely had a single hair left on her head, just a few thin strands that waved about like feather fluff whenever she moved. The veins in her head shone through her scalp and she wore a thick pair of glasses that swelled her eyes two sizes too big. It was saddening to even look at her, but listening to her was unbearable. She loved to talk Jesus, never would shut up about that water walker. Every time Aiden was there it was all he could do to get away in an hour for the likes of all her preaching, but he had to stay for the whole sermon to score the dope. She said she sold the pills to raise money for the church, all that cash funding Jesus's doings. "I can take the suffering now," she'd say, "just knowing what awaits."

What awaited Gerty Brinkley was Bennie Hazel, and he'd been up a week straight. They said he beat her until her head was just as flat as cube steak. There were times when Aiden had thought of robbing her, but the few beliefs he had kept him from acting. There was a part of him that had always believed in God and the devil. But when Bennie Hazel did that to Gerty Brinkley, that was the day Aiden McCall did away with God. If there was a God, He wasn't worth a damn. The devil wins out every time.

Aiden always cared about everything in this world a little too much, like at any minute this old hunk of rock might go spinning off its axis and shoot off into the Milky Way somewhere. Those thoughts kept him up at night and perhaps that's why he preferred pills. He liked downers and Thad liked uppers. Uppers made Aiden think too much, and him thinking too much had always been a dangerous thing. But ever since Gerty died, there hadn't been much in the way of pills. There for a while the doctors had prescribed Thad some pretty good painkillers for his back, but when they called him in randomly to check his script and all the pills were gone, that free ride ended fast. Now Aiden did whatever was on the table.

With the house Aiden and Thad stripped, they took 243 pounds of copper. The rate was $2.83 per pound, their haul worth nearly seven hundred dollars at the scrap yard. But they couldn't go to the scrap yard. The boys who ran the scales snitched to lawmen on those who tried to make an honest living stealing from millionaires and banks. The way Aiden saw it, he and Thad weren't stripping the houses of hardworking families. They stripped foreclosures, and, in winter, the second homes of millionaires who had the gall to use copper for gutters and downspouts on a mountain where most folks survived on winter gardens and canned meat. Those assholes had it coming.

Since the scrap yard was out of the question, he and Thad sold their copper to a general contractor named Nicholson, who, despite the slow business of others, seemed to keep a full calendar of remodels and, because of that, had a reason to haul truckloads of copper to the yard. Nicholson was a businessman and he knew they had no other option, so he offered two fifty and Thad shook his hand. The whole thing made Aiden sick.

The dope house marked the dead end of a long, muddy cut that ran three miles from pavement. There were trailers scattered along the first mile, but after that a long stretch of woods and rutted trail swept into the holler. The tweakers in those trailers were customers just like Aiden and Thad, and as the two drove by, those wild eyes stared down on them from porches and windows like owls. Late at night, those addicts would stumble down to the road and stand peering into headlights to decipher friend from fiend. But there was still an hour or two of evening light and they knew Aiden's ride, so there'd be no warning calls sounded.

At the house, the tweakers were always lit. Sometimes there were loads of them bouncing around the property like a circus of fleas, and it wouldn't take long till Thad jumped onto his pogo stick and sprang right alongside them. The world was already spinning fast and so Aiden had always preferred dope that slowed that whirling to molasses. But life was too slow for Thad, and he loved how buzzard dust mashed the gas.

Two girls, one tall and skinny and a fat gal wearing a nightgown, slinked along the edge of the woods. A wiry man with his shirt off and lightbulbs for eyes came toward the Ranchero as Aiden and Thad pulled up. The man stared into the cab, his face pitted with acne scars and his sunken jaw working like his mind held all sorts of ideas. Aiden watched him closely, but the man walked past and his stringy mullet never turned. He headed further into obscurity and joined those two girls along the muddy drive.

"Where y'all going?" Thad hollered. He was already drunk again, almost too drunk to stand, having bought another bottle of whiskey just as soon as the money touched his hand. The booze was nearly finished before they left the trailer. Thad had drunk faster than usual, knowing that as soon as he got the dope up his nose his mind would even out. He was always loud when he and Aiden went to see friends, just wouldn't shut the hell up to save his life, but he was especially bad around women. Thad had the door open and stood on the doorjamb with his upper half waving above the cab, as he banged on the roof and yelled, "Nose to nose my toes is in it, and toe to toe my nose is in it. There's plenty to go around!"

The two girls glanced back and the fat one snickered like that just might suit her, but it was that wiry, wide-eyed boy that stopped and turned. He stood there and didn't say a word, his eyes aglow from fifty yards like an animal's. Aiden stepped out of the car and glared to where he stood. They watched each other for a moment, but the man turned, and he and the two girls disappeared like shadows.

The dope house was an old white one-story built like the homes in a mill village. The white paint had aged to the chipped and crackled color of bone. Tall windows were set one on each side with a small porch centered between. The front door was open and light shone through the windows and doorway, making that place look like a skull with a candle burning inside.

Wayne Bryson was on the front porch, shaking a two-liter bottle filled with a bright blue liquid that sloshed and fizzed like some childhood science experiment. He twisted the top and burped the bottle after every shake to ease the gas building inside. His eyes stayed fixed and he never blinked, as if a moment unfocused would crash the spell he cast, his hands whirling household chemicals into crank.

"Who was the legs?" Thad asked as he walked toward the house.

"Shit, that's Julie Dietz, and that thing'd look like a wagon track through a cow pie." Wayne's words blew against a red bandanna he had tied around his face. He flicked his eyes to where the three had vanished, but snapped his stare back onto the bottle and stopped shaking as the plastic swelled tight. White chunks that looked like rock salt washed around in the bottom, and lithium strips melted into a copper film on the surface. Wayne unscrewed the cap, burped the bottle again, and an acrid gray steam seeped into summer air. "My cousin fucked her and he said she don't even trim down there."

"You don't like hair pie?"

"I don't like it looking like a stump full of spiders. That's damn near thirty years of growth, boys. I'm talking granddaddy longlegs."

Thad laughed, and he and Aiden stood there while Wayne worked the bottle until crystals formed.

"Who was that with her?" Aiden asked.

Wayne kept focused on his potion but answered with a nod. "The fat one?"

"No, that wiry boy."

"That's Doug, Dougie Dietz, Julie Dietz's brother. Why?" Wayne spoke speed track sentences that took a second or two to untangle.

"You remember him, Aid. He was the one they caught fooling around with that little girl when we were in high school. It was all over the papers. Her daddy, I can't remember his name off the top of my head, but he found them back behind the barn and Doug Dietz had that girl mashed up against an old Farmall."

"What little girl?"

"I know you remember. It was all over the papers. I can't think of that man's name to save my life." Thad looked straight overhead as if God alone could give him the answer.

"Murphy," Wayne said.

"That's right. Something Murphy. Lives down there by Ken's Grocery in that trailer park. Lays rock. He lays rock for a living."

"I don't know him."

"Well, he caught that son of a bitch with his little girl and he damn near beat that Dietz boy's brains out. Wish he had. I'd do it myself." Thad toppled forward and put one foot on the wooden step to catch his balance. "And I bet you that's why his sister right there don't shave her puss, Wayne. Reckon if she had that thing skinned that old nasty son of a bitch wouldn't be able to keep his hands off her. That's how them pedophiles are, I'm telling you. Fuck their own sister if they get the chance."

"I didn't like the way he was looking at me."

"Aw, Doug, Dougie don't mean nothing, man, Dougie just looks like that. He looks like that all the time." Wayne burped the bottle, shook it once more, and studied what floated and sank as if it might offer some glimpse into the future. "And he swears up and down he didn't do that."

"Well, fuck him's all I know." Thad slapped the rotted wood railing leading up the front steps and stomped the planks beneath him. "The real question is how much longer you got to dick around with that bottle before you can sell us a bag?"

"Almost there, Mr. Broom. This shit takes time."

A year before, there was a man named Charlie McNeely who had Jackson County gourded on some of the finest dope to ever hit the mountains. He had crystals as big around as his thumb and just as clear as quartz. How the law told it, Charlie's son stabbed his old man to death, then took out a deputy or two in a murder-suicide that played out in their front yard. After that, once the McNeely dope dried up, the whole scene turned wild. There was at least one person in every holler who cooked dope, and the folks who finally took the reins were the ones who controlled the medicine. The trick was to build an army to buy every box of pseudoephedrine from Arden to Murphy. The feds had an eye on what was being sold, but if a man had enough people, the ingredients could be walked right out of Walmart. Wayne Bryson had done just that.

When they made it inside, there weren't enough holes in Wayne's house to air out the ammoniac stench that settled on windows and walls. He left every yellowed windowpane lifted, the doors opened, and box fans blowing loud as warehouse exhaust, but none of it did a thing to soften the smell. It made Aiden's eyes water and nose burn like a tomcat had marked every square inch of the house, but Wayne didn't even seem to notice anymore.

Wayne untied the bandanna from his face and shoved the rag down the back pocket of his jeans. The crystal had started to deepen the shadows of his face, a fast-paced hollowing of features that uncovered a man's skeleton. He'd always been wiry, but the dope burned off any lean muscle he'd ever had and now he was as scrawny as a gutted squirrel. Even his pile of greasy hair seemed too big for his head. The motor-oil-speckled jeans cinched tight to his waist had at least four inches to give, and the WrestleMania shirt he wore with cut-off sleeves damn near swallowed him.

Wayne hit the power on his stereo, a Drive-By Truckers album Aiden hadn't heard in ages coming over the speakers. "Have a seat," he said, slapping his palm against a coffee table by the couch before he disappeared into the back of the house.

Wayne came back into the living room with a half-filled ziplock bag, at least an ounce of yellow crystal coarse as pea gravel. He tossed the bag onto the coffee table the way a man might toss his car keys, and slid a stamp-sized baggie from underneath an ashtray. When others stopped by, the bags were already filled, and Wayne swapped them fast for crumpled wads of cash. But he'd known Thad for a long time and for whatever reason trusted him, almost seemed to look up to him, especially once Thad came back from the Army. So Wayne always weighed what Thad and Aiden bought in front of them.

He brought out the big bag of higher-grade dope he usually saved for himself. There was no reason in the world he should have believed Aiden and Thad any different from the others, but Aiden thought, in that line of work, a man might be searching for at least one friend, one person he believes won't slit his throat, and, for Wayne, that was Thad Broom. Aiden would've dug Wayne's grave in a heartbeat, never even thought twice, but Wayne's dope was as clean as any shake-and-bake meth coming out of Jackson County, so Thad made Aiden promise to keep his hands to himself.

"How much y'all want?"

"A hundred a gram?" Thad asked.

"Got to be a buck twenty."

"One twenty? You hear this shit, Aid? Skinning us."

"Anybody else'd be one fifty."

"That ain't my problem."

"And it ain't mine whether or not you find that other twenty."

"Just a gram, then." Thad looked to Aiden as if he might give him the okay on buying two, but Aiden wasn't ready to drop all the cash they had. It was hard enough to save anything, but there was no telling when the next payday would come.

Wayne swung his rag of hair out of his eyes and shoveled crystals into the baggie with a plastic spoon. He shook a little back out, flicked the corner of the bag till the shards settled, eyed it, sealed it, and tossed it onto digital scales.

"Why you weighing that shit in the bag?" Thad hollered.

"Why you always asking questions?"

"I ain't trying to buy plastic bags."

"Bag's a gram. Dope's a gram. Ought to weigh two." Wayne pointed down to the scales where numbers bounced back and forth between 2.2 and 2.1 on an illuminated blue screen. "A cunt's hair heavy, if you ask me."

"Heavy my ass." Thad reached down and snatched the bag before Wayne could even think of shaving it back.

Wayne laughed under his breath, reached over, and killed the power on the scales. "Do a rail right fast?"

"Out of your bag, we'll do as much as you want." Thad counted out six twenty-dollar bills and handed them over. "What you say, Aid?"

Aiden nodded and Thad tapped out half the bag onto the table. He drew his billfold from his back pocket, slid his expired license from a sleeve, and started to mash crystal into powder beneath the card. Aiden watched him closely as he ran the butt end of a cigarette lighter over the top of the card, crunched shards into dust, and when it was ground as fine as he could get it, he cut the dope into two lines.

"That ain't enough to cook a toad," Wayne said, then spooned more from his bag and piled it between the lines Thad cut. "Divvy it up."

Thad went back to grinding, pushing, and turning the butt end of that lighter like he was milling medicine with a mortar and pestle. Aiden studied him as he raked the pile into three rails and scraped each across the table till they all had a thick trail of dope carved in front of them. Wayne snatched a straw from the table, slid his sodbuster from the side pocket of his jeans, and snipped the straw into thirds with the knife blade against his thumb. They each took a straw, Wayne counted down, and when liftoff came, they bowed like a family in prayer and walked their noses straight through dope as fine as broken glass.

The crystal burned them all the same, lit spot fires like a drip torch in each of their noses, and Aiden cleared his throat loudly with his eyes bulged to try and snuff it out. Thad howled over speakers rattling the Drive-By Truckers' "Puttin' People on the Moon," and Wayne sparked off the couch with his head jerking from side to side.

"Got something you boys got to see to believe," Wayne yelled before he shot off for his bedroom. "This shit's going to blow your minds."

Aiden's mind was already blown, running sprint car laps around the dirt track of his skull, when Wayne Bryson popped out of the bedroom with guns strapped all over his body. There was an AR-15 assault rifle aimed downward from his chest in a military sling, the black grips of a pistol peeking from his waistline, some long-barreled stainless revolver shoved in his belt and dangling down his leg like a machete, a pistol-grip pump shotgun in his left hand by his side, and some skinny carbine rifle he balanced against his hip and aimed toward the ceiling.

"Ready for war!" Wayne screamed at the top of his lungs. "Goddamn Booker Branch Rambo!"

Thad was laughing hysterically as Wayne stood by a doorway right next to where a bar split the living room and kitchen, then waddled toward them with his legs bent wide so the pistols wouldn't slide loose from his waistline.

"Where the hell'd you get those?" Aiden asked.

"Scabs'll steal anything." Wayne swung the shotgun up and tossed it Thad's way. "I'll take a gun over money any day of the week."

Thad snatched the shotgun out of the air, shouldered it, and stared down iron sights like he just might blow off the bottom halves of Wayne's legs. The gun seemed some natural extension of his body the way he handled it. He yanked back on the pump and a shell flipped into Aiden's lap. "Might ought to tell somebody there's one in the chamber." He slid forward and yanked again, pumped till there were no more to give. There were six shells scattered across the couch, three red and three yellow.

Dope had a way of running Aiden's mind full of some of the

clearest thoughts that ever lit in his head, and right then his mind fired those thoughts from a Gatling. His mind thought things and saw things a second before they happened, and trying to make sense of it made his muscles twitch.

"Buckshot and slugs," Wayne said. "I always go with the buckshot first. What you think, Mr. Broom?"

"I think I could do a lot of damage in close quarters with this thing, but in the long run I'd take that AR." Thad reloaded the tube, racked it on the fifth to make room for the last shell, and set the shotgun on the grimy carpet. Wayne drew the long-barreled revolver from his belt and laid it on the coffee table, but Thad couldn't leave it alone. He seemed to find something humorous about the size of the weapon and picked the revolver up, waving it over his head, hollering, "Nobody move!" before bursting into hysterics.

"Smith .500," Wayne said. "Dirty Harry ain't got nothing on that."

Thad pulled the hammer back just a fuzz with his thumb and spun the cylinder like a little boy playing with the wheels of a toy car.

"You ever seen one of these?" Wayne asked, and shook the tactical rifle that he held down his side. "This Kel-Tec folds plumb in two. I'm talking you could shove that son of a bitch down your britches." Wayne pushed down on the rear of the trigger guard and folded the barrel back over the stock, and the skinny rifle doubled in half. He placed it on the coffee table in that fashion, then pulled the pistol from his waistline and settled one hand on the grip of the AR. "But you're right about this AR. These two, now, these two are my babies. This here's the Colt my daddy carried in 'Nam." Wayne raised the pistol and pointed it center mass on Aiden's chest.

"Don't point that thing at me!" Aiden rose off the couch and had split the distance between them before Wayne's eyes even focused. Aiden's thoughts were coming clear. He was seeing the future.

Wayne flipped the barrel toward the ceiling. "Calm down, Aiden. Ain't nothing in the hole." He hit the release on the side and the magazine fell to the floor. "It's empty."

"You point that thing at me and I'm going to shove it down your throat." The dope had Aiden all funny and he was losing control quickly. The world was speeding up and speeding up and he was just about to kick it all into oblivion. Thad was still just laughing.

"Just calm down. Ain't a thing in it." Wayne cocked the hammer and raised the pistol to his temple. "See?" He pulled the trigger and the far side of his face blew off. A thrash of blood, chunks like grayed hamburger, let loose across the room. His arms dropped to his sides, his right hand still clenching the Colt, and he held there for a second or two before he toppled stiff as a tree face-first into the coffee table, rapping the bridge of his nose on the way to the floor.

Thad jumped up from the couch with his hands up around his face. "What the fuck just happened? What the fuck just happened?"

"Cocksucker blew his brains out! He blew his fucking brains out!" Aiden tilted his head so he could see around the coffee table, then kicked at Wayne's shoes, Wayne's bottom half trembling. "He's deader than hell! I'm telling you, that motherfucker's deader than hell!"

Wayne Bryson lay there with his gnarled face flat on the floor. His body blew a slow foam of bubbles where the hollow-point ripped apart his left brow. His mouth was slightly open. His eyes were closed. Blood pooled around pieces of him the same pale yellow hue as thrush.

"We need to get out of here, Aid." Thad started panicking, yanking his head every which way, looking everywhere to try and make sense of something that had happened as fast as a balloon popping. Thad snatched the crumpled twenties he'd paid Wayne from the table and shoved the money in his pocket. He grabbed the bag of dope and that long, shiny revolver, settled his eyes on Aiden with his jaws sawing back and forth. "We need to get the fuck out of here."

Faster and faster, the world was cooking now. Aiden followed Thad out the front door, knowing there wasn't a thing he could do to stop it.

(5)

WHEN AIDEN'S FATHER PULLED THE TRIGGER, HIS HEAD seemed to follow that bullet as it passed through the roof of his mouth and then the roof of his skull. His head slapped back violently and his body collapsed beneath him like some invisible puppeteer had pulled a knife and severed the strings to the puppet. Aiden figured that's how it always happened, but now he knew differently. Wayne Bryson stood there for a second or two, just stood there, head drooping with part of his face gone before gravity got the best of him. Felled him like a goddamned tree.

"I've never seen nothing like it," Thad said. "I've seen some fucked-up shit, but in all my years of living, I ain't ever seen nothing like it. Have you, Aid?"

"No," Aiden said.

"I mean one second he was talking, and the next second that shit blew out of him like he'd sneezed. That gun went off and his brains . . ." Thad shook his head like a madman. "Fucking chunks, I'm telling you."

Thad rocked on the couch in the living room of the trailer. He kept standing up and rubbing his hands down the thighs of his jeans like he couldn't get the sweat off his palms. He yanked the cigarette he smoked out of his lips and flicked ash in a spasm, tapped at the filter until bits of burning tobacco peppered the carpet around his feet. Then he plopped back onto the couch and hot-boxed another two or three drags, stood up, and repeated that series of movements over and over. Up down, up down.

Aiden's mind already ran faster than he could stand, and all of Thad's jumping around poured gas on the fire. Aiden's brain ran so quickly that there seemed to be a sound to it, a low ringing in his ears like feedback. He already wanted to come down, but there wasn't any hope for that. He hated the way crystal made him feel, but it never stopped him from snorting it or smoking it or anything else so long as there weren't needles. Time and time again, he'd get down, and when that mood hit him he'd do anything to feel different, any kind of different, anything at all.

Loretta Lynn was on the couch beside Thad, her straw-colored coat almost camouflaged against the fabric, and she kept nodding her head, panting, and sniffing like she thought the jig Thad danced was for her amusement. When the cigarette had burned down to the filter, Thad scooted to the edge of his seat and smashed the butt into an ashtray on a round plywood table that centered the room. The table was the size of a tractor wheel, an empty conduit spool Thad and Aiden salvaged from the scrap pile of a construction site.

As soon as they'd come inside, Thad dropped Wayne Bryson's bag of crystal and his long-barreled revolver on the tabletop, and now he was on his hands and knees digging a pinch of meth out of the bag. He patted his back pockets for his billfold and threw it onto the table when he found it. He scanned the room, slapped his hands against his chest with his eyes squinted, like he was trying to find something.

A thought seemed to light in his mind and he jumped up and stomped through the trailer into his bedroom.

Staring at the ounce of crystal on the table, Aiden knew right then he needed to take that shit and run. His mind had gone mad, but he understood two things. He knew that the dope would be Thad's end. He knew that if there was no running out, there'd be no coming down, and that could end only one way. But he also knew there was at least twenty-five hundred dollars in that bag, and that amount of money could be the start of getting off that mountain, so he moved quickly. He came out of his chair, swiped the dope, and was to the door in one clean motion, but even that was not quick enough.

Thad came back through the kitchen with a small glass pipe to his lips. His cheeks swelled as he blew into the stem trying to clear resin left from whatever they'd smoked last. Aiden had one hand on the doorknob and the other holding the bag, and he froze when their eyes met.

"Where the hell are you going?" Thad asked. He had a metal clothes hanger unwound and ran the straightened end in and out of the pipe a few times before blowing again to see if he'd cleared the clog, a slight whistle sounding from the steamroller.

"I'm going to run out to the car right fast," Aiden stammered. He hoped Thad hadn't seen the bag, and from his question, Aiden didn't believe he had.

"Hurry up," Thad said as he circled the wire inside the pipe. And about that time Aiden heard the glass crack. The steamroller was broken in Thad's hands and he stared at what he held as if he couldn't believe what had happened. He reared back and shattered what was left against the wall, screamed "Goddamn it!" before stamping back into his bedroom. But Aiden didn't stick around to see what came next. He was already out the door and gone.

. . .

AIDEN DIDN'T SEE HER when he hurried inside and rushed to the bathroom to hide the drugs. He was flat on his back on the tile floor with his head in the cabinet, trying to balance the bag of crystal on the trap under the sink. When the dope was hidden, he shimmied out and discovered her hovered over him. Seeing April there caught him off guard, and he hammered the back of his head against the edge of the cabinet in surprise.

"What the hell are you doing?" April asked. She was wrapped in a navy-blue robe, and from where Aiden lay he could see that she didn't have anything on underneath. Her hair was pulled into a ponytail, one blond sliver of bangs cutting across her stare.

He scrambled from the floor and they were chest to chest as he tried to back her out of the bathroom. "Nothing."

"Sure as hell ain't nothing," she said. The two of them were wedged in the doorway. She glared like she might be able to decipher the riddle from the way he looked at her. "Tell me what you were doing under there."

Aiden stuttered a lie about checking to see if the pipe was leaking, and not one word of it sounded believable because what came out was jumbled and his eyes looked like they were going to pop out of his head. She was just about to scoot into the bathroom and check for herself when the front door slammed against the living room wall.

"What did you do with that bag, Aiden?" Thad met them as they came out of the hallway. He stood barrel-chested out of breath with Wayne Bryson's revolver white-knuckle tight in his hand. April started to scream about the gun and what Thad was doing in her house, and he told her to shut her mouth without even glancing to where she stood. "Answer me, goddamn it!"

"I don't know what you're talking about," Aiden said. He had his arm stretched across the hallway so that April couldn't pass, and Thad came forward, raised the pistol, and pressed the barrel straight into Aiden's forehead.

"You're going to tell me what you did with it." Thad cocked the hammer with a look in his eyes that said he was seconds away from pulling the trigger.

"You better get that goddamn gun out of my face," Aiden said.

"I ain't doing nothing till you tell me what you did with that bag."

"Thad, I'm telling you, if you don't get that fucking gun out of my face I am going to beat your brains out with it." Aiden could feel the rage building inside of him, and it was one of the oldest feelings he knew. Those who had known his father said that Aiden's mother had been cheating, while others simply said she'd had her fill of his shit and was ready to leave, but the real reason didn't matter. What mattered was how Aiden's father had snapped. It was that unshakable volatility that carried into Aiden. It was that spark-away-from-burning-the-world-down that had always scared him to death, and he was almost there.

Thad prodded the muzzle into Aiden's forehead, Aiden snatched hold of the barrel, and April ducked under Aiden's arm before he could even try to stop her. She was between him and Thad with her finger jabbing at Thad's chest with every word she said. "I don't know what in the hell the two of you are talking about, but you're going to get out of my house!"

There hadn't been more than a few words between them in the two years since Thad had been home. Though they spent every day with nothing more than a hillside between them, April and Thad existed in two different worlds, and it had been that way for more than a decade. The tension had only worsened in the past year, after she'd put the property on the market. Since sixth grade, Thad lived in that trailer, and he was very clear in his belief that the place was just as much his as hers. Aiden didn't blame him for thinking that. April had always seemed to see her son as a burden. She didn't say a word when George Trantham moved Thad into the trailer. It was as if she believed that if it hadn't been for Thad she would've wound up someplace better than this. More than that, Thad seemed to know that's what she thought. So the two of them stayed at each other's throats and Aiden trod the ground between.

"I'm not leaving here until that son of a bitch gives me what he stole," Thad said. He still hadn't lowered the gun.

"I didn't steal a fucking thing." Aiden's mind was wild. He kept telling himself, Thad won't pull the trigger, there's no way he'll pull the trigger, but the more he thought about it, the less he was sure. Aiden was filling up inside, moving closer and closer to that threshold, and once he crossed over there would be no turning back. He'd never been able to stop himself once he'd started. Blank thoughts would wash over him, and he would not come to until it was over.

Thad clenched his teeth with his mouth open so that he looked like some growling dog with squinted eyes. His head slowly wrenched up to the side until he could turn no farther. He exhaled in one long breath, lowered the gun as he did, then dropped the hammer back down to rest.

April shoved hard against Thad's chest and he looked for a second like he might hit her as he took a step back, but she refilled the gap between them and shoved him again. "I told you to get out of my house."

Thad slapped her hands away when she tried to push him again. "And I told you I'm not leaving until that son of a bitch gives me what he stole."

April turned and stared at Aiden, those jade-green eyes taking him hostage when she did. Ever since the first time she brushed her knuckle down his cheek, she'd had control. The truth of it was she'd had a hold on him long before that, but after that first time, she owned him. She knew it and he knew it and neither one of them seemed to care because both were getting something out of the deal. "Tell me what he's talking about, Aiden McCall."

Aiden looked at her, but did not speak.

"Now," she said.

And though Aiden didn't want to say it, he knew silence wouldn't end the draw. They'd reached a stalemate, and explaining what had happened was the only way he could see the game ending. So Aiden told the story, and after what seemed an eternity, it was all spelled out nice and clear, from the way Wayne Bryson had turned his brain into sausage to how he and Thad had torn out of there before the gunshot finished bouncing around the holler. Aiden said he hid the dope because Thad was going to kill himself with that much crystal in his hands, and Thad told him it was none of his goddamn business. Aiden explained that he knew someone who just might buy that bag outright, that there was at least twenty-five hundred dollars' worth of methamphetamine and that it was a whole lot easier to divide money than drugs. He told Thad that once it was divided, Thad could spend it any way he wanted, and that seemed to suit him just fine. April just stood there listening until he had finished.

"I've only got one question," she said when everything was finally spread on the table and Thad and Aiden had reached some kind of common ground. Her eyebrows scrunched her forehead, and she hooked strands of hair that had fallen and framed her face back behind her ears. "What else you think he had stashed in that house?"

<h1 style="text-align:center">(6)</h1>

THE SUN ALWAYS TOOK ITS PRECIOUS TIME TO SET ON
this place. In the longest days of summer, the sun might dip its yellow face behind the peaks at seven o'clock, an invisible glob of molten orange that dripped behind the mountain, until all that was left
was red, as if a drop of blood had soaked back into the earth on the
other side. That lolling sometimes lasted until nine thirty before the
wick extinguished into darkness. Everything seemed to drag on forever, nothing in any sort of hurry. But it was finally dark.

April watched the taillights of Aiden's Ranchero stare back at her
as the car wound down the drive until they were swallowed completely by the laurels lining the road. She was uncertain of what Aiden
and Thad might find at Wayne Bryson's. It had been unlike her to
make that type of suggestion, just as it was unlike her to say it was
okay to keep the drugs in her house. There was a look of confusion
on Aiden's face when April asked what might have been left behind,
but Thad seemed to think it was the only sense his mother had ever
made. The answer was simple: money. If that bag was worth twenty-

five hundred, then what if there were two bags? Three bags? What if there was a pile of money rolled up in his sock drawer? If Aiden and Thad wound up finding drugs or cash, they'd be that much closer to having what they needed to leave, and them leaving would mean one less thing for her to worry about when she sold the house. Though Thad would've never believed it, April did worry what would happen to him and where he'd go when the trailer was gone. She knew Aiden would be just fine, but there was no telling with Thad.

She could hardly remember Aiden McCall before he came to live there. She knew he'd been missing when Thad brought him out of the woods and put him up in the trailer. She knew he had run away and that the sheriff's office was looking for him, and she knew what his father had done, because it was the gossip all through Little Canada. Even the gaggle of old women at church whispered back and forth in the pews on Sunday mornings about what had happened, saddest thing they'd ever heard. So when Thad brought Aiden home and George Trantham called the law and a convoy of patrol cars came to take Aiden into custody and hand him off to social services, April thought it was probably for the best until she watched it unfold.

When the deputies went onto the porch at the trailer, Thad met them at the door with a .410 shotgun he used to squirrel-hunt. He screamed that they'd have to drag Aiden out of that trailer, but he was just a twelve-year-old. The deputies barged inside and Aiden shot out of the front door and into the brush like a rabbit. After a few minutes, the deputies came out of the woods with muddied uniforms, dragging the boy by his arms.

That night, April convinced George Trantham that letting Aiden stay might keep Thad out of their hair. Maybe if Aiden was around to keep Thad busy, she wouldn't have to relive the darkest hour of her life every time she looked at her son, and maybe George wouldn't get so pissed at Thad that he drank till he couldn't stand, then beat her till she couldn't either. She signed the stack of paperwork and Aiden was back within a few days. From then on, the two boys raised themselves in the trailer, and she stayed cooped in the house until the good Lord finally answered one prayer and ate that drunk son of a bitch up with cancer, killed George Trantham before he could ever hit her again. But the boys were practically grown by then.

When Thad left for Fort Bragg and Aiden stayed behind, she watched him come and go for months before a word was ever spoken between them. She was lonely and he was there, and that's how it started. He'd always been able to make her laugh, and she needed that. One evening, she walked down to the trailer with a plate of food and a bag of weed. They sat on the front steps and passed a joint back and forth while lightning bugs came out of the ground and gradually floated into the trees. After that, she gave him odd jobs and asked him in for supper. She enjoyed his company. She liked the way he made her feel. Aiden wasn't like any man she had ever met. He was polite and timid and always waited for her to say the first word or make the first move, and so one night she did.

After he'd washed the dishes, he sat at the kitchen table smoking a cigarette, and she sidled up behind him and ran her hands down his chest. As he turned toward her, she kissed his ear and his neck, then led him to her bedroom. When it was just the two of them, she almost forgot about everything bad that had happened in that house, everything bad that had ever happened to her on that mountain: from the times in high school when her stomach started to show to the day her parents told her she was dead to them. There were so many things she carried, memories that lay heavy as stone. All of those things stayed bottled and building. All of those things had damn near broken her in two. She welcomed any chance to forget.

(7)

THEY WERE HALFWAY BETWEEN CHARLEYS CREEK AND Booker Branch when Thad finally said, "I want you to look at this," but Aiden did not turn to face him. He kept his eyes on the road ahead and tried to block out the fact that Thad was in the car at all. "You need to look at this, goddamn it," Thad said. And it wasn't so much the sternness of Thad's voice as the clack of metal that grabbed Aiden's attention.

He turned and looked to where Thad had the revolver pointed dead between his eyes, the cylinder opened to the side. Thad spun the wheel and Aiden could see gaps of light flicking by like an old film through the empty chambers.

"There wasn't a thing in it," Thad said. He dug around in the side pocket of his jeans and came out with five cartridges cupped in his palm, those .500s looking as long and fat as Swisher cigars.

"I don't give a fuck!" Aiden yelled. Until then he'd been chewing at the inside of his cheek, nervously trying to figure out what had gotten into April. The dope always made him grind his teeth, that chewing seeming to be some physical thing that tried to keep up with how fast his mind raced. "I don't care if it wasn't loaded, Thad. That's twice today. Two fucking times that somebody has pointed a gun at me. And both of those times the one pointing said, 'Aww, it ain't loaded.'"

"I had the shells in my pocket—"

"I don't care, Thad. Wayne Bryson said the same goddamned thing, and you saw what happened. He blew his brains out."

"Wayne Bryson was an idiot, Aiden. Always has been. You know that," Thad said. "He shot himself in his own leg with a twenty-two when we were in high school. I ain't Wayne Bryson. I know my way around guns and you know it. You know I wouldn't have pointed it at you if it was loaded."

The truth was, Aiden wasn't quite sure whether he knew that or not. He knew Thad was as close a thing to family as he'd ever had and he knew Thad would've regretted anything he'd done just as soon as it happened, but he also knew Thad Broom was just like him, so short-fused that nothing was ever out of the question. There'd never been anything between thought and action with either of them, and that's what Aiden had worked so hard to change. All their lives, they snapped time and time again. A thought would come and they would act. Nothing in between. Not a moment. Not a second thought. Nothing. So Aiden *wasn't* sure Thad wouldn't stick a loaded gun into his forehead. All Aiden knew was that he'd felt the blood run up into his face and his palms go sweaty. All Aiden knew for sure was that his mind was whirling out of control.

"I shouldn't have pointed that gun at you, and I'm sorry, I really am, but you don't know what it's like, Aiden. You *can't* know what it's like. You might like getting fucked up, but mine ain't a want, mine's a need, and that's a big damn difference."

"I'm going to go ahead and tell you right now, Thad, you ever stick a gun in my face again and one of us is going to be burying the other."

"I said I'm—"

"I heard you the first time," Aiden said.

Thad sat rattling the pistol cartridges in his hand like he was about to throw dice, and neither spoke for a good while. They rode along steep highway cut into the side of the mountain, rock face and trees towering to one side, a steep descent into the gorge below. And when the tension finally seemed to have eased just a hair, Thad broke the silence.

"Who you think's got enough money to buy an ounce of dope?"

Aiden glanced over and didn't say anything at first. He knew his answer was one that wouldn't sit well. "Don't worry about it."

"Don't worry about it? You tell me you've got somebody that'll buy a whole ounce of dope, damn near twenty-five hundred dollars' worth of crystal, and then say don't worry about it? Who the fuck's going to buy this shit, Aiden?"

"Leland," Aiden said.

"Bumgarner?" Thad squawked.

"Yeah."

"Goddamn, Aiden, are you kidding me?"

"If there's anybody on this mountain that knows where to unload an ounce of crystal, it'd be Leland."

"And if there's anybody on this mountain that'd fuck his own family over for a dime, it'd be Leland too. That rotten son of a bitch tried to dicker the doctor down when his wife was in the middle of popping out that kid of theirs. I'm telling you we might as well just flush it down the toilet."

"You know anybody else?" Aiden asked. He stared at Thad for a short moment, and when it was obvious there would be no reply, added, "Then Leland's the only shot we've got."

"Just don't say a word when he winds up dicking us over."

"He ain't going to dick us over."

Aiden and Thad knew just how snaky Leland Bumgarner could be because they'd always been friends with him. They'd sat back and laughed as he fucked over everyone from kids at school to his own lazy-eyed mother. Every man has something that makes him tick, and ever since Leland was old enough to pickpocket kids on the bus for nickels, it had been anything that would spend. He and Thad had a mixed history of horse trading and fistfights, and the conclusion Thad drew was that Leland couldn't be trusted. There was no arguing there. Aiden agreed wholeheartedly. But Aiden also understood that Leland was the only chance they had at making money off that bag, let alone money off whatever else they might find lying around Wayne Bryson's house. They were only a mile or so away now and Thad was still shaking those cartridges around in his hand nervously.

"Now, when we get back over there, I want you to stay in the car till I make sure that house is empty," Thad said. "You just stay out in the car and keep an eye out in case somebody comes riding in on us." Thad dropped one of the shells into the floorboard and he hunched over, rummaged through the trash between his feet, and came up with the cartridge pinched between his index finger and thumb, the other four shells still clamped in his hand. "You just wait out in the car and I'll clear the house," he said, half talking to himself as he slid each shell back into its chamber and slapped the cylinder closed with a flick of his wrist. "You understand?"

Aiden just nodded and stared up the road.

In the headlights, two orange eyes glowed in all that darkness like the lit ends of cigarettes, and Aiden couldn't make out if it was a possum or coon dragging a mangled hide of flesh and fur from the roadway. Whatever kind of animal it was slunk into the ditch, nothing more than a high-shouldered shadow, before Aiden could make it out. A thought struck him as he veered to straddle what the animal had dragged between the Ranchero's tires, and he steered on around the next curve. It wasn't just possums and coons that learned to eat what's left behind, that learned to make meals off scraps picked from bone. A man who spends enough time at the bottom learns to do the same. They were all alike in that way. Everything was feeding off another. It's the scavengers that turn predators to prey, he thought, and if a person can't see that, he's probably the one being taken.

WAYNE BRYSON COULDN'T SEE anything anymore. He just lay there by the coffee table on his stomach, his head cocked to the side, exit wound up. Where the bullet had twisted out of him, the flesh was gnarled, skin lapped, folded, and curled around a dark hole, but most of the blood seemed to have dumped from the other side of his head because of how he fell. The blood hadn't so much pooled as thrown a sticky mess across the carpet around him. What poured from the exit wound had washed Wayne's face red, like it might've been painted. His mouth hung open, dumbstruck. His eyes were closed. Aiden was thankful his eyes were closed.

The stereo had been on repeat since they left, the same Drive-By Truckers album still playing. There was no telling how many times it had played through in the hours since, but it was almost finished again. Patterson Hood was singing "Lookout Mountain," and there wasn't but one song after that. Aiden knew this because the last cut on the record had always been his favorite.

When they arrived at Wayne Bryson's, the front door was open, and neither Aiden nor Thad could remember if they'd left it that way. Thad told Aiden, again, just to stay in the car until he'd cleared the house, and Aiden watched Thad go inside. He didn't lower the revolver from the time he was out of the car until he'd checked every room. But only Wayne was there and he was no different from how they'd left him. Aiden and Thad just stood over his body for a second before Thad seemed to remember why they'd come.

"You just going to stand there staring at that son of a bitch or you going to help me?" Thad sidled past and grabbed the tactical rifle Wayne had folded in two from the table, slid that carbine and the digital scales into a black book bag. He and Aiden both brought bags to loot Wayne's house. Aiden's was still empty. Thad knelt between the couch and coffee table, snatched the pump shotgun from the carpet where he'd set it, and held it toward Aiden, pistol grip first, the barrel pointed back toward his own stomach. "Snap out of it and carry something."

Aiden took the shotgun from Thad, let it hang by his side, and Thad scuttled along the floor, running his hand beneath the couch to search for anything hidden. He came up empty-handed and pushed back to his feet. When Thad rounded the table and stood sandwiched between the body and Aiden, he unsheathed an old oak-handled knife that always hung fastened to his belt. That drop-point, Queen fixed-blade was what Aiden had given Thad when he headed off to Fort Bragg. The edge could carve calluses as thin as deli meat. Thad kept the knife that way. Almost every night he swiped the blade against whetstone, never even gave it a chance to lose its edge. He crouched beside the body and ran the blade under the nylon strap lashed over Wayne's shoulder and across his back to just under his opposite arm. Thad pulled the sling tight against the blade, swiped the knife back toward himself, severing the nylon clean in two. Only the buttstock of the assault rifle showed from underneath the body, and that's what Thad grabbed.

"What are you doing?" Aiden hollered. "Don't move him."

"He don't care, Aiden. He's dead." Thad yanked on the rifle and it nudged a little farther from beneath Wayne's body. "Take that pistol out of his hand."

"There ain't no way."

"Get the pistol, for fuck's sake." Thad sat on the carpet, braced the soles of his boots against Wayne's shoulder and ribs, and jerked as hard as he could, as if he were trying to pull a post from the ground. The rifle slid out from underneath Wayne's body, the upper and lower receivers and the hand guard greasy with blood that hadn't had the time or air to dry. Wayne's face skated across the carpet till his neck was cocked at a horrible angle, his whole torso contorting. When the rifle came free it dragged across Thad's pants and shirt, the severed sling painting him with bloodstains.

"You've got blood all over you."

Thad glanced down at himself, then settled his eyes on the pistol in Wayne's hand. "You going to grab that gun or not?"

"No. For God's sake, no!"

"And why the hell not?"

"It's a suicide, Thad, and that don't leave questions, but the minute you take that gun out of his hand, you've got a man with his brains blown out and no reason for it. Now, get up."

Thad stood, walked past Aiden, and turned into the bedroom just ahead of where a bar separated the living room from the kitchen. It wasn't so much a bar as a large opening cut into the wall. From the couch, where Aiden had sat earlier, he'd watched Wayne go through the kitchen to get the drugs. Wayne had moved through quickly and cut into a room that Aiden couldn't make out from that angle, but that's where Wayne got the dope from. That's where the stash would be if he had any more.

Aiden could hear Thad rummaging through Wayne's room, kicking at things on the floor, shuffling papers, and yanking drawers out of the dresser. Aiden only glanced in as he passed. Thad was turning Wayne's room inside out.

The kitchen was floored with yellowed linoleum, indented square tiles framed in green with a picture of arranged fruit centered on each. The linoleum curled against blackened baseboards beneath cabinets washed with a mossy green stain. Wayne's whole kitchen seemed eaten with green: the cabinets wrapping the room, the outlines on tile, even some ivy border running the tops of the walls against the ceiling.

On the stove top next to dirtied cast-iron skillets stacked three high stood the bottle Wayne had used to shake and bake crystal. A two-liter bottle that had the top cut off and turned upside down like a funnel was on the counter beside the stove. Coffee filters had been fitted into the funnel, and Wayne had spooned what he'd cooked into the filters to separate the dope and let it drip-dry. The filters slumped into the bottleneck, all of the liquid having seeped through since they left. The smell that filled his house was concentrated in the kitchen, all of it hovering around that stove top and those bottles. When Aiden breathed through his mouth he could taste it like floor cleaner. He stood there with his eyes watering for a second before he remembered the room behind.

There wasn't a door into the washroom, just a doorway. The small square floor was slopped shin-high with unwashed laundry. Both the washing machine and dryer had lids opened, but nothing inside. A narrow shelf ran above the appliances at eye level on the back wall with an opened box of powdered detergent and a stack of dryer sheets at one end of the shelf. On the other end, two tall olive-drab ammunition cans stood side by side. Aiden closed the dryer lid and set the pump shotgun there, slid the cans down from the shelf. Both were latched shut. Both had the same yellow letters stenciled on the sides:

100 CRTG .50 CAL
LINK M9
BALL M33

He unlatched the first can and opened the lid against a stiff hinge. The inside smelled of dirt and rust the way clumps of bolts and screws come to smell inside coffee cans once time has welded metal together. The can was filled nearly to the brim with blister packs of Sudafed. Aiden had no clue what the medicine would fetch, only that it'd be easy to sell. He latched the can shut and opened the second.

From the looks of it, Wayne Bryson had kept his entire business inside those two cans. Aiden's first thought was how stupid Wayne had been to leave it all out in the open, but then again, he never left his house. His business came to him and his business never left the front room, so anyone who made it to the back of the house would've had to go through him. At that point, it wouldn't much matter what he was hiding.

There were two ziplock bags filled just as heavy with crystal as the one Aiden and Thad had taken. Three rolls of money, bills coiled and banded as wide as beer cans, separated the two bags from a handful of small, square packs already weighed and measured for sale. There were fourteen or fifteen grams ready to serve to any tweaker who had a buck fifty to blow. Aiden was no good at math, but if every one of those packs was a gram, and if both those bags plus the one they already stole each held an ounce, then Wayne Bryson was sitting on nearly a quarter pound of methamphetamine when he put that pistol to his head and pulled the trigger. They'd never get top dollar, but with that cash and that dope, there was more than ten thousand dollars in drugs and money.

As fast as Aiden's mind was already running, the thought of that much money sent him into a panic. He reopened the first canister, dumped the dope and cash on top of the medicine, snapped the can shut, swung it by his side like a briefcase, and headed out the way he'd come. Thad stood over Wayne Bryson's body when Aiden came into the room.

When Thad saw Aiden there, he focused on what Aiden held. Standing at the threshold into the kitchen, Aiden had the shotgun in one hand and the can in the other. "What the hell is that?" Thad asked.

"Everything," Aiden said.

"What do you mean everything?"

"The dope, the money, every-fucking-thing."

Thad stood confused for a moment or two before he recognized the look in Aiden's eyes and knew he meant it, an excitement coming over him then. Aiden was grinding his teeth and could hardly keep still. "Goddamn Lonely Love" was midway through on the Truckers album. It was the last song to play. It was Aiden's favorite song. Thad tore out of the house and the screen door slapped closed behind him. Aiden stepped over Wayne Bryson's body and took one more look at his face, one more look at where his brains had blown out of him.

(8)

THE JURY-RIGGED BRIDGE THAT CROSSED THE HEAD OF Woods Branch might've fallen to pieces when Aiden hit it running wide open out of Wayne Bryson's drive. The warped planks and railroad ties that made up the bridge played like piano keys under the Ranchero's tires, but he never let off and damn sure didn't stop to check for damage. They were nearly back to pavement when Aiden almost ran her over. He thought someone had put a scarecrow in the road when the headlights hit her. Not until she waved her arms did he know she was real.

Aiden slammed on brakes and what little bit of gravel was left on the road kicked into dust that rose and rolled like fiddlehead ferns above them. She waved her hands to try and keep the dirt out of her face, but it didn't help. She just stood there coughing.

They'd never met, but Aiden recognized her from earlier. Julie Dietz was one of the lankiest women he'd ever seen. She might've dressed out at a hundred pounds, but that weight was stretched in every direction. Her shoulders stayed curled back, arms half bent in front of her. A purple tank top that looked like it was made for a child was fitted around her chest. The shirt rode high and showed off loose skin that looked like it was melting down her stomach. She wore cut-off blue jean shorts that should've fit tightly but didn't. Pencil-thin legs stabbed at the ground like stilts as she walked up to the car and placed one hand on the hood.

"Where the hell did she come from?" Thad asked.

"I ain't got a clue." Aiden revved the engine and lurched forward a few inches, nudging her a little farther down the gravel. They were past the houses on Booker Branch, the lights from a single trailer up the hillside the only sign of anyone within earshot, so Aiden wasn't worried about drawing attention. He laid on the horn and Julie winced, then he rolled down the window and slapped hard against the outside of the door yelling, "Get the fuck out of the road," but still she didn't move.

"Hold on a second, Aid," Thad said, opening the door to step outside. "Let's at least see what she wants."

"We ain't got time for this. We got to get the fuck out of here."

"It won't take a second," Thad said, and before Aiden could respond, he was already out of the car.

Aiden couldn't hear what was being said, but he could see the way that Julie was smiling, the way she slipped her hand onto Thad's stomach, and that shit-eating grin that immediately came over Thad's face. His first thought was to drive off, tires spinning, and leave both of them standing there in the dust, but he'd never left Thad behind, not once in their good-for-nothing lives. No matter how deep things got, it had always been the two of them, and no matter how bad Aiden wanted to, he would not leave him now.

Julie pointed to someplace up the ridge, and Thad turned to look where the trailer lights were shining through pin oaks and poplar.

She walked over to the edge of the road and Thad came around to where the passenger-side door stood open.

"I'll be back in a minute," Thad said, reaching in for his pack of cigarettes and shaking one loose into his lips.

"What the hell do you mean you'll be back in a minute, Thad? Get in the goddamned car and let's go."

"Won't take a minute, I swear," Thad said. He grabbed the lighter from the bench seat and struck fire to the end of his cigarette, his face lit a bright yellow for a brief moment.

"Get in the car and let's get the hell out of here," Aiden pleaded, but nothing.

"I'm just running up there to her house right quick." Thad pointed up the hill. "It's right there. Hell, you can see it from here. I'll be back in a second."

"Goddamn it!" Aiden yelled, hammering his fists against the steering wheel, but Thad was already gone.

They pushed through a thicket of laurel at the road's edge, and Aiden watched as they weaved back and forth up the ridge along a game trail to where the lights were shining. The creek cut away from the road, but Aiden could still hear water moving over stone somewhere down in the woods where Thad and Julie disappeared up the hill. Aiden didn't like how still the night had suddenly become. He didn't like being trapped there waiting. He was jumpy and felt like he was being watched. Sounds became more startling. He felt exposed. His mind flashed to all sorts of scenarios: What if some tweaker came up to the window with a pistol? What if Julie was just a diversion, and all of this was a setup? What if the law was hiding and spotlights flashed the woods into a sudden brightness and the bulls came barreling off the hillside as if from out of the sun?

The ammo can and guns were locked in a toolbox that stretched across the bed of the Ranchero, and Aiden thought it might be wise to step outside, grab one of those guns, and get ready. He didn't know what he would do when it unfolded, what might happen when the pin hit the shell. All he knew for certain was that he was absolutely scared to death, and he sat there clenching the steering wheel as hard as he could, his knuckles like white stones as he stared into the darkness ahead.

(9)

HALFWAY UP THE HILLSIDE JULIE DIETZ SPUN AROUND and pressed so close to Thad's chest that he was sure she was going to kiss him. He was about to try when she raised one finger to his mouth, bit her bottom lip, and slid her other hand down the front of his jeans.

"You sure you've got enough for all of us?" Julie asked.

"There's plenty," Thad said. He could feel all the blood leaving his head and pumping down to where she held him.

"Show it to me," Julie said, tightening her grip around him.

"It's in the car." Thad smiled, but Julie just squinted her eyes and shook her head.

"You better not be playing with me."

"I ain't playing with you at all."

"Exactly how much y'all got?" Julie prodded.

Thad's mind started to go places it had not gone in some time, and for a second or two he almost forgot where he was and what he was doing. "We need to get on up that hill," he said. "You grab that friend of yours and you'll see exactly what we've got."

Julie smiled like she knew she had him, pulled her hand back out of his pants, and the two of them made their way up the hillside out of the woods onto a scraggly strip of yard to the trailer. When they reached the small square of decking boards and stood in the porch light, Thad breathed against her ear. "Hurry up in there. I ain't waiting much longer."

Julie grabbed Thad's hand and leaned back until he was the only thing keeping her from falling. She laughed and let go, opened the door, and went inside, and Thad turned his back against the trailer. He had his head to the side, ear pressed against the metal so that he could hear the muffled television and Julie's voice.

That night in Wilmington Thad told Aiden about was the last time a woman had touched him. That had been almost six years before. Thinking back on it, Thad knew that even that night was a fluke. Maybe the girl had been looking to get back at her old man or maybe she just wanted to fuck, but she walked into the bar that night looking for someone to take back to her bed and there hadn't been but three men in the whole place to choose from. One was Chaz Johnson, who had a birthmark that painted half his face purple, and she wouldn't hardly look at him. Todd Cunningham, a farm boy from Alabama with muscles that carved shadows into his shirt, would have probably been her first choice, but he was head down on the table, drooling out of the corner of his mouth. That left Thad, and so he went home with her, and though it hadn't been all that good and she passed out sometime in the middle, she was the one he thought about the whole time he was gone. There were nights he wondered if she remembered him, and other nights that he just didn't care.

Julie came outside and introduced Thad to her friend. Her name was Meredith, and she pulled the door shut as she stepped onto the narrow porch. She whipped a long braided ponytail that hung down her back like rope across her shoulder. A loose T-shirt hung over her like a nightgown and almost covered the ragged pair of cotton boxers she wore for shorts. Her legs were welted with mosquito bites, maybe fleabites, maybe just scabs, but whatever it was speckled her shins with dark pocks. Looking her over, Thad wished he'd just told Julie to hop in the car when he had the chance. But it was too late to turn back so he just led them down the hill.

Meredith smiled at Aiden with a mouthful of tobacco-stained teeth as she slid in beside him on the bench seat, her dimpled thigh nudging against his leg. Thad took the window and Julie climbed onto his lap, and he slammed the door, packing the four of them inside the cab like potted meat. The engine cranked and Aiden hit the headlights and Thad watched as Meredith put her hand on Aiden's knee and ran her way up his leg. Aiden turned with a look like he just might kill them all, but Thad laughed and gave a lazy wink. He moved his hand under the front of Julie Dietz's shirt and said, "These girls say they want to party."

JULIE DIETZ WAS down to her panties and strutted around the trailer like a lanky crane as soon as they hit the door. She plopped beside Thad onto the stained couch and crossed her legs, stroked her hand along his spine, and flipped her hair out of her face. Loretta Lynn stood by Julie's ankles and watched her curiously.

Thad slid his license out of his billfold and rolled a dollar bill into a straw, set them side by side on the table in front of him where the revolver lay. He lit a cigarette from his pack and blew a heavy cloud of smoke into the center of the room.

"Let me get one of those," Meredith said from the edge of a ladderback chair between the couch and kitchen. She hunched over with her elbows rested on her knees.

Thad shook a cigarette free, just the filter extended from the open end of the pack, and offered it toward her. Meredith snatched the whole pack out of his hand, bit the butt between her teeth, and tilted her head back until the cigarette was free.

"Lighter," she said, her eyes wide and brow raised, as if even having to ask were some great burden.

An orange Bic was on the table, and Thad threw it like a dart into her shoulder. She sneered and leaned down to retrieve it from the floor, lit her smoke, and tossed the lighter back into his lap without ever saying a word. With his face toward the ceiling, Thad leaned back and rubbed his hands anxiously along his thighs.

The door opened and Aiden stood over the threshold with his right hand balled into a fist outstretched into the room.

"You ain't coming in?"

Aiden shook his head no, but didn't speak.

"Well, shit, Aid." Thad rose from the couch and ashed his cigarette onto the floor, a tiny speck of fire smoldering on the carpet for a second before burning out. He walked over to where Aiden stood and spoke with his cigarette jumping about his mouth. "What gives?"

Aiden looked past Thad to where Julie sat on the couch, then cut his eyes over to Meredith, who was drawing puffs of smoke like she was at a poker table, a long fingernail of ash curving from the end of her cigarette. Aiden still didn't say a word.

"You girls make yourselves comfortable," Thad said, looking back into the room as he ushered Aiden onto the porch and pulled the door behind him.

"You got anything to drink in here?" Meredith shouted just before the door shut.

Thad poked his head inside. "There's water in the sink," he said, shooing her toward the kitchen.

He and Aiden stood on the porch as Meredith tromped her way across the inside of the trailer. The scratchy drone of crickets hummed everywhere, as if the night were comprised from that sound.

"What's wrong with you?" Thad asked.

"I think you've lost your mind bringing those two down here."

"Why?"

"You don't know them two from Adam."

"What the hell you think's going to happen?"

"I'll tell you exactly what might happen. They could rob you blind, or more than likely walk around getting a good look at everything and then talk somebody else into robbing us. They could get picked up for something petty and go telling the law anything to keep from getting pinched."

"They ain't going to rat on us."

"And why the hell not?" Aiden's voice was suddenly loud, and he clenched his teeth as if to try and keep his voice down so the girls inside wouldn't hear. "You tell me one good reason why those two in there wouldn't rat us out to keep themselves out of trouble. Hell, everybody on this shit goes to blabbing before they're even cuffed up. What makes you think them two's different?"

Thad didn't answer.

"All I know is there ain't anything good coming out of this."

"You worry too much, Aid." Thad smirked. "Ain't nothing going to happen."

"What about that other girl? What you going to do with her when you're in there with that scrawny one?"

"What about her?" Thad shook his head and laughed. "I sure ain't about to roll her around in flour and find the wet spot, Aid. Is that what you think?"

Aiden stood there with a look on his face like he thought Thad was the dumbest person on the face of the earth.

"Ain't nothing going to happen tonight except for a good time." Thad held out his hand and waited for Aiden to give up what was clenched in his fist. Thad felt like he could do anything. When he wasn't high, life seemed fenced in, but on dope, the world opened up. Everything felt good for a little while. He smiled at Aiden and laughed. "Hell, I bet that big girl in there would let you run it right up her pipe chute. No questions asked."

Aiden didn't laugh. He just dropped the bag into Thad's palm.

"You ain't a lick of fun no more."

"And you've turned into about the dumbest son of a bitch I know," Aiden said.

"What the hell's that supposed to mean?"

"It means you need to grow the fuck up."

"There ain't nothing wrong with letting your hair down. All these years you'd have been right there beside me, and now look at what she's turned you into." Thad pointed up the hillside to his mother's house. "She's done turned you pussy."

"You're twenty-four years old and still acting like we're in tenth grade."

"That's exactly right. I'm twenty-four years old." Thad stood there shaking his head.

Aiden looked at him and Thad thought for a second that Aiden was going to say something, but he didn't. He just rubbed his forehead and stared at moths that orbited the porch light like dusty planets around some electric sun. Without muttering a sound, Aiden turned and headed down the steps and crossed the yard to the Ranchero. Thad watched him take the book bag filled with guns over his shoulder, the ammo can held by his side as he slammed the lid of the truck box. April's lights were on up the hill and Aiden headed toward them.

For the life of him, Thad couldn't understand why Aiden was so worried. Wayne Bryson was dead, but it wasn't like they had anything to do with it. He and Aiden hadn't done a thing other than take what would have wound up in an evidence locker when the cops found the body, and that's chancing some of the scabs right there along Booker Branch wouldn't have wandered in and made off with it themselves. Dumb luck. Nothing more than dumb luck.

There wasn't a reason in the world to let Aiden's mopey ass ruin a good time. There was a bag of dope in his hand, he was already halfway to the moon, and now there was a girl inside who wanted to party. He hadn't been with a woman in six years, six fucking years. She might just be the best he'd ever had, he thought. Julie Dietz might know things that'd make him forget there'd ever been anyone but her.

(10)

APRIL LEANED OVER THE BATHROOM SINK WITH HER nose just inches from the mirror and stared, puzzled, by the way she'd fallen apart. She wondered what had happened to the girl who was pretty, the one who was chosen homecoming queen at Smoky Mountain High that first year after Camp Lab and Sylva-Webster merged into one school. That was twenty-two years ago now, and seemed like another life altogether.

Raising her eyebrows, she watched the furrows crease her forehead, then smiled a fake smile to see how the lines cut her cheeks. Her mother had always told her that cigarettes did something different to women. We wear it on the outside, she'd said, those words some cruel omen come true. A small jar of Maybelline was on the sink, and April dabbed her fingers, rubbed the aging cream onto her cheeks, then wiped it down her face with opened hands. She tried to smile again, but it was just the same sad face. She almost felt like crying but didn't. She just lit a cigarette and blew the smoke against the ceiling above.

The front door opened and April leaned into the hallway and saw

Aiden make his way through the front room toward the kitchen. He was on the phone with someone, his voice low and indiscernible. All she had on was a T-shirt, so she went into the bedroom to throw on a pair of shorts. Though she'd never say it, she was happy to see him. Aiden always made her feel good about herself, and even if those feelings were short-lived, it beat the hell out of how she felt right then.

In the living room, a cheap desk catty-cornered a wall that separated the room from the kitchen. April leaned down and shook the computer mouse to wake the screen on her desktop. There were no Facebook notifications, but she wasn't surprised. The only reason she used Facebook at all was to spy on people she'd grown up with, to glimpse into lives that made her jealous. There'd been a time when everyone was jealous of her. She opened a second tab in the browser to cover the smiling faces of *friends* in her newsfeed and to search for a Dolly Parton playlist on YouTube. In April's mind, Dolly was the ideal woman: strong, beautiful, independent, fearless. She was from just over the ridgeline in Tennessee and represented all of the things that April believed she might have been capable of if the circumstances had been different, if the world hadn't been so set in stone.

April was raised to believe women had roles, and they were primarily to meet a man, settle down, and give him children, preferably boys, bread earners. The mountains had started to change now and girls were going off to college, some even leaving for good, but that wasn't the case when April was growing up. When she got pregnant with Thad at eighteen and there wasn't a man taking responsibility, her life was pegged. She was used goods, an eighteen-year-old kid trying to raise a baby she couldn't bear to look at. April clicked a video of Dolly singing a duet of "Just Someone I Used to Know" on

The Porter Wagoner Show, cranked the volume on the computer speakers until all she could hear was the song.

When she came into the kitchen, Aiden was slapping twenty-dollar bills onto the table and the bills curled from how they'd been rolled together. The tabletop was nearly covered with money and he was adding more to the pile as quickly as he could count, but she was fixed on the bags of dope.

"Who was that on the phone?" April asked. She sidled up behind him and ran her hands down his chest.

"The boy I'm hoping can get rid of this."

"You really think he'll buy it?"

"Leland wouldn't say it on the phone, but he told me to meet him at his house tomorrow, and if there's anybody in the world that can move this shit, it'd be him."

"Who's Leland?" She slid her hands up his chest, then rubbed his shoulders for a second before she took the seat beside him.

"Leland Bumgarner," he said. "Me and Thad went to school with him and then I worked with him on some jobs. Runs an excavating business, but he can sell anything. He'll know how to get rid of it."

"What's it worth?" she asked. Leaning across the table, she picked up one of the bags and noticed how the crystal looked like shards of glass cupped in her hand. She'd seen Aiden on dope a dozen times, watched him split locust posts for a week straight, high as a kite, but she'd never actually held meth in her hands.

"I know what I think it's worth but we won't get that. We'll be lucky to get half."

"How come?" she asked as she slid the bag back across the table.

"Because we'd have to sell it ourselves to get all the money out of it. Anybody buying that much dope ain't looking to use it. They're looking to sell it. And so Leland's going to dicker us down as low as he can to get more on the back end, and that's fine by me. The faster we get rid of it the better."

"You don't think you could hold out, see if you can't get a little more out of it?"

"We keep this more than a week and Thad'll get us locked the hell up," Aiden said. "Hell, he's down there right now laid up with two girls from Booker Branch."

"He's got what?"

"He's got two skanks piled in that trailer that are liable to steal anything he's got, or worse yet get the law called. I bet he ain't been to sleep in a week."

"Jesus, Aiden. You need to get them out of—"

"I've tried. For God's sake, I've tried. But he won't listen." Aiden was still counting money, his eyes cutting back and forth as he muttered numbers under his breath. "Damn it!" he yelled and threw a handful of wadded bills onto the table. "I can't keep count! I keep losing fucking count!"

"Well then just don't worry about that right now." April leaned over and put her hand on top of his, traced across his knuckles with the tips of her fingers.

Aiden glanced over at her, but didn't say anything. She could tell how quickly his thoughts were racing. She could see it in his eyes, and when she realized he wouldn't speak, she took his hands and guided them onto her face and neck. She watched as his expression turned to a different type of confusion, then she stood, still holding on to his hands, and guided him to his feet as if they were about to dance. He leaned in to kiss her, but she pulled away and led him out of the kitchen toward the bedroom just like the very first time. She told herself she was doing this for him, but that wasn't true. Maybe part of it was about Aiden. Part of it was about getting his mind off things, calming him down. But it was just as much because having someone touch her the way that Aiden did would make her forget how she'd felt just minutes before. She needed him right then. As shitty as it might've been, she needed him to make her feel worth something.

Piano and pedal steel guitar harmonized with Dolly Parton for the opening of "It's Too Late to Love Me Now," as April showed Aiden into her bedroom, flicking on the light switch, and sliding out of her clothes so quickly that there seemed to be no transition from clothes to skin. She pulled his hand onto her breasts and he fumbled hopelessly with his belt as she lay back on the bed. Then he was on top of her and April winced at how it hurt for just a second when he pushed inside. She gasped and he said he was sorry, but she just settled her thighs into his ribs, interlocked her ankles at the base of his back, and pulled him deeper.

April called him "sweet one." Every man she'd ever been with had forced himself onto her. Every man she'd ever been with had hit her. But Aiden seemed almost scared to touch her. He was unlike any man she'd ever met. The way he spoke to her and the way he waited for her permission gave her control. She felt powerful when she was around him, and that was a feeling that she'd never known. Even hurried by drugs that seemed to have his body moving in some frantic pace that his mind couldn't keep up with, he was gentle.

Just before he came, Aiden pulled out and rolled onto his back and lay there with his toes curling and legs trembling against the bed. He panted for air and stared at the ceiling, finally standing up when his senses seemed to return. Cupping his hand at his stomach so as not to make a mess, he hobbled into the bathroom. She clenched a pillow tight against her chest and didn't move.

When he came back to bed, she curled against him. She nuzzled into his chest and felt him bury his face into the top of her head, her hair smelling like mint. He breathed deeply through his nose and kissed the crown of her head. They lay there for a while in silence, and only when his legs quit shaking did she move.

April leaned across him and opened a drawer on the nightstand beside the bed. A glass pipe still filled with half a bowl pack from earlier that afternoon was in the drawer, and she felt around until she found the lighter and took them out for a nightcap. She sat up and struck fire to the bowl, took a long drag, let her thumb off the carb, and squinted as she held her breath. There was hardly any smoke left when she finally exhaled. She offered the bowl to Aiden but he said he didn't want any. His heart was beating wildly in his chest and she could hear it as she settled her head back against him. April asked where Aiden wanted to go once he had the money to leave, and he told her that he wanted to move to Asheville, but that it didn't much matter so long as there were mountains and so long as it wasn't here.

"You ever noticed how turkeys make a big circle?" he asked.

She shook her head no.

"Well, turkeys have this way of making a big loop that might take them a month or so round trip," he explained. "They might start in a field down there in Tuckasegee and wander up into a cove off Rich Mountain, then make their way along the ridgeline to Wolf and follow the river back down to where they started. You can sit right there in that field, and if you'll wait long enough, right there they'll come."

"I don't know what you're getting at," April said. She lifted her head from his chest and looked into his eyes.

"We ain't all that different's what I'm saying. All of us are just scraping by until we make our way back to where we started," Aiden said. "But for me that circle ain't ever been wide enough. What happens to turkeys if they don't have a big enough spread is they either run out of things to eat or they make easy pickings, but either way it ends the same."

The way he made it sound like his life was determined was comical to her, and she almost told him he didn't know a thing about it. He wasn't but twenty-four years old, maybe twenty-five. Just wait till you pass forty and the best years of your life are behind you and you've never been off this mountain before you start talking about a place not being big enough. But she didn't say it. She wouldn't say that to him. He just didn't know any different.

The fact that he was so young was part of the reason April didn't want to tell him the news. She didn't know how he was going to take it. She knew what Thad would say, but not Aiden. Either way, she didn't want to tell him right then. He already had too much on his mind and the day had been too long. Tomorrow she would paint the only other room in the house that needed painting, because, the day after, the real estate agent was bringing someone by to look at the property. No one had come to look at the house in months and she'd almost given up on the idea, almost decided that after forty years maybe she ought to just call a spade a spade. Finally she had something to hope for again. If she could sell the place, she was gone.

April looked up at Aiden and he was staring straight at the wall with a look like he was trying to solve some great mystery. "I just don't know if I can get Thad to go," he said after a few minutes of just sitting there.

"You don't need to get Thad to go."

"Of course I do," Aiden said.

"Why?" she asked, as if what he was saying made no sense at all.

"Because it's always been me and him," he said. "Always has."

"And things change, Aiden. People change." She sat up and took another hit from the bowl. "Look at me. You don't see me hanging out with any of the people I grew up with, do you? You grow up and you grow apart and that's just the way things happen. Twenty-four is a lot different than fifteen and forty's a whole lot different than twenty-four and that's all right."

"I ain't going anywhere without him."

"That's just silly," she said. "He sure went off and left you and didn't think a thing of it."

"That was different," he said, and she could tell that she'd struck a nerve. "I couldn't go with him."

"And that still didn't stop him from going, now, did it?"

"Well, no."

"And that's what I'm saying, Aiden."

"What's that?"

"That sometimes you have to do things for yourself, entirely for yourself. You'll waste your life waiting around on somebody else."

"You're one to talk," he said angrily.

"What's that supposed to mean?"

"It means for someone who sat around getting the shit kicked out of her her whole life, that's the pot calling the kettle—"

"Don't start that."

"I'm just saying. You want to talk about doing something for yourself."

"You ain't got a clue why I made the choices I made." There was a slight smirk on her face as she shook her head. "Now, I don't want to fight with you. Not tonight."

She had been sleeping in the bed she made for a long time. It hadn't started off as a choice. When she kept her mouth closed the way she'd been told to do, her parents disowned her. It was shameful enough for a girl that age to get knocked up when she wasn't married, but it was unforgivable the way she kept that secret. Her parents left Little Canada and there April was, just a kid with a kid, so when George Trantham came along and offered some kind of out, she took it, partly for her and partly for Thad. Waiting on folks at Waffle House wasn't any sort of living, and so maybe she did have to take things that no woman deserved to take from that asshole, but it beat scraping by. April didn't want to think about that, though. She was tired.

Settling her head against his chest, April ran her hand across his stomach and asked Aiden if he could go anywhere on earth where it would be, but he didn't know. He was wide awake, but it didn't take her long to doze off against him, her mind washing back and forth between consciousness and dream. Aiden ran his fingers through her hair, and that felt nice, and she slipped further to sleep. In one of the last flashes of thought before she drifted off, she shifted her head against him until she was comfortable and asked, "What about if you could have anything in this world, what would you want, sweet one?" He didn't answer right away and she was quickly dreaming.

"Family," he finally said. "Family."

But she was already asleep. She never heard a word.

(11)

HALF AN HOUR INTO FUCKING JULIE DIETZ FOR THE fourth time that night, Thad knew he could keep on driving into that train wreck until the cows came home and it wasn't going to do him a lick of good. Those first two times he came easy, but by the third go he was pounding Julie Dietz more out of sheer boredom than anything else. And, looking down on her now, listening to her wheeze and moan like some dying animal, Thad was pretty sure this was a wasted effort.

A low blue glow came through the curtains and it wouldn't be long before the sun was up. Thad stared at the wall and tried to conjure some image that would get him off, but that sunlight had made him lose focus. He turned back to Julie, who squirmed beneath him. She clenched the sheets in her fists behind her and shook her head wildly as her rib-slatted torso contorted away from the mattress. He thought for a second that, given the right circumstances, she could've been pretty, but the dope had eaten her alive. Thinking that, he just felt sorry for her so he pulled out altogether and left her lying on the bed.

In the living room, Meredith was sprawled on the couch staring at the ceiling, but wallowed up when Thad came into the room. She squinted her eyes, then opened them wide, as if to try and decide if Thad was real or just some redheaded hallucination. Thad shook his head and wandered into the kitchen. He opened one of the cabinets and reached behind a bag of cornmeal to where he'd hidden a Slim Jim beef jerky from Aiden a few weeks back. He wasn't so much hungry as just knew he needed to eat something. Thad peeled the wrapper back, bit the beef stick between his teeth like he was chomping a cigar, and slapped the cabinet door closed.

"Where the hell was you hiding them?" Meredith shouted. She'd just lit a cigarette and tossed the pack and lighter onto the table in front of the couch before leaning back to get comfortable.

"I ain't have but one," Thad said.

"You got any more?"

"You deaf or something?" Thad stood there looking confused. He could hear Julie blowing her nose in the bathroom as he chewed a bite and loped into the living room. He grabbed his pack of cigarettes from the table and tried to shake one loose, but the pack was empty. "You smoke every cigarette I had?" Thad asked.

Meredith just sat there with a look on her face like so-what-the-fuck-if-I-did and took a long drag.

"You better hope to God there's another pack out in the car," he said, slipping his feet into his boots by the table before heading for the door.

There was a slight chill in the air outside even though it was the middle of August. Thad headed down the steps and tromped across dew-covered grass to where Aiden's Ranchero was parked in the yard. They always kept a carton of cigarettes slid under the bench seat, but there weren't any left, so Thad checked the packs littered around the floorboard and came up empty. There wasn't a thing in that car but an ashtray piled high with stubbed-out butts and one half-smoked Doral 100 that Aiden had left burning when he went into the Sylva Roses a month before. Stale as hell, but it'd do, he thought. Thad lit what was left with a lighter on the dash, slammed the car door, and headed back inside.

Julie Dietz stood in her underwear by the edge of the couch with twisted wads of toilet paper shoved into her nose. Thad walked in right in the middle of something, both Julie and Meredith going still as stone with eyes wide when he barged through the front door. Julie had just handed something to Meredith as Thad came in, and now Meredith was doing everything she could to keep it cupped in her hand so that he couldn't see.

"What are you doing, baby?" Julie asked, and as Thad turned to face her he caught Meredith, out of the corner of his eye, try to slip whatever she was holding into the waistline of her boxers.

When Thad looked over at Meredith, he could see the corner of the bag of dope peaking out of her waistline. He turned to the table to try and find the one thing he'd need, but it wasn't there.

"What's wrong, baby?" Julie asked.

And all of a sudden Thad remembered that he'd taken that revolver into the bedroom to be on the safe side. Aiden was right all along. A man couldn't trust a soul in this world.

(12)

THE FIRST SHOT SOUNDED RIGHT OUTSIDE THE HOUSE.
Aiden had been staring at the ceiling all night and was delirious as he
threw back the shades to April's bedroom window and saw Thad
standing in his boots and underwear on the porch of his trailer waving the long, shiny revolver above his head like he was flagging traf-
fic. Julie Dietz and the fat girl were in the yard. Julie was doing her
damnedest to pull clothes over her bones, while Thad yelled something too muffled to make out from inside the house. April had just
gotten up and was in the shower singing "My Blue Ridge Mountain
Boy" at the top of her lungs.

The gun's report had barely finished bouncing around the cove
when Aiden came onto the stoop. The second shot hit the ground
like artillery just to the right of Meredith's feet, and Aiden heard the
bullet whiz up past April's house and bury in the hillside by the radio
tower.

That's when Julie Dietz rushed Thad. She made it up two steps
before he kicked her right square in the stomach and sent her sliding

on her side across dew-covered grass. His boot came off as he kicked, and though she coughed like she just might hurl, Julie Dietz crawled in a frenzy, grabbed Thad's boot from the base of the steps, and threw it out into the yard. That's when the third shot came. Grass and dirt clods blew up just on the far side of where Julie Dietz stood. She twisted and grabbed her left arm.

The bullet must've winged her because she didn't go down, but she screamed, "You shot me! You shot me!"

"Next one's between the eyes!"

Loretta Lynn was on the porch beside Thad and she yapped as loud as the rest of them. Julie kept screaming, "You shot me! You shot me!" and Loretta Lynn darted down the steps, bit into Julie's ankle, and started to tug at her leg like a rope. Julie punted Thad's dog into the side of the trailer, and Loretta Lynn thudded against the aluminum like a dirty snowball. The pup limped back onto the porch, panting so hard that it looked like she might trip over her own tongue. The dog had one burst in her and was spent.

Aiden knew Thad wouldn't have exploded so violently if Julie Dietz had stabbed April thirty-seven times in the stomach with a shiv, but the fact that she'd touched Loretta Lynn pushed him over. He marched down the steps and into the yard in nothing but that yellow-tinged underwear. Hobbling with one untied boot, he rose and sank with each set of strides. She cowered just as he hammered the barrel of that pistol across the side of her face. She was on the ground and he straddled her around the rib cage, slapped his empty hand back and forth about her face as if he were shooing flies. Julie's head flipped side to side with no restraint. She was unconscious.

Aiden had almost forgotten about Meredith until then. The girl had the size for middle linebacker at any school in the SEC, and when she blindsided Thad in the back, he howled in pain. The two of them rolled around in the grass for a second or two before she mounted him and rammed him again with her shoulder as he tried to regain ground.

Thad no longer had the gun. Meredith had knocked the revolver loose when she tackled him. From where he stood, Aiden couldn't see it, but the revolver had to be on the ground somewhere near where Julie lay cold in the yard. Up until then, he'd kind of enjoyed watching it unfold. He'd warned Thad to tell those girls to shove off and Thad hadn't listened. But the fact that the gun was no longer in his hands left the door open to disaster. The fact that any minute Julie Dietz could come to and find that revolver right beside her with two more shells to give meant things could turn ugly fast. It wouldn't take but one squeeze of the trigger to field-dress him, leave his brains and blood dripping down the side of that trailer like rust stains running from screws.

Meredith hammered away at Thad's face as Aiden started barefoot down the hill. Damp grass squished between his toes and his heels sank into the soft ground that rose between the trailer and house. The driveway cut a wide switchback around the hill, but he walked that slope at least twice a day, having long since scored a trail into the ground. He was almost down the bank when Julie Dietz squirmed on her back like a waking baby. She rolled onto her side and found the revolver within reach. Julie took the gun in both hands as she staggered to her feet, and Aiden jumped the split rail fence and rushed to catch her.

Slowly making her way to where Thad was being pounded, Julie aimed as best she could, and Aiden got to her just before she reached them. He grabbed hold of her wrists and lifted the gun into the sky. She pulled the trigger and a bullet fired off into the fog, the barrel hammering back into her forehead, her wrists too small to handle the recoil. Digging his fingers into the tendons of her wrist, Aiden forced her grip loose. He took control of the revolver, shoved her to the ground, drew sights where she lay, and told her to stay put. Tears and blood streamed down her face. Her left eye had already begun to swell, a mound of tight, shiny flesh along that whole side. Blood ran down her arm where the bullet had grazed her. Fear turned her into a statue.

Aiden walked behind Meredith and pressed the barrel into the base of her skull. "That's enough," he said. She clobbered Thad once more across the face and Aiden jabbed the barrel into the soft place at the tip of her spine. The click of the revolver being cocked froze her solid. "I said that's enough."

Her hands pressed into Thad's shoulders, pinning him to the ground, and she stayed there panting until Aiden told her to rise. He thought it amazing how slow people moved when a gun is aimed at them. She came off the ground and he kept his distance in case she got stupid. Aiden ordered Meredith to stand beside Julie, and Meredith did as she was told. Thad was on his hands and knees beside him.

"The two of you need to just get the hell on out of here," Aiden said. No one spoke another word. He just motioned down the drive with the pistol.

Julie Dietz spit a thick line of blood in front of her, wiped her mouth with the back of her hand, the whole left side of her face swollen ripe as a purple tomato. Meredith was still sucking air. They both turned and trod down the gravel. The fog held tight to the mountain and the morning sun shone like a flashlight through smoke. Aiden never took the gun off of them until they disappeared behind the laurels hedging the drive.

"What the hell happened?" Aiden asked.

"That scraggly bitch was trying to steal what was left of that gram you give me." Thad was resting on his knees, trying to brush the grass from his arms and shoulders. He winced and rubbed at his back. "She gave it to that fat one and that fat one shoved it down her britches."

"That girl was giving you a run for your money." Aiden started to laugh and Thad stuck out his jaw with anger.

"Well, goddamn, that bitch had me by a hundred pounds. Easy."

"That she did."

"That Julie hit me in the back with a frying pan when I was inside. I'm telling you I can't hardly get up."

"She hit you with a frying pan?"

"Why, yes. Goddamn cast iron," Thad said. He stood up and walked over to where his boot lay at the base of the trailer, and Loretta Lynn hopped down the steps to stand at his side. "Then when that fat'n hit me . . ." Thad stood there shaking his head and rubbing at the base of his back. "I'm telling you my back is about to give out."

Aiden reached into his pants pocket and drew out his pack of smokes. He lit one and started to laugh.

"It ain't funny."

"I don't know about that." Aiden held out his pack of cigarettes and offered one to Thad. "You've got to admit, that's pretty damn funny."

"What?" Thad took one of the USA Golds and bit the filter between his teeth.

"That girl having you on the ground about to beat your ass." Aiden laughed so hard he could hardly get the words out. "I told you those two were trouble."

"Well, you was right, by God." Thad huffed through his nose and smiled as he shook his head. He walked over to the steps and sat down on the edge of the porch. Loretta Lynn put her front paws on his leg and leaned up toward his face to get him to pet her. "Did you ever talk to Leland?" Thad asked.

"Yeah," Aiden said.

And the two of them just sat there smoking cigarettes as the sun burned off the morning.

(13)

TWO BARE-CHESTED BOYS WITH MUDDIED ELBOWS AND scabbed knees wrestled each other on a lopsided trampoline missing a third of its springs in Leland Bumgarner's front yard. The older boy had the little one by at least twenty pounds and was wringing a head-lock deep into his kid brother's neck. But what the little one lacked in size he made up for with sheer meanness. He trudged forward with bare feet kneading into the trampoline till his older brother back-stepped onto a drooping crescent of mesh, the two of them collaps-ing into the mud like a trapdoor had just opened beneath them.

"Cut that shit out now," Leland hollered from the porch, "before one of you breaks something we can't afford to fix." Leland's brow held his eyes in shadow. The two boys cut the horseplay long enough to offer a quick "Yes, sir," before going back to pushing one another when their father refocused on sharpening a lawn mower blade with a bastard-cut mill file.

Leland Bumgarner could sell ice to an Eskimo, or fire in hell. He'd always been that way. Growing up, him, Aiden, and Thad all rode the same school bus, and Leland would talk kids out of the best things their miserable lives offered. If a kid got a new Case XX for his birthday—carbon blade, jigged bone handle, the whole nine—Leland would dicker that son of a bitch out of it with nothing more than a busted flashlight, always something dopey. He had a way of convincing folks that what they had wasn't nearly as good as what he could give them, and someone who has that type of magic-bean salesmanship always has the upper hand. That's why Leland came to mind when Aiden thought about selling the dope and medicine.

Leland crinkled an empty can of Milwaukee's Best in his fist and tossed it onto the steps. He sat on the edge of the porch and kicked his heels against shabby lattice that fenced off dusty clay beneath the house. He pulled a few strokes down a goatee that hung to his chest, a habit he repeated over and over when he was in thought, then set back into filing the lawn mower blade without even acknowledging that Aiden and Thad were there.

"How you doing, Leland?" Aiden asked.

"Without," he said, not looking up as he made another pass with the file.

The screen door swung open and slapped against the clapboard house as Karen Bumgarner tramped onto the porch past where her husband sat and down the steps into the yard where Aiden and Thad stood. She slid her arm into the leather handles of her pocketbook and flung the heavy bag over her shoulder. Karen had always been the prettiest girl they grew up with, all of the boys hell bent on taking her out. Somehow or another, Leland won, and they all believed he must've conned her.

Karen stopped in the yard halfway between Leland and Aiden. Two children and a life she never meant for had worn her down, but she was still gorgeous. She cocked her hip to the side, a fat bottom sitting ripe in tight pink shorts, thick legs as brown as tung-oiled walnut from hours spent in the tanning bed. Her hair was short and dyed black with blond streaks, a hairdo that all the girls were wearing but which made no sense to men who dodged skunks with their pickups nearly every time they drove.

"I'm going into town to get some groceries. You need anything?" she asked.

"A carton of smokes and some beer."

"Anything else?"

"No," Leland said. He still hadn't looked up.

Karen spun away from him, sighed under her breath, and rolled her eyes.

"You going to take the boys with you?" Leland asked.

Karen looked over to where their sons were killing each other. The older one was holding his kid brother upside down, then dropped to his knees and pile-drove the little one's head into the ground, his neck surely breaking on impact. Karen didn't even blink. "You keep an eye on 'em."

Leland just grunted.

Karen glanced over at Aiden and Thad, flipped her bangs to the side of her face, and her blue eyes shone like sapphires in the sunlight.

"Well, ain't you just as pretty as always," Thad said.

Karen scrunched her face and shook her head. "Fuck you."

"You hear that? You going to let your old lady talk to me like that, Leland?"

Leland didn't say a word.

Karen stared at Thad like she might kick him square in his balls.

"Still a firecracker, ain't you?" Thad said. "A goddamn pistol, Karen."

She walked over and stood right between Thad and Aiden. She met Thad eye to eye and spoke in a low, sharp tone. "Don't you ever come back to my house all gooned out on that shit, you hear me?"

For once Thad seemed speechless.

"I've got enough trouble raising them boys already without folks like y'all poking around here." Karen stood there for a few moments just staring at Thad, daring him to say something smart-assed back to her, but he didn't. She walked off and climbed into a light blue Chrysler minivan with paint peeling to the primer on the hood. She drove out of sight and Aiden found himself wondering if she'd ever come back. If he were her, he wasn't sure if he would.

"Still a pistol, ain't she, Leland?" Thad walked over to the porch.

"You ain't telling me nothing," Leland said, and spit into the yard.

"Hell, maybe he had to haul her down to Harris and have her sewn back up, Aid." Thad laughed. "Maybe that's why she was so pissed off."

"What did you say?" For the first time since they'd arrived at his home, Leland looked up. He glared at Thad and clenched his hands around the tools he held: the mill file in his right, the sharpened lawn mower blade in his left. Aiden knew that Leland heard what Thad said, but he was giving him a second chance.

Leland Bumgarner had the biggest pecker anyone had ever seen. One time he and Aiden were working for a cheapskate contractor who wouldn't put diesel in the trackhoe to carve a ditch. Instead, he made them dig with pickaxes and shovels. Leland stood right up and said, "If he's going to work us like mules, then by God I'll look like one." He dropped his overalls in the middle of the gravel road and there he stood with his dick halfway down his thigh like a horse. The other men joked from then on that if they had knee knockers like that they'd flop them out in wheelbarrows and haul them all over town for the world to see.

But Thad brought up a story Leland told one time in the locker room when they were still in high school, a story about how he'd accidentally hurt Karen. He said her parents had to take her down to Harris Hospital and have the doctors sew her back up. Aiden used to joke behind Leland's back that he didn't know how Leland slept at night knowing good and well he'd put a hole like that in his old lady. But those types of jokes don't fly once a girl goes from being someone a buddy's banging to the mother of his children.

"I said you must've had to take her down to Harris and have her sewn back up, the way she was acting." Even when everything seemed to suggest that he should keep his mouth closed, Thad never shut up. It was worse when the dope had him. A day without sleep, and he spoke every word that crossed his mind. He'd been up nearly a week.

Leland stood from the porch and calmly set the mill file onto the planks. He traded the sharpened lawn mower blade to his right hand, the edge he'd filed shining white as mirror glare, and ran the blade against the hairs on his left arm. The blade scraped, hairs flicking into air then disappearing, leaving bare skin behind the pass. Leland looked down at what he held in his hand and shook it like he might try to guess its weight as he took a few steps closer. "I'm only going to say this once, Thad." Leland held the lawn mower blade in front of him, aimed it square between Thad's eyes. "If you ever say another word about my wife, I will open your head like a watermelon."

"I ain't mean nothing." Thad shifted uneasily where he stood, flicked his eyes back and forth from Leland to the ground. "I was just giving you a hard time is all."

"Do you understand me?" Leland still held the blade outstretched. His expression had not changed and he waited for Thad to look him square, to tell him he understood.

"I was just joking around. That's all."

"One more thing before we do business." Leland put the lawn mower blade on the porch beside the file, then looked at Aiden. Leland talked more to Aiden than Thad now. "Just like Karen said, I don't want neither one of you to ever come here again all gooned out on that shit. Not around my boys."

"We ain't all gooned out, Leland." When Aiden said those words, he knew they weren't true, but he was only twenty-four hours in and it could've been worse. He was more tired than anything, though Thad had obviously kept the pedal to the floor all night.

"Y'all's eyes are about to pop out of your heads. Thad there has been scratching at his arms like he's eat up with chiggers and you're grinding hell out of your teeth, so don't tell me that. I don't care what either of you do, but don't come acting like that around my boys." Leland looked out into the yard to where his oldest son wrenched a figure-four leg lock into his wincing brother's ankles. The little one slapped at the ground to cry uncle.

"We're sorry, Leland," Aiden said. "It won't happen again."

Leland Bumgarner stepped between Thad and Aiden and led them around the side of the house to where a shipping container was buried in the hillside out back. Years before, some businessman in Sylva had a lead on shipping containers for a few hundred dollars apiece. Folks all over the county nabbed those containers and buried them into hillsides to use as root cellars. The heavy steel was almost bulletproof and would probably survive the rapture.

Only the blue doors shone on a hillside blanketed with curly dock and lamb's ear, sedge shoots and oat grass. The container ran straight back into the mountain. Leland worked a combination lock free and unlatched the steel bar holding the doors closed. He stretched a pull cord from overhead at the entrance and a lightbulb flicked on. Thad and Aiden followed him inside. There was one more light at the far end of the cellar. Leland yanked the cord and a yellow glow bounced around the corrugated walls, colors blending into a stale green all around them.

Makeshift shelves lined with mason jars canning everything from dilly beans to bear meat ran the length of the left side. Dusty boxes, the tape that once held them closed now stringy as corn silk with dry rot, were stacked on the right. At the far end, where Leland stood, a table piecemealed together from two-by-fours and warped plywood stretched the width of the container. Above the table, a board at least five feet long crossed the wall with a timber rattler skin lacquered to wood, the scales tattered and flaking. Aiden walked over and set the ammunition can on the table.

"How many boxes you say you had?" Leland asked.

"I don't know how many boxes," Aiden said. "Its just blister packs."

"And what're you wanting to get out of them?"

Aiden popped the latches on the can, placed the three bags of dope on the table, and counted out the sheets of pseudoephedrine.

"Wayne Bryson used to give scabs twenty dollars a box," Thad answered.

"Cash or credit?"

"What are you talking about?" Thad asked.

"I mean was Wayne paying cash or trading dope?"

"Dope," Thad said. "That's all they was after."

"And that's a lot different than cash."

"There's a hundred and four packs so I'm betting that was half as many boxes," Aiden said.

"I'll give you ten a box."

"You're out of your goddamn mind!" Thad squinted his eyes and stuck his jaw out. "You hear this shit, Aid? Now I just told you Wayne Bryson was paying twenty dollars a box. Twenty dollars a goddamn box."

"No, Wayne Bryson wasn't paying twenty dollars a box," Leland said. "Wayne Bryson was trading a bunch of tweakers dope he already had, dope that he'd set the price on. Ten dollars a box is all I'm paying. Besides, y'all called me."

"So five twenty's the best you can do?" Aiden asked.

"I might go five fifty, but if Thad there don't shut the hell up, I'm more likely to tell you to pack your shit and head on down the road."

"I bet you would, you cocksucker." Thad was fighting mad.

Leland Bumgarner stood in the yellow light with a work shirt opened to the middle of his chest, and pulled long strokes down his goatee. His head was close-shaven, eyes green as dollar signs, and he shot them both a look like, Take it or leave it.

"And what about the dope?" Aiden asked.

"Ain't got no use for it," Leland said. "I won't touch it no more. But I might know someone who'd take it off your hands."

"You find somebody to buy the dope and we'll do five even."

"You kidding me, Aid?" Thad screamed. "Wayne Bryson got twenty dollars a box. Wayne Bryson got twenty goddamn dollars a box. Why don't you just give it away?"

"Shut up, Thad," Aiden said.

"You're just giving it away."

"I said shut up, Thad." Aiden turned and looked him dead in his eyes. Thad didn't say anything else. "Go call your boy, Leland. You find somebody to buy that dope and you can have it."

Leland stood there for a second, but it didn't take him long to figure what he'd make. He scooted between them and went to the end of the root cellar. Leland swung the doors open into daylight and walked out into the yard so he could get cell reception. He stood in white light that seemed too bright to be real and held the phone to his ear. The container door creaked closed, cut away more and more view from Aiden and Thad until it shut entirely and they could no longer see the day.

Thad wouldn't speak. He turned away and checked mason jars on the shelf, turned the glass in his hand, and surveyed what sloshed inside. He picked up a jar of bear meat and eyed where the fat filmed over the cubes. Old-timers said they could predict the weather by how the fat rose and sank. Thad stared forever like he might decipher the next time it'd rain. When he made up his mind, he turned and kicked at mildewed boxes that teetered against the opposite wall. He flipped back one of the box flaps and rummaged through the contents, slapped the box closed when he found nothing that suited him.

After a few silent minutes, Leland came back inside the root cellar. He nodded as he came toward them. "I've got somebody who said he'll take it all."

"Who?"

"A guy named Eberto that used to paint houses with me."

"A spic?" Aiden asked.

"Yeah. Good guy, though."

"You sure?" And it wasn't so much that Aiden didn't trust Mexicans as that he'd never had any dealings with them. All he knew was that the minute they poured into Jackson County, all the good-paying jobs for folks who worked with their hands had dried up. Why pay a white man double for what a Mexican would do just as well for half? Since then, working-class white folks had been in a war of sorts with the Mexicans whether they said so or not.

"He's the only person I know who can take that much dope off your hands in one go," Leland said. "He's connected to folks trying to get things back to how it used to be, get everything moving through one source again. When it all boils down to it, he's a businessman just the same as me."

"So he's going to pay us a third of what it's worth?" Thad shot another smart-ass one-liner. He'd been silent too long.

"He'll pay you what he pays you, but ain't nobody else in this county sitting on enough cash to take all of that off your hands at once." Leland looked over at the table to where the three bags of crystal sat beside the ammunition can.

Aiden knew Leland was right, but mulled it over in silence, and finally asked, "He coming over here now?"

"No, he said he'd meet you tomorrow."

"Where?"

"He lives down there in those apartments between Jimmy's and Ken's, right straight back across from the church."

"You going with us?"

"No, I ain't going with you," Leland said. "Ain't got nothing to do with me."

"What apartment?"

"He didn't say. He just said he'll come out when y'all pull up."

"And how the hell will he know it's us?"

"'Cause there ain't no other white folks driving back in there."

Thad shook his head like he and Aiden were about to walk in front of a firing squad. The whole thing sounded sketchy, but Leland was right. There wasn't another person in Jackson County with enough cash to buy a quarter pound of methamphetamine.

Aiden walked over to the table and pulled the blister packs of pseudo from the can, counted them out per five, and slid them stacked against the metal wall. Leland watched him work, tugged his goatee, and mouthed silent numbers as he counted. When all the packs were on the table, Leland took out a wad of folded bills from his back pocket, licked his fingers, and slapped twenty-dollar bills onto the table one after the other. He counted twenty-five, gathered them in his hands, and tapped them even against the plywood before counting twice more. When the cash was on the table, Aiden flipped through once for himself. They nodded at each other as Aiden threw the money into the can, dropped the three bags of dope on top, and latched the lid shut.

"A couple words of advice, and if I was you I'd listen awfully close," Leland Bumgarner said, his eyes as serious as Aiden had ever seen. "First and foremost, don't walk into any sort of business all gooned out. If it was anybody other than me, the two of you might not be breathing. Now, I'm going to give you a couple pills and I want you to take 'em tonight before you go to bed." Leland grabbed a bottle of Advil from the table and shook two capsules into his palm. "Hand me the cellophane off your smokes."

Aiden slid the plastic off his cigarette pack and handed it to him. Leland dropped the pills inside, rolled the packaging up, held a lighter to the edge, and dabbed it sealed between his index finger and thumb.

"What the hell is it?" Thad asked.

"I don't remember what he used to call them," Leland said. "The devil's something or another."

"I want you to listen to him, Aid. A nut job, I'm telling you."

"It's Ativan and Geodon," Leland said. "It'll knock the two of you off this binge you're on and put some sense back in you."

"I ain't ever seen Ativan in a pill like that," Aiden said. "Now, I've taken loads of it, but I ain't ever seen it like that. And I ain't ever even heard of Geodon."

"A buddy of mine made 'em," Leland said. "Six pills into each one of these. Six milligrams of Ativan and sixty milligrams of Geodon. That's six pills, sixty-six milligrams. It'll put your dick in the dirt. Back when I used to stay lit, that buddy gave me a batch of these to knock me down so I'd go to sleep, so as I wouldn't lose my job and Karen wouldn't leave my ass, and let me tell you, they work. The two of y'all take those tonight and you're going to wake up tomorrow afternoon feeling like daisies."

"If we wake up," Thad said.

"You'll wake up."

Aiden slid the cellophane into his pack of cigarettes. He lit one and watched the first puff hold on the still root-cellar air like breath in winter.

"Last word of advice," Leland said as he made his way to the door. "Don't take all the dope with you. About the stupidest thing you could've done."

"It's just you—" Aiden started to explain.

"It don't matter. You can't trust a soul when it comes to dope and money."

"But—"

"Your own family will put a knife to your throat." Leland cut Aiden's words short again, swung open the heavy steel door on the root cellar, sunlight blinding all three of them for a second or two, but only Aiden and Thad covered their eyes. Leland stretched wide in the summer air, stroked his goatee as he yawned. His sons were still playing outside. The older boy was chest deep in an aboveground swimming pool that stood beside the trampoline in the front yard. The aluminum sides of the pool bellied out like they just might blow apart any second. The younger son bounced around the trampoline, then cut a lazy flip in the air over the water. He splashed down on his ribs just shy of his brother. The older boy settled his hands around his little brother's neck when he came up for air, held him under while his arms flailed. "Sometimes it don't even take dope for them to do it."

(14)

THAD REPEATED THE SAME THING MULTIPLE TIMES BE-
fore Aiden ever threw the Ranchero in park: "I know I didn't leave the
door open." Whatever was used to pry into Thad's trailer had bent
the top corner of the thin metal door like a dog-eared book page.
Aiden imagined whoever broke in just reached inside, unlatched the
lock, and turned the doorknob after that. Neither of them said a
word when they walked inside, and they certainly didn't speak once
they saw the dog.

Loretta Lynn had a sixteen-inch flathead screwdriver pinning her
lifeless body to the plywood table in front of the couch. The wood
was muddied with blood, but the way her paws had raked and finger-
painted the puddle meant she hadn't died right away.

Thad collapsed to his knees beside the table, his upper half hunched
limp over the only thing that had made him smile for two years. He
looked too shocked to cry. He didn't make one sound. Aiden wasn't
even sure if Thad was breathing, and he wanted to walk up to him,
put his hand on Thad's shoulder, but that moment felt like glass. That

moment felt like any movement at all would shatter the whole world into a million fucking pieces.

The ratty couch with yellow flowers had been flipped onto its back, its cushions strewn about, with one balanced in an angle against the wall like the start of a little kid's lean-to. Past the living room into the kitchen, cabinet doors stood at various angles, everything inside ransacked and piled into a broken heap of dishes and glass, the shards dusted with cornmeal and slopped with spent cooking grease. A dust devil of fruit flies whirled up from the pile when Aiden scuffed through, but there was no absence of places to light, and in a split second the air was still.

Aiden peeked into Thad's bedroom at the far end of the trailer, but it was hard to tell whether the room was ripped apart or just how he'd left it. Navy-blue sheets bunched away from one corner of the mattress, the dark sheets splotched with dried gray stains. The bed was slung sideways, dirty clothes strewn carelessly about the room. Gun magazine centerfolds were taped to the wall. Drawers were ripped from the rails of the dresser. The closet emptied into a mixed mound of filth.

Down the barrel of the trailer, Thad was still hovering over Loretta Lynn's body. He was motionless, but the potential for him to ignite was packed in his gunpowder stare. Gravel spun beneath tires outside, just a dark blue blur as April's sedan shot past the open doorway, and that sound pulled the trigger.

By the time Aiden made it onto the porch, Thad was halfway up the hill. April was out of the car and slammed the passenger-side door with her free hand, a paint roller and tray balanced under her other arm. Cocked to the side by the gallon of paint she was carrying, she evened the load between her hands, but dropped it all when she saw her front door standing open. Her tabby cat, Mittens, wandered onto the stoop and circled lazily, back arched as he ran his body along the door frame. Thad was almost to the house, his fast pace and raised shoulders hinting that when he got there something bad was going to happen. Aiden took off after them and Thad followed his mother into the house just as Aiden crested the hilltop. When Aiden made it inside, they were already screaming.

"My house is ripped to shreds, Thad. Don't you think if I was here I would have done something?" April stood in the living room with her arms raised over the mess. Light yellow paint had dried in her hair, speckled her black tank top and loose-fitting carpenter's pants. She turned and looked around the littered floor. "I'd like to kill whoever did this to my house."

"Well, where were you?" he screamed.

"I went to get paint."

"Paint?"

"I needed more paint, Thad. Is that hard for you to understand?"

"You and this house."

"This house is all I've got. This house, Thad, is torn all to shit and I guaran-goddamn-tee it was some no-account you was running around with did it."

"What'd you say?"

"I said I'll bet you a million dollars this had something to do with those skanks you had piled in that trailer last night."

"Just shut the fuck up!"

"No, Thad. No. I won't shut the fuck up. I won't shut up and you know why? Do you have any idea why?"

"Why?"

"I'll tell you why. Look around, Thad. They broke my entire collection." April kicked at a broken figurine that used to sit on one of the shelves by the door. The knickknack shelves were smashed into jagged wooden scraps. The chalk statues were shattered over the carpet. "I've been collecting those my whole life. My mama and daddy gave me some of those when I was a little girl. You have any idea how much that collection meant to me?"

"Your collection?" Thad moved toward his mother.

"Can you really not understand what I'm saying?"

"Your collection?" He was almost to her.

"My—"

Before April could get another word out of her mouth, Thad grabbed hold of her face, mashed her cheeks and lips together in his hand. He kept forward until she was on the floor and he was on top of her, her eyes and mug still scrunched into a wrinkled wad in his hand like some chubby kid making faces. "They killed my dog!" Thad was screaming down at his mother words that broke apart and pelted her face. "They killed my fucking dog, you dumb bitch!"

Aiden loped forward and tackled Thad away from his mother, the two of them rolling into a knotted melee on the floor beside her. They wrestled around for a minute or two before Thad's rage gave him the upper hand. His knees dug into Aiden's ribs as he hammered square into Aiden's forehead. Thad brained Aiden again, and that second one dazed him for a moment, but when a clear thought came, it crashed like a meteor and lit Aiden afire. That's when Aiden rolled Thad onto his back and pinned his arms behind his head. Thad was trying to knee Aiden in his kidneys, trying to climb his way up his body, and it took almost a minute before he spent, that tantrum finally fizzling, him just heaving for air on the floor.

When it was over, Aiden twisted off and let go of Thad's wrists.

Thad spun to his feet and walked to the open doorway. He turned to face them. April sat beside Aiden with her arms wrapped around her knees and her head buried and sobbing. "Fuck you, Aiden," Thad said. His features were hidden in shadow, the world glowing white behind him. April looked up from her arms with her face sunken with tears. "Fuck you both," Thad said as he shook his head, turned, and melted into the sunlight with his mother and best friend speechless on the floor.

15

THE MEMORY OF HOW THAD CAME TO BE HAD NOT waned in twenty-four years:

Every night for two weeks April had gone to the church to practice piano until the song she would play that coming Sunday was something memorized in the tips of her fingers. She'd turned off the lights and was headed to lock up, the sanctuary so still that even her muffled screams echoed.

There was little light to be had, which made it hard to see who was holding her there, her vision so frosted by tears that everything blurred, impossible for her to see the man, just a shadow figure that smelled of corn liquor and Aqua Velva, the way he always did, the way he always did even on Sundays, even when he stood at the reverend's side and broke bread, even when he dressed up as Santa Claus that one Christmas when the congregation gathered in the fellowship hall and held a cakewalk for the Aikens, who'd lost everything in a fire. Booze and cheap cologne, he'd always smelled like that, and that's how she knew.

She didn't need to see his face. She could smell him. She could smell him as he moved over her. She could smell him as if her face were buried in him. She could smell him from then on. She could smell him in the fragrance aisle at Walmart when she went to town. She could smell him any time someone who'd been drinking breathed. It was something she hadn't forgotten, something she could never forget, not now, not ever, a smell nine months older than Thad, a smell that, to this day, left her helpless with fear, her body tightening to stone, her mind a furious turning.

The man who broke her had said to keep quiet, and she did. She kept quiet when her stomach started to swell and the kids she'd grown up with called her a whore. Having sex didn't make you a whore, but getting pregnant did. She kept quiet when her parents kicked her out of the house, and when they left the church and moved out of Little Canada from shame that they'd raised her. She kept quiet when Thad was old enough to ask about his father and she could barely look at him and all she could do was lie and say the man was Cherokee. When George Trantham forced her to go back to that same church on Sundays, when she had to look at the man who'd hurt her sitting piously behind the reverend, she shoveled it all deep inside and never said a word. But all of that anger and all of that hatred was reflected onto Thad, the one reminder that could not be buried.

April relived all of those feelings as she knelt on the floor and cried into her hands, a queasiness in her stomach that built till she was certain she'd be sick. The way Thad had rushed her and pinned her to the floor seemed some eerie revelation that her son's deepest truths were rooted in blood and could not be blotted out or erased. He was his father's son. In her mind, he was no different from the man who'd raped her. But for the first time in all those years, the sickness that rose with the resurfacing of memory filled her more with rage than fear. She stared through the open doorway into the light outside where Thad had disappeared and prayed that the sun would burn him alive. She prayed that he would be incinerated and in that moment her memory would be erased and it would be as if he'd never existed at all.

"I wish he were dead," April said under her breath, wiping the tears from her cheeks with both hands as if she were washing her face.

"What did you say?" Aiden asked.

Neither of them had moved from the floor since Thad walked out, and these were the first words spoken between them.

"I wish he were dead," she repeated, so matter-of-factly that it was clear how many times she must've thought it before.

"You don't mean that," Aiden said. He stood and looked down on her.

"I've never meant anything more in my life."

16

THAD BURIED HIS DOG ABOVE APRIL'S HOUSE IN A LONG sweep of yellowed grass that bent as stiffly as rake tines any time the wind blew. The radio tower reached into the sky over the mountain and broke apart late-summer sun with metal bones that cast a skeleton shadow down upon where he dug.

Each spring, creeping phlox spread a pale blue blanket over the hillside. The color always seemed to burst unexpectedly like some delicious explosion that happened overnight. Thad had always heard that dogs were color-blind, but Loretta Lynn seemed to see those flowers bloom. The minute she saw them, she sprinted for the hill as if the flowers were trespassing, and upon discovering they were only flowers, squirmed around on her back with her tongue lapping about her jowls, like the whole world suddenly made sense again. Watching her made Thad happy. Even though the world was tearing apart at the stitches, seeing her roll around in those flowers that spring had made Thad laugh.

That spot had to be Loretta Lynn's favorite place. That little patch of ground was probably the closest thing either of them would ever know to heaven, and that's why he buried her there. He didn't say a word as he dug. He didn't even notice that Aiden stood behind him. He just worked until the hole was deep enough. Then he wrapped her in a blanket, placed her in the ground, and covered her body with dirt.

When the work was done and he leaned over the shovel, the grayed wooden handle seeming to hold him up like a scarecrow, he glared stone-eyed down to where Aiden was standing. The white T-shirt Thad wore was stretched about the neck, and he lifted the shirt from his belly to wipe sweat from his face.

"You know she was right," Thad said after a long spell.

"What?" Aiden asked.

"She was right in there." He stared into the sky trying to make sense of something that lacked reason.

"I don't know what you're talking about," Aiden said.

"About all this having something to do with those girls."

"What makes you say that?"

"I just know it," Thad said.

"You think those two girls could do that?"

"Not those girls, Aiden, but that brother of hers, Julie's brother, that Doug Dietz, you're goddamn right I do."

"I still don't know what would make somebody do that."

"I do," Thad said. "And that's my fault."

"How the hell is it your fault?"

"Because I told them."

"You told them what, Thad?"

"I told Julie about Wayne Bryson. I told her about what happened and what we took."

"What the hell do you mean you told her?"

"I know I shouldn't have said nothing."

"Jesus Christ, Thad. Do you have any—"

"I know what I did, Aiden!" Thad screamed. "I'm the reason this happened. I know that." Thad braced the shovel across his shoulder, hung his arms over the handle, and made his way down the hill.

"Well, what the fuck are we going to do?" Aiden asked as Thad came near.

"Ain't but one way to make this right," Thad said without even turning to look as he went by. His eyes were set on nothing at all as he headed toward the trailer. Something broke inside him then. His mind retreated to a place more familiar. There was a sergeant who told Thad the infantry were the hands of God, and that idea made sense to Thad because it was no different from what he had heard all his life growing up in church. The old-timers said some prayers needed feet. But there was evil in this world that had to be strangled. And so it wasn't just a matter of giving those prayers legs. Sometimes a prayer needed hands just the same.

(17)

A TWISTED SPIRE OF FLAME AND SMOKE LICKED ABOUT the sky after Thad doused the cheapjack table with gasoline, tossed a struck match where oil and blood soaked the wooden top, and set the large spool ablaze in the front yard. The fuel spent fast, and within a few minutes the plywood had crumbled into a bed of coals. A few minutes more and nothing but a wide circle of gray ash and black earth lay in the yard like a tarnished coin flipped by the hand of God.

April watched Aiden and Thad from the stoop of her house. She'd yelled something when the column of fire first spiraled into the air. Neither answered her. When April wished her son was dead, when those words came out of her mouth, Aiden knew it was the most heartless thing he'd ever heard her say. Mothers weren't supposed to say things like that. Fathers, maybe, but mothers never. Then again, she'd never been much of a mother at all.

While the fire burned to nothing, Thad came up with a plan. He chose the shotgun and Aiden took the revolver. Thad made Aiden grab a fence-post driver to use as a battering ram. Once inside, they'd bind them with zip ties and duct tape. Force a confession. After that, Aiden was uncertain. Thad hadn't gotten that far.

The two of them waited for nightfall, and when that last bit of glow dissolved into the mountains, they drove Booker Branch without headlights, lowered their heads together, and snorted enough crystal to make sure it all happened in the blink of an eye.

They snuck through a laurel thicket and up the darkened hillside on a game trail that switchbacked three times to the trailer. The lights were on inside, and screamo music blared from busted speakers just behind the door. Aiden and Thad didn't check the windows. They just moved fast onto the porch. Thad shouldered the shotgun and readied himself to bum-rush whoever moved. Aiden slid the revolver down the back of his waistline, the barrel cold against his skin, and took the fence-post driver with both hands.

When Thad nodded, Aiden swung heavy steel into the door, just left of the handle, and the trailer lid slapped the wall behind before rattling loose on busted hinges. Doug Dietz jerked around with eyes wide and his greasy mullet slapping his neck. His pants were down by his ankles and he had the fat girl, Meredith, dogged over the couch, a ratty nightshirt pushed up her back. He was as deep as he could get, with one hand yanking her braided ponytail like a leash, when Thad and Aiden filed inside, Thad screaming, "Get on the goddamn floor! Get on the goddamn floor!"

They were dumbstruck as Thad moved into the house. He swung the buttstock of the shotgun into the base of Doug's neck before that son of a bitch ever let off. The blow knocked Doug unconscious, and he collapsed forward onto the fat girl's back, rolled to the side with his ankles tangled in denim jeans, and hit the floor like a lassoed calf.

Meredith crawled down the couch and scuttled toward the kitchen to get away. Her weight was forward as if she were already falling, and her arms circled around her sides like she was some storm-blown whirligig. Thad's pace never slowed. He kept forward past where Doug lay, and kicked her with a long, loping stride. She crashed headfirst into the base of a countertop that split the living room and kitchen. She was sluggish in her movements, but tried to lift herself from the floor. The thin, moth-eaten nightshirt was up around her shoulders, stretch marks squiggling her back. Thad stood over her and hammered down into the back of her boxy skull with the shotgun, but that first blow did not take her. It took him gripping the shotgun in both hands and raining down on her wildly with the stainless receiver before she melted on the floor.

Aiden yanked Doug's pants up and was securing his wrists behind his back with zip ties and duct tape when Julie poked her head out of the back room at the far end of the trailer with a bag of frozen corn pressed to her eye. She stood there in red sweatpants with Marlboro written down both legs in cracked white letters, a Slipknot T-shirt hanging loosely from her shoulders. Thad drew down on her with the shotgun, and she dropped what she was holding, tightened rigidly with arms half raised at her chest like some stiffened skeleton set to scare children in a haunted house. "Don't you fucking move," Thad said through teeth clenched tight, his words clear over the blaring music, as if no sound stirred at all. Unlike her brother, unlike Meredith, who lay sprawled between Aiden and Thad, Julie Dietz did as she was told.

Thad cinched a fistful of Julie's hair at the back of her head and led her through the kitchen. He threw her forward by that ball of hair and she tripped over Meredith's leg, collapsed on a coiled, woolen rug that centered the narrow living room. She turned glassy-eyed toward Aiden, her one eye still swollen purple where Thad had hit her that morning. Pushing herself from the floor, her shoulder blades cut sharply at the back of her shirt.

"Unh-uh," Thad grunted before she could rise.

Julie crumbled to the rug. Her eyes were set on Aiden as he finished binding her brother's ankles, Doug's feet now pulled up behind him and hog-tied to his wrists. Julie's dark, hollow eyes filled with tears. Her face scrunched before she broke, but Aiden paid her no attention and went on about his business. He bound Meredith just as he had Doug, though she was not near as limber and required a chain of zip ties to link her wrists and ankles. Both were hog-tied now. Both remained unconscious. Julie was the only one awake, and while Thad worked on her restraints, Aiden pulled the revolver from his waistline and checked the rooms.

The Dietzes' trailer had the same standard floor plan as most two-bedroom single-wides: front door opening into the living room, living room running into the kitchen, bathroom and narrow hall splitting the space between the kitchen and far bedroom, the other bedroom connected to the living room behind the front door, a bedroom capping each end. The living room and kitchen were open to view, but the bath and both bedrooms had yet to be cleared.

Aiden chose the bedroom behind the front door first. Music blared inside. A black light mounted over the bed colored everything ultramarine. A gallery of velvet posters glowed neon on the walls: a mushroom-laden fairyland, a drippy skull with a cobra slithering from one eye, a bearded wizard summoning fire from a dragon's mouth, and a naked sword-wielding woman whose nipples burned purple on tangerine breasts. All of that color seemed to make the place move, and Aiden felt dizzy. His mind raced, his heart pounded, and he felt for a second like he might black out. It was hard to tell if it was panic or the drugs. It couldn't be the drugs, he thought. He'd only been up twenty-four hours. He'd only done two rails of dope. He could always last at least two days before the panic set in, before the world fell apart. Aiden ran the pistol all over the room, but found nothing other than the stereo. He turned the volume down, the screaming finally slack. Everything slowed a bit then and he regained what little hold he had. There was no one in the room but him.

On the other end of the trailer, Aiden threw back the shower curtain in the bathroom. Red stains from hard water bloodied the shower, and his own reflection in the speckled mirror glass frightened him for a second. But there was nothing else.

The second bedroom was bigger, a room shared by the girls. Beds stood in each corner and a short table stretched between, with its walnut veneer torn to yellow particleboard. A puddle of scented oil melted in a heated dish on the tabletop, the oil filling the room with the fetor of baby powder. The ten o'clock news flashed by on a small television retelling another story of another man killing another man in another godforsaken town. Filling-station statuary of Indians with feathered headdresses riding horseback stood on shelves hammered to walls, and dreamcatchers twirled on fishing string from the ceiling having failed to catch this nightmare.

Thad yelled from the living room, his scratchy voice breaking some daze that'd come over Aiden. "See if you can't find some socks."

"Some what?"

"Something to shove down their throats."

There were dirtied clothes strewn about the floor, and Aiden scrounged some socks before moving into the living room. Julie sat on the far end of the couch with her ankles bound with zip ties, her arms cuffed behind. The way her arms were fastened hunched her forward, with her stringy hair sweeping her knees. Thad left her mouth uncovered, but had Aiden stuff wadded socks into the mouths of Meredith and Doug, seal their lips with strips of duct tape. Meredith started to wake up when Aiden did this, but she was woozy. The back of her head was soppy with blood. She'd yet to regain any sort of lucidity. With their mouths shut, she and Doug wheezed for breath, their nostrils flaring like sleeping animals.

Thad demanded that Julie tell him what had happened, and for a long time she kept saying she didn't know what he was talking about. But when he pulled out his skinning knife, pressed the flat side of the blade flush against her lips, and told her he would cut out every tooth in her head, she sang a different song. She told him they'd come for the drugs and the money. She told him they'd broken into the trailer and house. She told him that she and Meredith ripped the rooms apart while her brother searched for the dope, and when he came up empty-handed, that's what pushed him over the edge, the way that dog would not shut up, that's when Doug killed her. When she was finally done with all she had to tell, Thad stuffed her mouth with a sock until she strangled and wrapped tape around her head. Mascara washed over her cheeks like shadows until she no longer held tears to cry. She just sat there and choked on her breath, her body shuddering with each bit of air.

That's how Thad and Aiden left them when they walked outside. That's how Aiden planned to leave them altogether, but Thad didn't make it off the porch. Aiden was halfway to the woods, dragging the fence-post driver across a thin sliver of grass that separated the trailer from the hillside, when Thad called, "Where the hell are you going?"

Aiden turned around and stared to where Thad seemed some black silhouette carved in the porch light behind. "Let's get the hell out of here."

"What are you talking about?" Thad asked. "I ain't going anywhere."

"What are you going to do, Thad?" Aiden huffed as if it were a joke. "You going to kill them?"

"That's exactly what I'm going to do." Thad stood there, and though his eyes were wild, the methamphetamine and adrenaline raging inside, his demeanor was calm and collected. "Some people deserve to die," he said.

Aiden had known Thad his entire life and still could not believe those words. "And who makes that call?"

"God," Thad said.

"God? Do you hear yourself? You think it's God telling you to do this?"

"God doesn't have hands, Aiden."

"You're out of your fucking mind," Aiden said. "You know that, don't you? You have absolutely lost your fucking mind!"

"No. I don't think I have," Thad said.

"And what about the girls?"

"What about them?"

"Those two girls in there didn't do anything more than try to steal from us. That's all they did, Thad. That's it, and that's no different than what me and you have been doing our whole good-for-nothing lives."

"They're just as guilty as he is."

"You know that ain't true."

"You are the company you keep," Thad said.

Just hearing him say that sent Aiden into a rage. For a long time, he'd felt that anger building up inside and for a long time he'd done everything he could to keep that damper closed. But what Thad was about to do would be the end. This was just one more time around the circle he'd spiraled his entire life, and that broke Aiden's heart. He dropped the post driver and the revolver in the yard and stood there for a moment breathing heavier and heavier until all of a sudden all of that fire that had built inside let loose.

Aiden shot up the front steps and had his hands around Thad's throat before Thad could blink. He rammed the back of Thad's head over and over into the side of the trailer, and Thad didn't fight him. He just stood there taking it, and Aiden held Thad at arm's length and punched him as hard as he could in the side of the head. Aiden swung again, then stood there and looked at how Thad stared emotionless and unfazed. He lifted his fist and was about to swing again when Thad said, "That's enough," but Aiden reared back farther. "That's enough," Thad screamed. There was blood dripping from the corner of his mouth as he shoved Aiden across the porch and raised the gun.

"You going to kill me too?"

Thad didn't say a word, nor did he lower the gun.

"Then kill me, you son of a bitch." Aiden came forward until the muzzle was flush against his chest. "Pull the fucking trigger and kill me, Thad. Do it!" He was screaming at the top of his lungs and Thad's expression did not waver. "Do it!"

"Get the fuck out of here, Aiden."

"Do it!" Aiden screamed. And when he knew Thad wouldn't pull the trigger, Aiden slapped the barrel down away from his chest and glared with eyes frosted by tears.

"Get out of here."

Aiden backed away and stood at the edge of the porch, staring at the closest thing he'd ever had to family. He knew that once he walked away there would be no coming back, and he pleaded. "You're not going to be able to live with this, Thad."

"With what?" Thad asked.

"With killing those girls."

"You don't know what I'm capable of living with."

Aiden shook his head and walked out into the yard. He picked up the post driver and revolver, then turned back one last time. "That shit is going to eat you alive." But Thad didn't say a word.

Aiden pushed through a briary thicket of brush and limbs to find the trail that led down the mountain. He had never walked away from anything Thad had gotten them into, not once in their whole sorry lives, but he could play no part in this. He'd never drawn a line before, and maybe the lines weren't things that were consciously drawn. Maybe the line was there all along, deep inside, and no one knew exactly where it was until he was standing at the edge of it.

The woods were loud as they always were in summer, but when that first shot sounded from the top of the hillside, it frightened Aiden, as if it were the first sound he'd ever heard. He cowered into a ball on the ground. He did not rise until there was silence. Aiden turned and looked back to where he'd come from, and when that second shot sounded he cringed. When he made it to the car, he sat there without cranking the engine for a few minutes, waiting for the third shot. But he could have waited there forever, and it still wouldn't have come. So after a while, he had no choice but to drive away.

(18)

WHEN A FIREWORK OF BUCKSHOT OPENED AGAINST Meredith's back, something inside Thad came to life with horrifying intensity. So when he swung the shotgun to draw a bead on Julie, he didn't even focus on his target. Thad looked through her and pulled the trigger, everything deafening with sound thereafter.

The ringing made it seem as if he were inside the resonation of some giant bell, his entire consciousness having been swallowed by sound. The report slowly hummed away until the only thing left was the absolute truth of it all, some sort of full-color enlightenment. He'd felt this the first time he fired and his life depended on it, the first time that shot wasn't headed for a metal target down range, and the thing about it was he'd come to love that feeling, that adrenaline-fueled madness. He'd been missing and chasing that feeling ever since.

He stared down to where Doug Dietz was writhing on the floor. The gag Aiden had secured in his mouth capped everything inside of him, Doug's eyes bulging, his face flushing red each time he seized. Thad knelt beside him, held Doug's head as if he were going to scalp him, and forced him to face where his sister was lying. He wanted Doug to suffer. He wanted Doug to feel how he felt. "Look at what you've done," Thad said.

Doug shut his eyes and shuddered with tears running like tiny wet fingers down his cheeks. He coughed against what had been shoved into his mouth and seemed to struggle more and more to find a breath.

"No, you're going to look at her," Thad yelled. He shook Doug's head like a can of paint, then set the shotgun on the floor and used his free hand to pull back Doug's eyelids. Doug's eyes rolled back into his head until they were nothing more than smoothed pebbles as cloudy white as milk quartz. He was screaming now with all of that sound muffled, his flared nostrils blowing snotty breaths each time he ran out of air. Thad didn't want him to suffocate before he finished what he'd started, so he yanked the tape from Doug's mouth, and Doug spit the gag onto the floor.

"What the fuck did you do?" Doug screamed. He looked around the room and then directly into Thad's eyes. The words were loud, but still hummed within the ringing. "What in God's name did you do!"

"Don't you mention God to me," Thad said. He hammered Doug's head against the floor. "God has no mercy for people like you."

When Doug's breathing slowed, Thad stuffed the wetted sock back into his throat. He grabbed the roll of duct tape from the floor and wrapped Doug's head just as he had Julie's a few minutes before. Thad didn't want to question God right then. He knew he was right, that God didn't have mercy for people like Doug Dietz. But sometimes he questioned if there was any mercy at all. Those questions that came afterward were what haunted him most, so it was best not to think during the thick of things.

George Trantham had dragged Thad to church all his life, but Thad never believed in God until he saw war. Pinned behind a rock with PKM fire raining down, everyone came to believe in something. Thad believed because, no matter how hard he tried, nothing else made sense. There was only one reason some made it and some didn't. And ever since, Thad had been trying to imagine a God who would forgive the things he'd done.

With his hand clenching Doug's hair, Thad turned him so that they were staring each other eye to eye. He pulled Doug so close that he could feel him breathing. "There'll come a time when I ask forgiveness," Thad said, "but it won't be from any God who'd answer you."

(19)

THERE WAS MUSIC PLAYING WHEN AIDEN WALKED INTO April's house. His first thought was how strange it was that the computer hadn't been stolen or wrecked, but, then again, nothing was taken. What Doug and those girls were looking for was on the table at Leland Bumgarner's when they came. They hadn't even found the few hundred dollars Aiden had stashed in the front closet. Julie and Meredith had ripped the trailer apart while Doug searched for the drugs, but now there wasn't even proof they'd been at April's at all. The floor scattered with broken figurines and shelves just hours before had been cleared. The only real difference was that the walls were bare and the house smelled of paint.

Mittens rose with his back arched from the couch cushion where he'd been sleeping, and stretched his front legs with claws opened and catching in the thin sofa cover. The cat dropped lazily onto the floor and sidled over to where Aiden stood, ran his head and body against Aiden's shin. The cat followed him into the kitchen and leapt onto the table as Aiden shook one of April's cigarettes from the pack that lay there. He grabbed the lighter, lit his cigarette, and tossed the Bic back onto the table. The lighter slid to the far side and the cat batted it back and forth between his paws before both he and the lighter fell to the floor. Aiden watched without a thought in this world, the drugs and the days running him out of his mind.

He looked around the room, to how the stove top and counters were wiped clean. Even the edges of cabinet doors were absent the faintest smudge of dust. There were no signs left of the work she'd done, no dirtied paper towels, no smell from Clorox or 409. There was a fresh bag in the trash can, and Aiden thought for a second how April had seemed to spend her whole life cleaning up messes she hadn't made. There was nothing fair about it, but then again there was nothing fair about the world at all. Her hand was no worse than his own. She just seemed better at playing cards, better at her poker face, better at everything. The world heaped it higher and she shoveled as best she could, and she'd gotten pretty good at it, he thought, at least better than himself.

In the second bedroom he found her curled from exhaustion on the floor. When she'd spent a week holding paint swatches against each wall in the house, it was a pale, yellow shade of white called eggshell that she chose for the second bedroom. Aiden told her all that paint was a waste of her time and money. People looking to buy a house would have their own favorite color and wind up painting it over, but he couldn't help but think it looked good now. The room glowed with that color, her arms and face speckled with tiny dots that had spattered when she rolled the walls. The twin bed, the dresser, and the old treadle Singer sewing machine were pulled out, and she'd almost finished the trim. Aiden bent to one knee and dug his arms underneath her body. He brought her into his chest and carried her into her bedroom. Only in her bed, when Aiden pulled the wagon wheel quilt over her, did she wake for a split second.

"What time is it?" she asked.

"A little after one," Aiden said, walking out of the room. He flicked on the light and pulled the door closed behind him.

There was a little bit of paint left in the roller basin and Aiden used it to finish the trim. He moved a small stepping stool along the wall as he made his way around the room, and, somewhere midway through, that feeling like he might black out washed over him again. He felt heavy, but the painting kept him from thinking about Thad. He needed to stay busy, to do something with all of that restlessness, so he painted until the room was finished. When it was done, he peeled the blue painter's tape from the ceiling, baseboards, and window frame. He carefully slid each piece of furniture within an inch of the wall and then went outside.

The night was filled with the same sounds as always, though it seemed quieter than it ever had before. The world was muffled by the way he felt. He wandered down the hillside to his car and fished through the trash littering the passenger-side floorboard. The empty pack of cigarettes he'd crumpled on the way back held the pills Leland Bumgarner had given him, the cocktail of Ativan and some other drug Aiden'd never heard of at the time and couldn't remember now.

He opened the cellophane and took one of the capsules, rolled the other back up, and slipped it into the cigarette pack. Aiden was never one to swallow pills, preferring instead to let them dissolve in his mouth so that the drugs hit faster. With his head rocked back, he twisted the casing apart over his tongue. The crushed pills were bitter and he stumbled over to the side of the trailer to drink from a spigot that came out of the ground. Tomorrow Aiden would meet Leland's connection and sell everything.

When he climbed the hill back to April's, he didn't go inside. Instead, he sat on the stoop and stared at Thad's trailer below, stared at the way the moonlight made a scab out of the darkened patch of ground where they'd burned the table. That scar was a bitter reminder that all of this was real, and that realization made Aiden thankful that it didn't take long before the drugs began to come over him in waves. His mind overflowed with thoughts, thoughts about Thad, about what Thad had done and whether or not he'd gone through with it or whether those shots were just warning shots and where he was right then and whether there was any coming back from that place. Aiden thought about April too and what she'd do if anyone ever decided to buy her house and where she might go and whether after she left he'd ever see her again. He thought about all kinds of things, but the one thing he tried to avoid thinking about was himself. All of that thinking made him uneasy, but the drugs were taking hold and the thoughts seemed to ebb a little further away each time the waves came. The tide was going out and he welcomed that feeling. In a few minutes he was almost there.

He wandered into the yard and lay down in the grass, the dew soaking through his clothes and wetting his back. The ground seemed to buzz as if there was music buried there that he could now feel humming against his body. The way the earth tingled felt good to him and he let the ground take him deeper.

Above, the stars shone, and as he looked down over himself, the heavens came with him. The stars traced from the sky to his body so that he became a mirror image of what was above. He lifted his shirt and could see the stars on his skin. He could feel them. He could feel them touch him and he thought that this must be what it felt like to be touched by God. He fell a little bit deeper. A few seconds more and deeper still. He took in as much air as he could hold, as if he were about to dive into some bottomless pool, and he closed his eyes and right at that very moment he surrendered. Aiden let the ground swallow him whole.

(20)

A RED GEO TRACKER WITH ITS BLACK RAGTOP SUNKEN on the metal frame like hide over a skeleton was parked at the far end of the Dietzes' trailer. The plastic windows were opaque and torn. Mud caked the tires. Thad opened the driver's-side door and found the keys in the ignition. He tried to turn the engine over, but the motor wouldn't crank. He stamped the gas pedal a few times, rolled the key again, and on the second go the engine sputtered to life, a belt screeching beneath the hood before dying into a lower shrill. The small four-wheel-drive rattled, and Thad left it to idle while he went back inside.

On patrols, they bagged the heads of those they captured, black sacks over their faces as if they were trying to trick cats from finding their way home. The only thing the prisoners knew about where they were headed was in the jarring of Humvees traversing rocky ground. But the whole countryside was rocky, with one place looking and feeling no different from the next, so the only thing for certain was that the mountain at the end wasn't the same mountain as the beginning. This confusion kept the prisoners from running, which was a must, because orders stopped the soldiers from killing those detained. But there was nothing stopping Thad now. He had no need to put a pillowcase over Doug's face. There wasn't anyone to tell him no.

One slip of the knife and Doug Dietz was no longer hog tied. His hands were still bound behind him, but his feet were no longer pulled up and linked to his wrists. Thad slid his knife back into the sheath on his hip, then lifted Doug to his feet by his elbows and shoved him toward the door. He led Doug into the Tracker's headlights. From the passenger side, Thad slid the seat forward and crammed him into the back floorboard. Doug tottered about, tried to roll from his stomach, and managed to get onto his side just as Thad slammed the seat back against him. That fast, and they were off.

Left out of Booker Branch, headed east up 281, the road rose above Cedar Cliff Lake and alongside Bear. Thad drove past Christmas tree fields and a goat farm and swerved around a gaze of raccoons eating from a bag of trash ravaged across half the two-lane highway. He drove by ditch-side memorials where families put plastic flowers and white crosses and stuffed teddy bears in memory of their loved ones. He headed past hand-painted signs nailed to trees, signs with single words dripping down them, words like REPENT and JESUS bloodred on whitewashed scraps of barn wood. Charleys Creek Road shot off to the left toward home, but Thad kept going, rounding the next bend and crossing over Sols Creek and Neddy Creek, narrow troughs of water barely deep enough for deer to wet their noses and drink. Then he was at Grays Ridge Road and whipped the short-axled Tracker onto the cut at the right and felt the bald tires slip a bit around the switchback. He followed past abandoned shacks, past farmhouses and single-wides where good people eked out hard lives. The paved road ended at a small parking area where a gated gravel road wound farther into the valley. From here, they would have to walk.

Thad wore the headlamp, the lantern beaming square from his forehead so that when Doug Dietz looked at him Thad must've appeared as some hellish figure with a head made entirely of light. Yanking Doug from behind the seats, Thad pressed the shotgun into the back of his head. "You're going to walk, and you don't want to stop walking till I tell you. You understand?"

Doug Dietz turned and nodded. His mouth chewed behind the duct tape and his eyes were wide. The headlamp spotlighted his dirty face and grease-strung hair, and until right then Thad hadn't noticed just how blue Doug's eyes were.

With the shotgun prodded into his spine, Doug stumbled forward along the gravel road. Oat grass, sedges, and bull thistle leaned in from the ditches, all of it slick with dew that wet the two men up to their waists as they headed farther into the darkness. They were nearly a mile in when the sound of water overcame the usual nighttime chatter. At the metal bridge, current slipped over smoothed stones, dropped bench by bench down the mountain, and within the bigger pools the surface roiled in a reflection of the movement beneath. They crossed the bridge, and, reaching the other side, Thad grabbed Doug by the nape of his collar and guided him underneath the iron trestles to where an old roadbed cut farther into the mountains. The roadbed dead-ended onto one that was maintained and led to a transfer station the power company had built, just a small building and a tower. Thad's headlamp lit the eyes of a black bear in the middle of the logging road that moved further still. Doug froze in his tracks when he saw the bear watching them, but Thad kicked at the backs of his knees and shoved him forward with the barrel. The bear tore through the laurels and vanished.

The logging road curved and headed upward, but Thad pushed Doug to the right to follow the river. The name of the place was Bonas Defeat, and Thad knew the gorge well. This was where he'd come when his mind could take no more. Old-timers said the name came from a hunting dog, a Plott hound named Bona, that shot out of the yard after a deer one Sunday and wound up chasing the young buck through the bushes and over the cliff, both animals kicking wildly against the air until they hit bottom. Though everyone who grew up in Little Canada knew the place, very few ventured here. There was no reason to go.

Bonas Defeat was nearly solid rock, boulders as big as houses teetering with an unsettling stability after having been set there by water thousands of years before. A man couldn't plant a thing in this place, nor was it land to hunt, and though there were speckled trout in the stream, the number of rattlesnakes and copperheads denned up in this country made fishing too risky to be worth the time. The only people who ever came to this place were outsiders, thrill-seekers with a mind to climb a rock face or rappel into caverns, at least one or two killing off each summer in a fashion that left local men to risk their own lives to retrieve the bodies. People who grew up in this place didn't hunt for things like that. It was a burden on their neighbors, oftentimes their own blood, for men to come drag their body out of somewhere they had no business being to begin with. Living was plenty hard enough.

When they reached the start of this rocky place, Thad told Doug to sit and rest. They took a spot along the river where a large slab of granite lay flat. Thad peeled the duct tape off Doug's mouth and

Doug spit the sock into the water, the gag pale and waving as it moved downstream like a palomino trout in the nightglow. Doug flopped onto his side, buried his face in the river to drink, and when his mouth was wet enough for words he lay there and said, "I can't keep going."

"You'd be surprised what a man can do when he has to," Thad answered. He pulled a flat stone from the river and stroked his fingers across its face. The sound of water was so loud that to talk to one another they were nearly shouting. When Thad had the stone just how he wanted, he pulled out the skinning knife and swiped the blade back and forth to reclaim the edge. He was turned so that the shotgun across his lap stayed aimed at Doug, who'd finally managed to rock himself upright, his arms behind him and hunching him forward, legs spread in front of him. Thad stayed focused on the stone, that simple swiping of the blade having always been one of the things that calmed him most. Every night in the mountains of Paktika Province he'd stayed up and sharpened that same knife while the others took advantage of what sleep they could find. Thad didn't sleep, and running the knife's edge against whetstone became meditative.

"You know, there was these people in Afghanistan," Thad started to say, but stopped abruptly when he'd finally finished tuning the edge. He tossed the stone back into the river and checked the blade against a callus on his hand, the skin slicing clean as paper. "There was these hajj in the mountains there and everybody was scared to death of them. When we'd enter one of those villages the folks who lived there would get to telling stories."

Doug stared at Thad as if he were confused by why he told him this. He glanced to where the shotgun lay in Thad's lap, but darted his eyes away when Thad settled his hand onto the pistol grip and ran his finger over the trigger.

"There was this one story those hajjis told every time we started in on them," Thad said. "They told that same story over and over. It was why they wouldn't tell us shit. What they said was that there was this woman who got taken one time, and that woman had been talking to the Americans and the Taliban knew it. So they took her off into the mountains, and you know what them hajjis said they did to her?"

Doug shook his head.

"They cut off the soles of her feet and made her walk to her own grave."

Thad rose and pushed the gun into Doug's temple until Doug's head bent sideways. "I'm going to need you to get on your stomach," Thad said before kicking at Doug's shoulder, him tipping onto his side.

Doug Dietz rolled around for a minute like some grub having fallen out of its rotten home. He finally settled with his chest flat against the granite slab, his right cheek pressed against the cold, damp stone. Thad straddled Doug's body and sat where his hands were bound at the base of his back. He pulled one of Doug's feet toward his chest and Doug immediately began to kick and scream wildly. It took a second or two of fighting to lock Doug's foot against his chest, but once it was there Thad took the knife and went to work. When the pain overcame him, Doug passed out. Now there was only the sound of water, and Thad worked quickly until it was done.

DOUG DIETZ WHIMPERED SOFTLY when he finally came to. Thad was close by, with his legs hugged to his chest, and when Doug noticed that dark silhouette beside him he began to cry. Thad stood but did not speak. He simply bent down, hitched his arms beneath

Doug's elbows, and hoisted him to his feet with a heavy grunt. The second Doug was left to stand on his own, he screamed out into the night and collapsed first to his knees, then onto his face. Thad stomped one heavy kick into Doug's rib cage before he jerked him back to his feet.

"Now walk," Thad said, but Doug couldn't. He just fell back to the ground and lay limp. Thad knelt and whispered so close to Doug's ear that those first few words made him cringe. "You think you know how this is going to end and you think because it's going to end that way you might as well just stop doing what I'm telling you," Thad said. "Well, you're right about that ending, but you're wrong about having any sort of say. I can keep you alive as long as I want to, Doug Dietz. I can drag this ending out as long as you'd like. Now I'm going to stand you up and you're going to walk. You're going to walk on your own two feet to the very end."

Thad lifted once more, and as Doug stood bent-legged like some reptile, Thad severed the zip ties that bound his wrists.

"You can get up yourself from here on," Thad said. "Now walk."

Doug hobbled a few tiny steps but when his foot came down that third or fourth time it was like he'd stepped on a nail. His legs collapsed beneath him and he just lay there and shook and cried on the ground.

Thad did not feel the least bit sorry for him. Doug Dietz had killed one of the only things in this world Thad loved, and before that, even more unforgivable, Doug had taken the innocence of a child. In Thad's eyes, Doug was just the same as those towelheads who posed as unarmed shepherds, who strapped explosives to the chests of little girls and spent hours skinning prisoners before beheading them, hanging pieces of their mutilated bodies from tree limbs like wind chimes. He wasn't sorry then and he wasn't sorry now. There was wickedness in this world that swallowed any light that might've been, darkness that could be answered only with darkness.

"Get up," Thad said.

Doug trembled on the ground. "I can't," he muttered. "I can't!"

Thad stood a few feet behind while Doug repeated those words like a mantra, and in a few minutes Doug's breathing was heavy and calm, as if he'd fallen into some painful meditation. When Doug regained what composure there was to be had, Thad said again, "Get up," and this time he did.

They made their way forward across rocky ground, over a landscape constructed by stone and water. The river swept through spaces in a valley cobbled by monoliths, water dividing, then disappearing and running through hidden passageways that could be heard but not seen, a living river that split like veins, only to find some new convergence downstream. They crawled along the edges of great cairns, stones the size of houses balanced with an unfathomable gravity as if they'd been set just so by the hands of some watchmaker god. They moved beneath stone, through caverns created by granite overhangs, places that held the sound and echo of water and words and breath, hollows where they could hear the whispering of their own hearts. A mile in, they stood beneath a sheer rock face, a cliff that rose some hundred feet above them, its edge, in such darkness, marked only by the absence of stars. This was the cliff where the place had gotten its name, the cliff where Bona had chased the young button buck, its antlers burled under skin into velveteen knolls, off into the sky, off into nothing, off into forever. They stood there for a moment at the place where the world had fallen, and when they'd caught their breath, they moved on.

When Doug Dietz's body finally gave out, he screamed, "No more! No more! I can't go any goddamn further."

Looking down over Doug's sprawled body, Thad said, "This place will do just fine."

He allowed Doug to crawl those last few feet onto a rock that angled high above the others, the water somewhere deep beneath them. The river seemed to go underground, the current just a faint washing sound deep in the gaps left between rocks. It had taken them the entire night to reach this place, and Thad's body was nearly spent. Over the eastern mountains the darkness began to crack apart. It would still be hours before the sun rose from that jagged horizon, but when it did, Thad would be gone from this place and Doug would be gone from this world.

There were holes augered through the rock where Thad and Doug sat, similar holes in the rocks that surrounded them, some drilled straight through, others carving deep tubes and bowls into the stone. Thad pulled out his cigarettes and lit a smoke while Doug lay there so worn-out that, despite the pain and drugs, he was almost asleep. Thad remembered hearing one time how those holes are created, how stones get caught in depressions and how water washes those stones in circles and how given enough time—thousands of years, maybe—pebbles so small that you can hold them in the palm of your hand can bore through a rock the size of a house. Thad reached into a cup-shaped depression in the rock. The water that pooled there was cold, almost shockingly so, and he dug around till he found the pebble at the bottom. He pulled the stone out and turned it in his hand, a light pink stone not much bigger than a buckeye. He wondered if, given enough time, this stone might make its way through the mountain. He wondered how long it would take to burrow to the center of the earth.

(21)

SHE WHISPERED IN HIS EAR, BUT THAT DID NOT WAKE him. Aiden dreamed about the day the law had come to the trailer to take him to the group home, the day Thad Broom toed the line with a gun in his hand to keep Aiden from going back. "You're not going anywhere you don't want to go," Thad said, as he stood there with his single-shot .410 broken open under his arm and slid a shell into the chamber. Aiden could see in Thad's eyes that he meant it. There were crows cawing from the treetops outside, and for once, as he curled under the bed in silence, he felt protected. Everyone else he'd ever trusted had abandoned him, but Thad promised to keep him safe. Right then, Aiden put all his trust into one person and closed his eyes. He held his breath to keep quiet and in his mind he prayed.

He opened his eyes to fog. Clouds lowered onto the mountain, swallowed the ridgeline, and strung everything with tiny beads of dew almost every morning, the trees and leaves and grass shimmering as if they'd been given jewelry by the night. It had always seemed strange that what most people spent their entire lives staring up at actually pushed down on this place. Everything was always pushing down on them.

When Aiden's eyes settled on the woman who stood over him like a pale angel it seemed as if dream delivered him to dream.

"We need to get you up, sweet one," she said, but he didn't stir.

"It's nice here," Aiden said, and rolled his head against the grass and closed his eyes as if he might just go back to sleep.

"You can't stay in the yard. There're people coming. We need to get you down the hill, get you on the couch."

When she knelt beside him, he could finally make out her face. "I finished painting the room," he said.

"You didn't need to do that. I could've finished," she said. "Now, come on and let's get you up."

April took Aiden by the hand and he tried to come up from the ground, but his body was mush. When he finally rose to his feet, he was so dizzy he nearly fell over, but he blinked his eyes until the feeling passed, then stood drooping in the yard until he'd regained some sort of control. "Where's Thad?" he asked.

"Down there, I guess. But I don't know."

"I'm glad he made it home," Aiden said. April was beside him and Aiden put his arm over her shoulder so he wouldn't fall as he stumbled drunkenly down the hill. When they were to the trailer, April led Aiden inside and helped him onto the couch. The place was still ripped apart, but he was too out of his mind to pay any attention. April leaned down and kissed him on the forehead, and she put her thumb against his mouth and he puckered his lips to kiss her back. "Tell Thad I'm glad he made it home," Aiden said. And then he closed his eyes and was asleep.

(22)

A LIGHT DRIZZLE THAT SEEMED MORE TO HANG IN THE air than fall started around midday. It looked like Ireland, or at least that's what the folks who'd come to see the property said. April didn't know if that was true or not. She'd been out of those mountains only twice in her entire life.

Their names were Pat and Connie Lathan, and they were up from Atlanta. Pat had been a urologist and Connie had retired as the provost of the Savannah College of Art and Design, something she kept repeating as if her career had trumped her husband's. Pat was stubby and had a wild swath of hair swept across his head. He wore a pair of tortoiseshell eyeglasses with thick frames that circled his eyes and didn't seem to fit his style at all. Connie had undoubtedly picked them out. She was tall and lean and dressed to the nines with high-waist slacks and a thin silk blouse that made her figure stunning, even in her midsixties. Pat talked so fast that April had a hard time understanding what he said, while Connie's words rolled out of her mouth in a low-country drawl. April had neither met nor seen people like the Lathans in all her life. Nothing about them made sense. It was like she was looking at aliens.

"Dr. Lathan wants to plant that hillside with Christmas trees," Tom Rice said. He'd had the listing from the beginning and assured April that he could sell the property if she was patient and willing to negotiate. So far he'd only brought three people in a little over a year, but April was hopeful.

"Christmas trees, huh?" April ran her eyes over Pat as if she might have missed something, but she hadn't. She turned to Tom Rice, who stood before her, just a pudgier, balder version of the boy she'd gone to high school with. Tom had never been much to look at and she would've laughed at him if he'd had the nerve to ask her out back then. But now he owned a real estate firm that had made a fortune during the boom, and he'd lived far enough below his means that he hadn't lost his ass like all the others when the market tanked. She focused back on Dr. Lathan. "I think Christmas trees could do well here."

"You do?" Mrs. Lathan squealed in horror. She eyed April with a sneering skepticism, then turned that expression toward her husband. "I personally think he's gone batty."

Pat stood silenced and Tom Rice's eyes were wide like he hadn't the foggiest idea how to break the tension.

"I think they'll do just fine," April said. "The Hoopers have made a lot of money through the years growing Fraser fir just over that ridge." She nodded to someplace back behind the house that could've just as easily not existed at all for what the Lathans knew of this country. "You've got the Hoopers on that side and there are some Fowlers on up from there, and all of them got some of the prettiest trees in this country. Even had one in the White House one Christmas."

"The White House," Dr. Lathan said. "You hear that, hun? The Hoopers even had a tree in the White House."

"You're saying people have grown *presidential* trees on this property?" She stressed that word *presidential* as if to dismiss everything April said.

"Not on this property, no." April stared at Connie and did everything in her power to keep a smile on her face. She'd gotten up early, put on her makeup, curled her hair, and slid into the nicest thing she had, a pretty cotton sundress that fit her perfectly, but it didn't matter. There was nothing she could do to pass for anything more than backwoods to a woman like Mrs. Lathan. April was Kmart classy at best. "There hasn't been trees grown on this property, but we're right in the heart of some of the finest firs there are. That's a fact. And it might even bode well that the land hasn't been touched. The soil might be richer."

"The soil will be richer," Dr. Lathan repeated sternly.

April suddenly realized that they hadn't made it off the front porch. "I have some coffee inside if you'd like to come in and see the house."

"That's okay, dear." Mrs. Lathan squinted her eyes as if to get a better view through the mist. "And who owns that little trailer down there?"

"I do," April said. "The property runs past that and then cuts over through those trees for a ways and back up to the top of this ridge, then it kind of takes an angle down to the road where you came in. But the trailer down there, it's a part of the six acres. My son lives in it right now."

"Someone lives there?" Mrs. Lathan looked absolutely appalled.

Dr. Lathan seemed to pay attention only to the property lines April had drawn, appearing satisfied with what he envisioned.

"We really should step on into the house," April said. "There's no sense in standing in the rain."

"I kind of like the feel of it," Dr. Lathan said. "And, besides, we don't have any interest in the home."

April cocked her head to the side thinking she'd misunderstood.

"That's the thing I didn't get a chance to tell you on the phone, April. The Lathans are interested in the property, but just the property," Tom Rice tried to explain. "Not the house or the trailer. Just the land."

"I don't think I understand what you're getting at."

"We already own a home," Mrs. Lathan said. "It's in Wade Hampton."

"I know a girl who does some housekeeping there." April tried to make small talk, tried to say something that might make Mrs. Lathan look at her differently, but it didn't work.

"We divide our time between there and Atlanta."

"So I still don't think I understand," April said. "What interest do you have in this place, then?"

"Well, there's no land in Cashiers," Dr. Lathan interjected. "Our community is divided into small lots, see, and there's certainly no room for Christmas trees."

"I could die," Mrs. Lathan screeched. "Like I said, he has absolutely gone batty."

"What they're saying, April, is that if they were to make an offer on the property it would be for the land, just the land."

April stood there and tried to process everything that had been said. After a while, she pushed herself to grin and met eyes with Dr. Lathan. "Christmas trees, huh?"

"Yes, Fraser fir. Presidential trees in every direction." Dr. Lathan opened his hands out over the land in front of him. "I can see it now."

April laughed at his theatrics and it seemed to please him that she was amused. But really what she found amusing was what he thought he could do on this land. There was nothing simple about growing trees, and anybody with half a brain would've known that. Trying to farm trees on six acres was one of the stupidest things she'd ever heard. She certainly expected some highbrow doctor and his wife to have better sense than that.

Most of the families who raised trees in Jackson County had been cabbage farmers decades ago. When trees outpriced cabbage, they phased out their land year by year until the cabbage was gone and they had ten generations of tree stock, a transition that took a decade to make profitable and even then left them to scrape by. It was as if Dr. Lathan believed trees had to be easy work, a lot easier than, say, tomatoes or strawberries. After all, the woods were full of trees and no one toiled away to make them grow.

April was certain he'd roll a tractor onto himself or get bit by a rattlesnake, but she wasn't entirely sure if that would be all that bad of an end. If he cleared all of the land this fall and managed to get trees in the ground, he'd be lucky if he ever got to see one tree wrapped in lights with an angel on top at Christmas before he killed off. The more April thought about it, Dr. Lathan's old lady was right.

"He's gone stark raving mad," Mrs. Lathan said, and they all stood there and laughed for a minute longer.

When the rain poured down, the Lathans and Tom Rice hightailed it for his notchback sedan, hollering they'd be in touch. April wasn't entirely certain whether that was something that pleased her or made her sad. She watched them drive past the trailer at the bottom of the hillside and she thought she saw Dr. Lathan wave at her. His wife beside him seemed to turn toward the trailer, where Aiden was still asleep, Mrs. Lathan probably questioning how the hell people could live like this. April thought about all of the time and money she'd dumped into the house. She and Aiden slaved away to turn this place into something nicer than it'd ever been. All of that work, and this place was nothing more than a joke to these people, a house to raze, a lot to clear-cut, and all for nothing more than shits and giggles, just a hobby. Dr. Lathan wanted to play farmer.

But April was over it. She didn't care what the Lathans thought about her or her house or this land or her life. She'd suffered too long to care anymore. She'd been cussed and hit and spat on for so damn long and all she had to show for it was a house and a piece of land that other folks wouldn't touch with a ten-foot stick. She was tired. And if those people wanted this mountain and they were willing to cut a check, then by God they could have it. She was sick of staying put and hoping for better. She'd been waiting on better her whole life, and better never came.

She was soaking wet and the rain was still coming and she no longer knew whether to go inside or just keep standing there. So she just stood there figuring why the hell not, and hoped to God they'd make her an offer, because if they did, she was done. She'd take the money and never look back.

(23)

THE SUN DID NOT RISE ON BONAS DEFEAT. BEFORE DAY-
light could climb over the ridgeline, clouds swept across the fracture
of sky over the gorge and brought an early-morning drizzle that
could be more heard in the trees than felt on the ground. Ashen-gray
clouds pushed against one another and built into a greater darkness,
and by noon the rain was upon him.

Thad was climbing a craggy path along the edge of the spillway at
the head of the gorge when the storm came. The spillway crumbled
into stones at the bottom, but the concrete slope up top was slicked
with green algae where a thin veil of water always flowed. The concrete quickly darkened from white to a leathery brown under the
rain. What first streaked by in heavy sheets soon became one solid
torrent. By the time he made it to the top of the dam, Thad's clothes
were soaked through.

The lake was low with a wide rim of clay-caked stone and sand
outlining dark water that seemed to steam as the rain fell. A murder
of crows strutted about like black chickens on the bank and picked

through litter discarded by fishermen: beer cans and pale blue containers that had held night crawlers, balled-up wads of fishing line, and an Igloo cooler busted to pieces against the rocks. Thad figured the lake was lowered so that men could work on the dam, but there was no one around, just a CAT bulldozer and trackhoe, their yellow paint chipping around scabs of rust, their tracks muddied with clay. He headed through the rain up a road above the spillway and did not see the fork until he was upon it. To the left the old logging road wound into the valley and came out at the metal bridge where he'd begun, and to the right the road led past Slickens Creek to where Highway 281 cut south toward Rock Bridge and Round Mountain and north around Tanasee Lake and Wolf. He kept right at the fork, his footsteps stamping brief impressions in the muddy gravel but soon washed away and gone.

Only the men who had been there knew how it rained in Afghanistan. Until he was there to feel it pelt his helmet and see it with his own two eyes, everything Thad had ever been taught as a kid made him believe that there was nothing but desert. That wasn't true at all. In Afghanistan, the rain had its own season.

Late October or early November a daylong sandstorm would blow in from the west to signal the start of rain. The temperatures would drop and then the rains would come, sometimes so much water that they would spend entire days filling sandbags and building retaining walls to divert what otherwise would have washed them away. All the year's rain and snow was contained in the months between November and April, and there were times that the men were hammered by storms. The wet season ran right into fighting season. Nothing ever eased up one bit.

It was the February before Thad came home for good when a blizzard struck and left sections of the mountains in six feet of snow.

There were standing temps twenty below and drifts so deep that even the Humvees became useless. When all of that weather hit so suddenly, the entire division out of FOB Rushmore added aid missions to their patrols. Thad's squad worked to get supplies—clothing and blankets, food and fuel—into mountain villages where barefoot children were frostbitten so badly by the time the soldiers reached them that there was no choice but to amputate. Thad remembered walking through draws where tribes of goats and sheep had huddled together to weather the storm only to freeze with open eyes and iced fur that cracked like bottle glass when he nudged at their bodies with the steel toes of his boots.

He remembered one time he dipped snowballs in water so they were hard as rocks and hid them behind a bank near the latrine. That evening he waited for Darnell Johnson to finish shitting out his MRE. When Darnell came out, Thad clobbered him in the side of the head with a snowball and had another one into his neck before Darnell realized what was happening. Darnell was a monster who'd played on the line at some all-black college in South Carolina before he joined, and the minute he caught sight of Thad, he barreled full speed and tackled him into the snow. They wrestled for a second or two, both of them laughing their asses off, before Darnell took control and shoved a fistful of snow down Thad's throat. When it was over, Darnell stood up and kicked powder onto him, and Thad just lay there in hysterics with his nose bloodied as he flapped the outline of an angel into the ground.

Thad laughed and turned around to say something, but there was no one there, just empty road and mountains. He was alone and this was not the place where his mind had wandered. Even through the gray haze of rain, this place was too green. He was in Little Canada, humping down Highway 281 with a shotgun in his hands.

Somewhere up the road, tires hissed across the wetted pavement and the car was nearly there before he heard it. A patrol car running the highway to the county line veered around the curve ahead, and Thad barely had time to jump the guardrail into the laurels before the headlights swept across him. He lay on his stomach in the wet leaves and ferns until the car had passed and then for some time after until he was certain they were gone.

Just before the bridge where Tanasee Creek emptied into the lake, a trail cut by pickup trucks and four-wheel-drives sloped away from the highway toward the creek. The grass between the tire marks was high and fanned out over the gravel so that he could hardly make out where the tires had been. By the creek, a rusted burn barrel dented and ragged with holes stood between two metal folding chairs. One of the chairs had bent legs and leaned toward a fire pit circled by stones, the coals now old and weathered into nothing more than blackened earth. Thad looked upstream. The creek wrapped around a sharp bend before a final plunge pool that slowed to slack water in the space between him and there. If he followed the stream far enough north, he would wind up on Charleys Creek, then home.

As he hiked upstream, Thad could tell by the way his bones ached that he was coming down. The dope always made his back hurt worse and he wished that he had some alcohol to numb the pain, but he didn't. So he trudged forward over the rocky back of a serpentine streambed that meandered between mountains for miles. Only when his knees felt like they would burst if he took another step did he stop to find shelter.

High water from weeks when the rain did not cease had cut a bank beneath the roots of two scarlet oaks that seeded so closely together in the beginning that time welded their trunks into a single tree. Pebbles made a bed that transitioned to a wall of dark soil, water dripping from the veined root ceiling above. Thad tucked himself inside the cut bank and watched as a crawdad backed away from him toward the stream with its claws raised and pincers opened. When its tail found water, the crawdad slipped into the stream and vanished. Thad scrounged for leaves and twigs to start a fire, and his body trembled from a day spent drenched with rain. His cigarettes were soaked through and the flint of his lighter would not spark at first. Midges and crane flies swooped down and lifted to light, their bodies hopping Us against gravity, until Thad finally made a fire and smoked them out of the cut.

The fire was small, but still it seemed to help him reclaim some of the heat he'd lost. He lay there and rolled a soaked cigarette back and forth in front of the flames, and when the paper and tobacco were finally dry enough to light, he tried to ease his mind, though it did no good at all.

The water in his clothes sank back into the ground as he lay there and remembered. Pulling guard was always the worst because one man was responsible for keeping everyone else alive while they slept. It wasn't all that much different from running point in that sense, but at least when everyone was on their feet, every man had a gun in his hands and a finger over the trigger; they could all keep an eye out for one another. Night watch was different because the trust was in one man when the others shut their eyes, even though they all knew that he was just as tired as they were.

What Thad remembered was a night when the Red Bull and the snuff couldn't keep him awake. He fell asleep on watch with a dip of Skoal wintergreen in his lip, and woke up to metal clanking and then the bawling of sheep. By the time he saw the small herd, he could also see the man who pushed the animals through the canyon. Thad barely had time to raise his gun before the first sheep was there. He screamed for the shepherd to stop and the others in the squad woke from their dreams and joined him with guns aimed until the ANA interpreter figured out the man was nothing more than a farmer who'd spent an entire day tracking down sheep that had run off and was now just trying to get home. The shepherd led his flock on through the canyon and the other soldiers cracked jokes before trying to get a few more hours' sleep, but all Thad could think about was how he'd failed them, how he'd fallen asleep on watch, and how if that shepherd had been anything other than a shepherd they all would have been goners.

It had been five or six days since he'd last slept and he was just as tired right that second as the night he pulled guard. With the shotgun hugged against his chest in the cut bank, he lay with his body shivering, the fire all but gone and nothing left dry enough to burn. His body was exhausted. The dope had taken him into a foggy space between waking and dream where his mind couldn't separate past from present. He couldn't make sense of where he was or how he'd gotten there. Everything seemed some strange vision, and he could no longer remember where he had been just an hour before.

Memories seemed as if they happened right that second, and in those flashes when he snapped back out of his mind, he was scared to death. He drifted into this sort of lucid dreaming where he was on patrol, always at some low vantage, trying to keep eyes on the hillside when the first crack of gunfire sounded, that crack snapping him awake. Thad stabbed at the coals to try and stoke any heat left in them, and then curled into a trembling ball and stared out into the rain. He let his mind wander back into that place that felt real, and he told himself that someone else was on watch. Someone else was looking over him, guarding him, and would keep him safe while he slept. And when his mind was there, he closed his eyes and fell back into that dream that washed him around and shook him awake with eyes wide and wild. He drifted in and out of his mind, in and out of this place, and only after a very long while did what he feared most find him.

(24)

THE FRONT DOOR CLACKED AGAINST THE WALL ON A howl of wind that blew rain inside the trailer. The pry job Doug Dietz did to get inside made it impossible for the door to hold shut, the dog-eared door now clapping against the wall as the wind blew off the mountain. Aiden woke from a dreamless sleep to the sound of the doorknob hammering the wall. Through the doorway, he could see the rain sweep across the yard in sheets. He did not move. He just lay there on the couch until his vision cleared and watched the wind turn loose paper across the floor, those tumbling pages a raspy clatter like dried leaves.

He knew neither how long he had slept nor whether the low, gray light outside indicated morning or night. The room seemed empty now without the spool in front of the couch. When he thought of the table Aiden thought of Loretta Lynn, and when he thought of the dog he thought of Thad. He wondered if Thad was asleep in his bedroom. He wondered what time Thad had made it home, if he'd made it home, and what he had done in those hours between when Aiden left him on the front porch of the Dietzes' trailer and now, however long that might have been.

Most everything in the kitchen had been thrown onto the floor and the same was true for the posters and photographs that had been tacked to the walls. The only thing that still held exactly where it had been was an electronic weather station hung on the side of the cabinet that showed sunshine and thirty degrees rather than rain and whatever temperature it was. He paid no attention to the forecast. What he was interested in seeing was the date and time because they were accurate.

The screen said it was Saturday, August 21, and almost eight o'clock in the evening. That meant Aiden had only slept the day away, which was good, he thought. Leland had told him to meet his contact that afternoon, but going a little late wouldn't be a big deal. He and Thad could be down there before eight thirty or nine. After wading the trash piled in the kitchen floor, he stuck his head into Thad's bedroom to see if he was in bed. He wasn't. The room was empty and just how Aiden had seen it the afternoon before, the bed pulled away from the wall with navy-blue sheets in a bunched mess.

This worried him, but he always got ahead of himself, so he tried to stay calm by thinking that Thad could've just as easily come home and left again. There was no way to know. All he could do was take care of what needed to be done. There was a schedule that had to be kept, and though he hated to do it alone, he was already late. When he got back from selling the dope, if Thad was still gone, he could go look for him. If Thad wasn't back by then, Aiden was fairly certain he knew where to find him.

.   .   .

SOMEWHERE BETWEEN Charleys Creek and Tuckasegee, the rain shifted from a torrent that made it impossible to see the road to just a steady fall. Further still, the rain lessened into a hazy drizzle that steamed from the blacktop, as if the world were just shy of catching fire. Aiden cracked the window and listened to the hiss of his tires on the highway, lit a cigarette, and wished on his life that Thad were with him. The more he thought about where he was headed and what he was doing, the more his mind raced, and before long he'd worked himself into a panic.

He knew where to go, but not who was waiting there. He'd even forgotten the name that Leland Bumgarner gave him, but fortunately found it scribbled on an empty pack of cigarettes in the floorboard of his car: Eberto. That name was all he had, a name he'd written down as soon as he and Thad got back in the car. He didn't know Eberto, and he didn't want to know him. All Aiden wanted to do was sell the drugs and leave.

Jimmy's set on the corner where Highway 281 dead-ended onto 107. The mom-and-pop convenience store was the first place to stop for gasoline coming out of Little Canada. Most folks came in for Zebra Cakes and SunDrops, a box of Copenhagen or a carton of Dorals, but whatever they wanted to buy had to be purchased early because Jimmy's closed not long after the sun went down. A building next door had been a dozen restaurants in Aiden's lifetime, his favorite having been one called Granny's, where he and Thad would eat streaked meat and grits, sometimes biscuits and sausage gravy early mornings on their way to high school. Now the place was some Mexican restaurant with a name Aiden couldn't pronounce that served tamales and sopes to migrant workers who'd dodged deportation and had no plans to leave.

The parking lot was empty and he circled around under the covered island and parked at the pumps with the car facing back the way he'd come. The apartments where Leland had told him to go were just behind him through a copse of scraggly pines, but there wasn't any way in hell he would drive right up to the building. If a man wheeled in and things turned sour, there he'd be with no way to get out. Things could get hairy fast. So Aiden planned to leave his ride at Jimmy's and walk over to the apartments. Then, at least, he'd have a shot at running. If things went south, he could tear off through the trees and get back to his ride and the Ranchero would already be aimed where he needed to go. He'd just turn her over, dump her into drive, mash the pedal to the floor, and get the hell out of there.

Despite the ill feelings Aiden had for people with names like Eberto, spics he blamed for undercutting hardworking white folks right out of construction jobs, he put those feelings aside. Whether Eberto was white or Mexican or some yellow-haired albino with pink eyes, if he was the only man in Jackson County who could take that much dope off Aiden's hands, then that was exactly who he needed to meet. Money's funny like that. Bills spend just the same no matter what color hand slaps them on the counter. Green is green and that's the only color that mattered.

Just the same as he wouldn't drive into the apartments, he wouldn't walk in carrying the dope. Leland's last words of advice had been never to take all the drugs at once, and that made sense. Aiden stepped out of the Ranchero and unlatched the truck box behind the cab. He took out the ammo can, opened the lid, and grabbed the rolls of money, the digital scales, and the long-barreled revolver.

He emptied everything out of the can but the dope, then shoved the revolver down the back of his pants, held the ammo can at his side, and locked the rest back in the truck box.

The break in the rain was a blessing, especially now that it was dark outside. Toads hopped all over the pavement and made quick meals of earthworms brought out of the ground by the storm. About fifty yards north of Jimmy's on Highway 107, Tuckasegee Baptist Church sat directly across the street from the gravel entrance that led into the apartments. He would hide the drugs by the church. That was somewhere close enough to hurry over and grab it when the deal went down, but far enough away that it wouldn't be found if it came time to run.

There was a house and old shed by the road at the church, a trailer down below that. A mixed-breed heeler that was chained to a post in the yard made one hell of a fuss as Aiden walked into the church parking lot. There were cars at the house, but they appeared to be rusted junkers that hadn't been driven in years, grass grown up to the bumpers where whoever owned the place hadn't mown. The lights were off in the house and Aiden was thankful that no one was home to hear the dog, to peer through the windows and see him looming outside.

A streetlight at the far end of the church parking lot illuminated one corner of the building and the front row of headstones in the graveyard at its side. Aiden walked to the light and checked the names on the graves: Hooper, Woodring, Queen, Barnes, names that were tied to this place and its history. There was a tall, cobbled monument with REV. HOOPER stamped into stone, and he chose that marker to hide the ammunition can behind, setting it so that the only way to see it was from behind, nothing back that way but woods and river. He took a gram of dope in a little square baggie out of the can and pocketed it so that he could show Eberto what he had for sale. If that spic came up with the cash, Aiden would bring him the rest. But only once he had his hands on the money.

He would've given anything to have Thad there with him, but he was alone and the only chance he had to leave Jackson County rode on this one shot. With his palms sweaty, he pulled the revolver from the back of his pants and swung the cylinder open to see how many shells were left. Checking the gun hadn't occurred to him until then, and he quickly realized just how useless that monster was to carry. Four of the five rounds had spent primers. There was only one shot left. Aiden slapped the cylinder closed and held the hammer back as he rotated to find that one chamber. Hunched over, he tried to use what scant light the streetlamp offered to make sure he found the last round. When he was certain of it, he eased the hammer back down onto the shell and stuffed the revolver into his waistline. He should've brought another gun. He should've checked the one he had. But it was too late now. It was too late to go back and change a thing. He would just have to make do, hope he wouldn't need a gun at all, and if he did, pray to God one bullet would be enough. There was no place to go but forward.

(25)

APRIL LOOKED AT PICTURES OF HER HIGH SCHOOL BOY-friend, Ron Schiele, on his Facebook page, and gauged how his life had turned out. When they were in high school he played football and ran track and was cut with muscles. Halfway through tenth grade, he had a scholarship offer to run the hundred meters at some college in South Carolina. He had these blue eyes and a smile that held people captive, even the teachers, could get away with anything, the type of guy everybody knew would wind up perfect.

All the girls hated April's guts. They smiled to her face and told her they loved her earrings or her hair or her hand-me-down blouse or whatever it was they needed to love to play the game, but she saw the way they looked at her when they thought she wasn't looking. She saw them sneer when she walked by in his coat. She knew the girls who asked if she and Ron wanted to ride to the prom in the limousine one of their parents had rented were the same girls who spread the rumors about her. They were the same girls who wrote on the bathroom stalls how she'd given Ron head in the field house during homeroom. They made up all kinds of stories about her and smeared her name from Sylva to Andrews until the day came that there was something bad enough that they didn't have to make up stories anymore. She was pregnant.

Up until then Ron had never batted an eye to the stories boys told in the locker room. But soon as April started to show, Ron was quick to tell anyone who'd listen that the baby wasn't his because, despite what everyone believed, they'd never actually done it. Folks had assumed, and Ron was fine with those assumptions on the long bus rides to away games, but when she got knocked up, it was like he'd never even thought about it. "That thing would've eat my dick off," he'd say. "Only reason I was with her was because she swallowed."

April slipped one of her Dorals out of the pack on the desk and laughed. Turned out Ron Schiele's life hadn't wound up so peachy, after all. He drank himself out of that track scholarship in just under a semester and was back home working in the paper mill before Thad cut his first tooth. The trophy wife he scooped up at twenty didn't look so good at forty. The seven boys his wife gave him reaped hell on her body, and April figured that girl had either grown udders after the third one or more than likely her titties warped into something out of *National Geographic*. Ron hadn't aged well either. He was losing his hair and his teeth were bad and he'd eaten himself into a caricature of the war on poverty. Not even the insulin could save him now. He'd resorted to prayer from *friends*, and April laughed at his status: "Going to the doctor tomorrow to see if they'll have to take my leg. Please pray." She *liked* it.

It was funny how things panned out. Life had a way of rolling over like a lake in fall. All those folks who had everything in high school wound up with nothing when it mattered. And people like Tom Rice, who she'd seen get hit so hard in the chest with a rotten apple Ron Schiele threw one afternoon at lunch that he shat himself in the courtyard with the whole school watching, wound up being the ones who got away.

The phone rang in the kitchen and April ashed her cigarette into a cold cup of coffee that had been on the desk since morning. She took another drag and walked into the kitchen to grab the cordless by the stove. When she picked up and said hello, she was taken aback by the voice she heard.

"April, it's Tom," he said. "How are you?"

April started to say that she'd just been thinking about him, but then it struck her how weird that might sound, or maybe it wouldn't sound weird at all since he'd been there earlier that day. All of those thoughts hit her at once and tongue-tied her so that what she said made no sense at all.

"What?"

"I'm sorry. I'm, I'm fine, Tom," April stuttered. "How are you?"

"I'm well, April, but if I've caught you at a bad time I'd be more than happy to call back after the weekend. I know it's getting late and I probably caught you in the middle of something—"

"No," April interrupted, "No, I'm not doing anything."

"Well, good. That's good," Tom said. "Listen, I don't want to keep you, but I just wanted to call and tell you some good news. Some pretty good news, I think."

"What is it?"

"Well, the Lathans have put in an offer on your property."

"That is good news," April said. She took two quick drags from her smoke, then turned on the faucet and held the cigarette in the water. When it was out, she turned off the tap and walked over to the trash can to throw the butt away.

"The thing is, it's a lot lower than what you were asking."

"How much lower?"

"About a third," Tom said. "They're wanting to give you sixty thousand."

"That ain't even tax value on the land," April said, "let alone the house."

"I know it, but it's like they said when they were there, April. They're not interested in the house, just the land, and they're wanting to offer you ten thousand an acre."

April suddenly felt sick to her stomach and she wanted another cigarette, but her pack was in the living room by the computer. She walked out of the kitchen and grabbed the Dorals off the desk, the cordless phone going all staticky until she got back by the stove. The next words came from the corner of her mouth, a cigarette in her lips. "So did you try to get them to go any higher, or did you just turn over?"

"Of course I tried to get the price up, April. You think I want to sell low? I don't stand to make anything at that price, but I just know how long you've had the property on the market, and so at the very least I thought I'd put it on the table."

"The county's got these six acres valued at a hundred thousand dollars, Tom. A hundred thousand dollars, and that ain't even counting the house," April said. "Between the land and the hundred twenty they've got valued on the house and the thirty thousand on the trailer, I'm paying taxes on a quarter million dollars of property every year. What they're offering is a slap in the face, and the fact that you're putting it on the table—"

"Now, I'm going to have to stop you right there," Tom said. His voice was stern and it was obvious to April she'd ticked him off. "You and I both know the value the county has on that land is high. The last time property was assessed was at the height of the market, and that place isn't worth half that now. I'm sorry to put it like that, but it's just the truth. The property is not worth that. So to be completely frank, I think ten thousand an acre is a generous offer, and I think if you're really wanting to sell it right now, at the very least, you need to entertain it."

"And what about the house?" April asked.

"They told you. They're not interested in the house. To be honest with you, they'd probably offer a little higher if the house wasn't there. The Lathans are going to have to tear down that house and that trailer and haul it off the property to do what they want to do. It'll probably cost them twenty thousand just to get that piece of land anywhere close to how they want it."

"You don't think you can talk them up to a hundred?" April asked. She was hot-boxing the cigarette nervously and tapped her nails against the metal sink.

"There's no way."

"Well, I'm not selling for sixty. I'm just not," April said. "You think you can get them up to eighty?"

"I don't know."

"Seventy-five?"

"I can try."

"Just ask," April pleaded.

"I said I'll try," Tom said.

"You just tell them I ain't selling for sixty, and that they're going to have to come up if they want to make a tree farm out of this place."

"I'll see what they say, but you think about what I'm saying to you. If you want out, then you need to think long and hard about what that's worth."

When he was gone, April hung the cordless back on its charger. She leaned with her butt against the countertop and took a long drag from her cigarette, the ash breaking away and peppering the tile between her feet. Mittens jumped onto the counter and purred loudly as he rammed his face against her arm and back, tiptoeing a tightrope along the edge of the counter. For as far back as she could remember this place had been the very thing that haunted her. Every ridge, every road, every room, every face held memories. When she looked at her son or drove by the church or passed her parents' old house, where she'd grown up, all April could see was the worst moment of her life. And when she lay in that bed just down the hall or stood there where she stood right then, all she could think about was the times George Trantham had taken every bit of hatred he had for this world out on her.

For a long time, all she'd wanted was to move to someplace that held no memories. All she wanted was to head off to some town where she knew no one. With the land sold she could go anywhere she damn well pleased: Savannah or Charleston or maybe Atlanta or Memphis, it just didn't matter so long as it wasn't Little Canada. So the question Tom Rice raised was a good question to ask, and she wasn't quite sure of the answer. How much was it worth?

(26)

BEFORE THE APARTMENTS WERE BUILT, TOMMY PRESS-
ley kept the Mexicans stacked in buses like cordwood. For years, his
family had brought the migrants in at seed and harvest, worked them
to the bone for wages no white man would have broken a sweat over.
They housed the workers in the same buses used to haul them from
field to field. That was the start of it. That was when the Mexicans
first came to the mountains and to Jackson County.

They could just as easily have been Guatemalan or Honduran or
Salvadoran or Colombian or anything else, but none of that mattered
to people who'd never seen them before. They were Mexicans. They
were farmhands who worked spring and fall, and outside of those
times were nowhere to be found. Then one year, Tommy Pressley
got the bright idea to build dormitories that later became apartments. The idea came to him just the same as it had to mill owners
who built the houses where the workers lived and paid them in scrip.
Build the world they live in and they wind up handing back the same

money they're paid. That was the idea, that's what he'd done, and that's how it started.

The problem was that once those Mexicans had places to live that weren't just seasonal, they had to find ways to earn a living outside of farming. Most had trades they'd learned back home, trades like Aiden, who mostly laid rock, but could do about anything with his hands. They were stonemasons and plumbers and framers and painters and electricians and roofers and operators, and some hung drywall and some hung gutters and some hung hardy board and some did grading and some poured concrete, and all drank Tecate and shared lunches of beans and spiced meat with tortillas and two liters of orange soda. Their work was just the same as any white man's and they did it for eight dollars an hour at first, then negotiated to ten, which was still a break because none of the locals would even think of lacing up their boots for anything less than fifteen. This meant higher margins for contractors, so they came to prefer the work of Mexicans to white men: two-thirds the wages and no need to pay taxes or 1099 them. Done deal.

Aiden still found work when the market was strong because there was just that much work to be had. Developments popped up along every ridgeline in Jackson County faster than contractors could pull permits, so fast that the county had to build a second permitting office at the southern end just to try and keep up. But when the market crashed and the plug was pulled and construction sites dried up overnight, leaving houses that were half-finished abandoned like the end of the world had come, the white jobs were the first to go and the Mexicans lost theirs not long after.

None of that mattered because they were there by that point, whole families filling every trailer park and apartment slum from

Cashiers to Cullowhee. Cantinas popped up all over the place and their parking lots were always filled with foreign cars with South Carolina tags, all of those Mexicans learning quickly that they could register the cars they shared in the state below without a lick of insurance. If one of them crashed drunk at night, he'd pop the tag off with a screwdriver, leave the car in the ditch or wrapped around a tree, run like hell, and have the same plate on a new ride by morning. All sheriff deputies had were blood trails that trickled out away from the crash. Nobody to arrest. Nobody to charge. Just a mess to clean up.

There were some jobs starting to pop back up now, two years after the housing bubble burst, but that same pattern from before now worked in reverse. The first jobs went to Mexicans who'd do the work for half the price, and so the market coming back didn't mean a thing to Aiden. He was still out of work and carried all of that hatred with him as he headed up the gravel drive to the apartment building where Eberto lived.

Dim yellow lights over doorways lit the ground floor and the balcony above, a group of men on the second floor talking loudly and singing. One of the men tossed a bottle down into the parking lot, where the glass shattered any stillness there might have been and sent a stray cat hightailing for shelter. Another group of men huddled together at the corner of the building and didn't make a sound, just stood there. They were the first to notice Aiden as he came up the drive. The group of men opened up, most of them wearing canvas pants, dirtied T-shirts, and work boots, their clothes caked with dried plaster and concrete and paint. One man wore a pair of clean blue jeans and a nice button-down dress shirt tucked in, a straw cowboy hat on his head, with the tips of his boots and his large belt buckle catching all light there was to be had. There was also an old lady toward the middle of the building who snapped beans from a metal folding chair. She was hunched over by age and work, and never even looked up until Aiden was directly in front of her.

"Do you know which apartment Eberto lives in?" Aiden asked.

"No," the old woman said without lifting her eyes. She pulled another string from a pod, snapped the bean in three places, and tossed the quartered sections into a plastic grocery bag at her feet.

"There's supposed to be an Eberto lives here. You don't know anyone named Eberto?"

"No Eberto," the old woman said, and just then a small girl cracked the door behind the old woman and peered out at Aiden with curious eyes. The little girl looked to be five or six and had her hair pulled up into two loose pigtails that ran to her shoulders. She wore a bright red T-shirt with a cartoon dog on the front, and the shirt was too small, her brown stomach lifting the fabric at the bottom to where Aiden could see her belly button. The old woman turned and shouted something in Spanish and the little girl cowered back into the apartment. Her eyes caught something behind Aiden and she looked frightened just before the old woman yanked the door closed, and Aiden felt the burlap sack yanked over his face.

The sack smelled of potatoes, the porch light checkered through the loose weave. Two men had Aiden's arms and he felt someone yank the revolver from the back of his pants, the front sight raking his skin as the gun was ripped free. Aiden tried to pull away and scream but it did no good. Then he felt something heavy hammer him in the back of his head, a white light flashing in his eyes and a fire burning over his scalp. Then they moved him forward. He stumbled over his feet and tripped onto stairs, and they yanked him back up and led him farther to someplace he couldn't see. He heard a door open and the heavy two-beat bass of music coursing from speakers on the other side of a wall, and he knew he was inside because he could smell food and marijuana smoke as whoever held him pushed him into the room. He started to scream and was hit again. This time the blow knocked him to his knees and he thought for sure he would go unconscious. Falling forward onto his chest, his face against the floor, he could feel something wet and cold moving over his scalp, his hair slick with it. A knee was in his back and those same hands hadn't moved from his arms, though he felt a new pair of hands rummaging through his jeans and pulling everything he carried out of his pockets.

Aiden heard three or four voices shout things in Spanish and then he was rolled onto his back with his arms and legs pinned to the floor. He bucked his head wildly, but could not get the sack off his face. There was a light above and a dark figure that hovered over him, but everything was broken into a crosshatched blur.

"Where's your partner?" someone asked with a thick Hispanic accent.

"I'm by myself," Aiden grunted.

"Leland said there were two of you."

"Leland doesn't know what he's talking about." Aiden felt a boot press down on his cheek, and his head turned beneath it.

"That's where *you're* wrong," the voice spoke. "He wouldn't lie. Not with what he stands to make. So I'll ask you again, where is your partner, your *compañero*, friend?"

"I've done told you, you cocksucker, I'm by myself." The boot vised down onto Aiden's face, and he knew then that he'd been duped. Leland Bumgarner had been a snake since they were children, but until right then Aiden and Thad had never been the mark. They'd always been friends, or at the very least they'd always been in on the joke, the three of them laughing at whomever Leland swindled.

"Where are the drugs?" the man asked.

"Fuck you!" Aiden yelled. He thrashed his head back and forth to try and get free, but he couldn't move against the hands that held him. Suddenly he felt something hot burn into his forearm, someone putting a cigar or cigarette out against his skin, and he screamed like a child, though his screams were met only by laughter and the repetitive thump of music that played on the other side of a wall to his left.

"You tell me where the drugs are or else I am going to castrate you like a *becerro*." The voice was calm and collected, those words spoken like dinner conversation.

"Fuck you!" Aiden said again.

This time his words were met with someone pulling his shirt up his chest, and a sharp pain dug into his stomach. He knew he was being cut slowly, a knife carving something into him. He tried to say something, but couldn't put words together, just broken profanity and grunts as he felt the blade press deeper into his skin.

"I will ask you again, my friend, where are the drugs?"

The pain was unbearable and Aiden could feel the muscles in his stomach tighten. Blood washed over him and wet his pants and underwear, and he knew he could not get away. All he could do was tell them what they wanted to know and hope that was enough. "Just don't kill me," Aiden said. "Just don't kill me." The knife kept cutting.

"Where are the drugs?" The voice stressed every word, as if each were its own sentence.

"At the church!" Aiden screamed. "At the fucking church!"

"What church?"

"Across the street."

"Where?" the voice yelled angrily.

"I told you, across the street!"

"Where at the church?"

As the man spoke, Aiden felt the knife or razor or whatever was being used to cut him dig deeper, and he suddenly knew that the man who spoke was the same one who cut him because of how the blade seemed to punctuate his words. "In the graveyard," he screamed. "In the goddamn graveyard."

"You're going to take me there."

There was one final slash across his stomach and Aiden was jerked to his feet. He could feel the blood run down the front of him into his pants. He could feel the shirt now wetted against him as the men turned him and led him into the night. He kept tripping over his own feet and fell to his knees, and he almost tumbled down the stairs, but the arms that held him caught him as his legs swung free. Once they were on the ground, he could hear the gravel crunch beneath his boots and he knew they were leading him across the parking lot, the world darker. The rain was falling again, the break in the storm now over. He heard a car pass on the highway, the hiss of tires, then silence as the ground changed from gravel to pavement. Then he could see a light up ahead and he knew that it was the streetlamp at the side of the church and he knew they were almost there and he hoped that the drugs would satisfy them, that they'd leave him there alive and breathing, anything but dead. Aiden was in the light now and the ground softened beneath him. The headstones were barely visible, but he could see their shapes.

"What grave?" the voice said.

"Hooper," Aiden answered. "That tall one with river rock. Reverend Hooper." He heard someone move past him and shout something in Spanish from up ahead and he knew that whoever it was had found the ammunition can behind the grave because even from where he stood he heard the heavy, rusted latches pop and the hinges creak open. There were a few more words in Spanish and then the voice spoke again.

"Don't come back here," the voice said, just as calm as before. "You come back or you try to sell anything and I'll kill you. *Muerto. Estarás muerto.* Do you understand?"

There was a sharp kick to the backs of Aiden's knees and he collapsed to the ground. He could feel the earth seep into his pants and then he was stomped in the back and fell to his stomach. There were kicks all over his body, every square inch of him on fire with pain. No one held him now and he turned, trying to fight his way off the ground, his hands ripping at the sack on his face, but the blows only came harder. Finally he was in too much pain to move and just curled into a ball and covered his head the best he could. He could barely breathe, and when he did get a breath, it felt like a spear point jabbing into his ribs and the breath shuddered out of him. All of a sudden the burlap sack was ripped off and his vision was blurred and the night seemed blinding the way the rain pelted his face. He tried to see the shadows that moved around him, tried to make out their faces, but he could not see a single thing, just figures. And then there was one final crack to the side of his head, the toe of a boot driving hard into his temple, and the world went white.

WHEN AIDEN REGAINED CONSCIOUSNESS, the rain came down so hard that it seemed to pin him to the ground. His first thought was to burn the goddamn place to the ground. If he couldn't be certain of who had done this to him, then his best bet was to set fire to them all. He would pour gasoline around the entire apartment building and burn them up like a nest of yellow jackets.

But then Aiden thought of the little girl who stood in the doorway just before the sack was cinched over his face. All he could think about was that little Mexican girl with pigtails and a belly and dark eyes that had looked so scared at what she saw as the door was being closed in her face. When he remembered that little girl, he knew that he could not go through with it. He knew he would not be able to bear knowing that one of the screams was hers. What needed to be done was something he could not do alone. He needed to find Thad. Everything would be okay if he could just find Thad.

Aiden tried to stand, but fell back to his knees when a sharp pain pierced his side. He struggled to get to his feet and found that if he stayed hunched over, with his body cocked just so, he could keep the pain in his ribs at bay. That's how he managed to stagger out of the graveyard into the light. He was covered in his own blood, the white shirt he wore now red with it, the front of his jeans darkened almost purple. Blood and rain soaked his clothes and he stood there for a minute in the streetlight in front of the church looking over his body, amazed at what had come out of him, and unable to comprehend how anything could be left inside to keep him alive. His stomach burned as he lifted his shirt, the fabric tight to his skin and making the pain worse, and when it was lifted to his chest, he could see the dark lines carved into him: XIII. A deep X and three lines had been cut into his skin, the last slash hurried and not nearly as deep as those preceding it, the bottom of the line tailing off toward his waistline. He had no clue what it meant, the roman numeral thirteen carved into him as if he were a tree.

At the road's edge, Aiden could see the yellow porch lamps that looked like a strand of Christmas lights strung along both floors of the apartment building through the trees. He could barely make out the building other than those lights, and he certainly could not see if anyone still stood outside, but that didn't matter. He would not go back alone. Down the road he hobbled with the rain against his body until he reached his car. He patted his pockets to try and find his keys, but they'd taken his wallet and his pocketknife, the change he had, and the gram of dope, everything. The windows were fogged on the Ranchero and Aiden checked the door. Luckily he'd left it unlocked and there were spare keys in the glove box.

The wipers had dried to the glass, so that the first swipe when Aiden cranked the car split the blade on the driver's side, the torn rubber wagging about wildly with each stroke. The thin strip of rubber lashed about the windshield like a baby blacksnake he and Thad found slithering through the yard one time when they were thirteen or fourteen. It reminded him of how the snake's pencil-thin body had whipped about the ground after Thad chopped its head off with a hoe blade. He could still see the snake's decapitated head with those black, unblinking eyes as it snapped its mouth open and closed and tried to bite whatever came close in those last seconds of life, a hatred for the world right up to the bitter end. He and Thad prodded sticks into the snake's mouth until it finally quivered closed, with the top jaw crooked over the bottom.

Aiden always found himself thinking about times when he and Thad were kids. The simplest things triggered flashes of memory. Those times when they were children stayed so clear to him—the images and the sounds and the smells, the way those moments had tasted—but yet he could not remember a single detail of a single afternoon from times when Thad was gone. He wondered if there was anything worth remembering anymore. He wondered where the hell Thad was in that darkness. Everything would be okay if he could just find Thad.

Pulling out of Jimmy's, he could barely make out the road ahead through heavy rain and fogged windows. When he passed Booker Branch, he thought that he never should have left Thad behind, but he had, and now he needed him. He remembered where Thad had gone those few months he disappeared. Bonas Defeat was hell on earth, but if Thad had run, that was exactly where he'd be. So Aiden paid no attention when he reached Charleys Creek and the road home shot off to the left. He just kept on Highway 281 deeper into Little Canada.

Through the rain, Aiden drove more by memory than road signs or landmarks. He barely had time to read the white letters spelling names like Dark Cove and Old Mill Road and Neddy Mountain and Wolf Pen on green signs as he came upon and passed them in the same instant. He knew the Mathis family had tree farms just through the woods to the right and that Fraser fir stretched in rows from the creek to the ridgeline. Turkey loved to walk through those trees all year long, and Goob Coward got lawed for shooting a hen through the neck with a .22 lever-action one spring. The tree farm had been there ever since Aiden could remember, and Goob Coward poached turkey and speckled trout off the Mathises' land for years before he finally got caught. Aiden knew that a little farther up the road the Messers had cattle and goats and two great big blueticks named George and Stella that walked all over the pasture with their noses to the ground and broke off into sprints, chasing the goats, when the mood struck them to do so. The Messers had always raised goats and cattle there, and they'd always had blueticks that took ribbons in the Mountain State Fair every fall. Nothing about this place had changed in all of Aiden McCall's life, and maybe that's why he'd come to hate it so badly. Everything was exactly how it had always been, the haves having and the have-nots starving to damn death. Few in Little Canada had much, but they were salt-of-the-earth people for whom church and work and family were enough to make life worth scraping by. But none of those things had ever belonged to Aiden. Every year bled into the next and the next, just on and on until the day he'd die, and maybe that was all there was to look forward to anymore. Maybe that's all there is to this old life, just waiting around to die.

When he came to the end of Grays Ridge Road, his headlights swept across the back of a red Geo Tracker and he remembered having seen that little jeep outside the Dietzes' trailer. He left the Ranchero running and the headlights on, stepped out, having almost forgotten how bad his ribs hurt until then. He stumbled over to the Tracker to look inside, but there was nothing to be seen. When he yelled out for Thad into the night, he knew there would be no answer. He knew how far the trail stretched ahead and how rough the country was through the gorge. There was no chance of finding Thad then. Aiden was unsure if he could even make it home.

APRIL FLASHED A LIGHTER TO THE END OF HER ONE-hitter and took a toke. Mittens sat like a statue on the kitchen table in front of her, the cat's posture like those concrete lions people with gates on their driveways set on brick pillars by the road. She set the pipe on the table, watched it roll a radius across the wood, and stared blankly as Mittens strolled over and casually slapped the pipe onto the floor. She didn't even bother to pick it up. April was just glad to finally stop thinking for a minute or two.

Ever since Tom Rice called she'd been at the table running figures through her mind, ciphering numbers on a notepad, and trying to imagine how long the money would hold out. She wondered what kind of life she might have if she took the offer and left. April was still too young to collect survivors insurance from Social Security as a widow, but there was a thousand-dollar check that came on the fif-teenth each month from an insurance policy George Trantham had for years. That check would keep coming until the policy ran out, but that wasn't near enough to live on. The seven hundred fifty she'd taken in each month as a lease on the land for the radio tower is what made her lifestyle viable after George died. Between those two checks, she took in $21,000 a year, which might not sound like much, but when the farm's bought and paid for and all you have to do is sit on your ass and collect, there are worse ways to make a living. If she sold the property, that lease check was gone, and that meant she'd drop to $12,000 a year. The question became how long the money Trantham had in the bank and the money from selling the property would last. She figured she could make it years if she was smart. Worst case, she could get a bartending job or wait tables. She didn't have the body she'd had at twenty years old, but she'd held up better than most and could still turn heads. Flirting with old men for tip money might just be worth it to leave.

She took a sip of coffee, lit a cigarette, and walked into the living room to get on the computer. She thought she might look into some places on Tybee Island, see how much it would cost to rent an apartment. That was one of the few places she'd ever been, and she'd fallen in love with that town when George took her and Thad there not long after she married him. There'd been some sort of pirate festival going on that weekend and there were all these ships built onto trailers being pulled through the streets. There were men dressed up with tricornes on their heads and buckles on their shoes and one with a peg leg and one with an eye patch and even a midget waving a curved saber that was longer than he was tall. There were women in blouses with ruffled sleeves and corsets pressing their breasts up to their necks, and some wore their hair braided and some wore bandannas as skullcaps and one turned up a bottle of booze and blew a mouthful of liquor into a ball of fire. April wondered if she could do that—not the fire breathing, but riding on one of those ships in the parade and playing dress-up and throwing candy and beads down to kids in the street. She guessed most everybody who lived there played a part in the parade. She guessed all she'd have to do was move down there and make friends. She wouldn't have to tell them where she was from. She could make up a name if she really wanted. Start from scratch.

The front door flew open and April almost came out of her skin. The rain was still pouring outside and Aiden walked into the house with water dripping from him, his pants and shirt and face covered in blood. She gasped when she saw him standing there like he'd been in a car crash, and maybe he had.

"Jesus, Aiden. What happened?"

He didn't say anything at first. He just stood there as if he were about to collapse.

"What happened, Aiden?" April walked toward him.

"I got robbed," he said. "That son of a bitch Leland Bumgarner sent me to meet . . . they beat the shit out of me. Robbed me fucking blind."

"Where's Thad?"

"I'm going to kill them," Aiden screamed. "I'm going to kill those motherfuckers and I'm going to kill Leland Bumgarner for setting me up."

"Where is Thad, Aiden?"

"I don't know where he is," Aiden said.

"He didn't go with you?"

"No, April. For fuck's sake, I told you." He walked to where April had been sitting at the computer, grabbed her pack of Dorals from the desktop, and lit a cigarette.

"Your head's bleeding." She moved around to the back of him to get a better look at the cut on the crown of his head.

"Don't you think I know that?"

"You need to get to the hospital."

"I ain't going to the hospital. They'll ask all sorts of questions. They'll have the law in there before you can bat an eye. I ain't going to no hospital. Period." He plopped onto the office chair and bent forward with his face in his hands. The cigarette between his fingers trailed smoke against his face, and April watched as a drop of blood ran through his hair, slid along his jaw, and dripped from his chin to the floor.

"We got to get you cleaned up," April said. "We need to see how bad it is."

She hurried down the hall into the bathroom, shoved the rubber stopper into the drain at the bottom of the tub, and cranked the water. The bathtub started to fill and she headed back into the hall to the linen closet for more towels and washcloths, old ratty ones she wouldn't mind throwing away. Under the sink, April rummaged through the cabinet for medical supplies. There was a bottle of iodine she'd had since Thad was little, a bottle of alcohol, and a half tube of Neosporin pinched flat. She slapped the cover down on the toilet seat and piled everything on the lid. There were some large square gauze pads, a small tin of Band-Aids with only the sizes and shapes that no one ever used, and a roll of brown elastic bandage with little silver clips that had started to rust. That was everything she had. She didn't know the first thing about stitching him up.

In the living room, Aiden was still hunched over in the desk chair and the cigarette had burned out between his fingers. He'd thrown up on the floor between his boots and he looked like he was asleep, and those two things worried April to death because, while she knew little about bandaging someone up, she knew a lot about concussions. She'd had three that she knew of, one that kept her throwing up for two days after George Trantham came home staggering drunk off white liquor and damn near beat her to death. The few times it had been bad enough that she had to go to the hospital, the doctor told her not to go to sleep because a lot of times people wouldn't wake up after going to sleep with a head injury, after having *fallen down the stairs*. She rushed over and shook Aiden by the shoulder and he raised his head slowly toward her.

"Let's get you back there in the tub," April said. "We need to get you cleaned up."

Aiden didn't move, just kind of blinked his eyes in a daze.

"Come on." She prodded. "Get up, Aiden."

She led him down the hall slowly. He hobbled on heavy steps, and when she got him into the bathroom, she had him stand there while she undressed him and eased him into the tub. He slid down into the water, the cuts and blood on his stomach immediately spreading a cloud of red into the bath like drops of dye. Those marks and that gash on the back of his head seemed to be the only places he was bleeding, but from the looks of his clothes, he'd been bleeding awhile. There were marks all over him, places that were red and blue. A bruise that looked like a birthmark as big as a quart jar was stamped across his ribs.

April dipped one of the washcloths into the water, and as she dabbed at the cuts along his stomach, he sighed a bit. But when she squeezed a washcloth full of water over the cut at the back of his head, he winced.

"Goddamn," he yelled. "That hurts like hell!"

"I know it does, but I can't see it till it's cleaned up," she said. "You need stitches."

"No, it don't."

"Trust me, it needs stitches." April took another washcloth full and this time pressed it directly on top of his head to let the water run down through his hair and wash the blood away. "Now, who did this?"

"A bunch of spics," Aiden said. He was deep in the bathtub with water lapping at his chest. His feet were up against the tile by the tap handles, with his legs bent out of the water.

"And you don't know who they were?"

"I ain't see them."

"What do you mean you didn't see them?" April asked.

"They put something over my head."

"Who did?"

"That spic," Aiden said, opening his eyes for a second or two this time as April rinsed more water over the cut. "Some spic named Eberto, or at least that's what Leland said his name was."

"But you don't know him?"

"For God's sake, April, are you not fucking listening!" he screamed. He'd never raised his voice like that to her in all those years.

"Don't talk to me like that." April was shaking. "I'm just trying to help."

"Well, can't you fucking listen," Aiden said. "I told you I don't know who they were. If I knew, I'd tell you."

"I don't need this," April said. She stood up and dropped the washcloth onto his chest. "I've got enough already. I don't need this anymore."

Aiden mumbled like he was talking in his sleep, and April couldn't make out what he said, but it didn't really matter what he said. She didn't care to listen. She was tired of always worrying about someone else's problems.

The more she thought about it, the more it didn't matter how little those assholes from Atlanta wanted to offer her for the land. She'd take it. She'd take the check out of their hands with a smile on her face if it meant getting the hell off this mountain. She didn't care if she had to get a job and survive off tip money like those first few years with Thad, those years before she married George Trantham just so she wouldn't have to struggle. She didn't care about having to leave Aiden behind, because she'd done everything she could to try and help him. No matter what she said, he still did the same things over and over again. Her out was here and she had to take it, or live with the fact that it might never come again. That made the decision easy. April was done with regret.

$$(\textbf{28})$$

THAD DREAMED ABOUT WATERBOARDING A MAN WITH diesel fuel. He dreamed this because it had happened. It was something he'd done. He was given a direct order and he poured the gas, and ever since, he'd tried to forget the smell and the sound of that man gagging and the way the fuel felt cold on his hands as he shook the metal can empty.

The man might've been thirty years old, though he could have just as easily been younger. Unlike most Afghani men, he did not wear a full beard. His dark face was patchy with hair and a scruffy mustache. Black hair draped the shoulders of his navy-blue thawb. Over the tunic he wore an olive-colored vest and on his head a Chitrali cap the same chestnut brown as his skin. He was kneeling in the middle of the road with a small trowel, like he might've been digging ramps when the patrol rounded a steep outcrop of sandstone. But that dirt merchant wasn't digging anything out of the ground. He was burying something.

There was nothing more cowardly than burying IEDs and running into the mountains to play shepherd. If Thad's patrol had come any later, it was likely the soldier whose boot found the trigger would have been killed and the rest would have been left to scour the ground for body parts to ship home.

They bound the man's hands with zip cuffs and bagged his head in a black sack. Sergeant Spencer Lawing gave Thad the order. While one soldier held the man's legs and another pinned his shoulders to the ground, Sergeant Lawing steadied the man's head and told Thad to pour. The ANA interpreter shouted and Sergeant Lawing directed the questions and the man cried, and every time an answer didn't suit the sergeant he simply hollered, "Gas!" and Thad would dump the diesel down the man's throat. The can glugged and thumped, and Thad kept pouring until all twenty liters was emptied.

The part that was different in Thad's dream was what came when the sergeant yanked the sack off the man's head. Instead of finding that scraggly jihadi with his face greasy with fuel, everything was reversed and Thad was now the one being tortured. He could feel the gas in his eyes and coating his mouth and throat with a thick metallic taste. The smell stung his nose and he felt like he was suffocating. He was staring into daylight and it was hard to make out who was standing over him because his vision was blurred, but when that figure finally came clear it was Doug Dietz. It was Doug Dietz smiling down at him and Doug tossed the empty fuel can to the side and fished a lighter from his pocket. That was the moment Thad gasped and his eyes shot open and he slapped around the wetted ground to try and separate dream from reality.

Seconds passed before he realized what he had dreamed was not real, minutes more to realize where he was, and until those realizations came, he just lay there shivering in the cut bank with the shotgun clenched tightly in his hands. The rain had stopped sometime while he drifted in and out of sleep, but it was dark now. The creek had risen and lapped at his feet. Random split-second showers sounded when something high in the trees buckled and sprinkled water onto leaves below. He figured daylight was close because a titmouse kept calling from some hidden perch. He thought about how many times in his life he'd woken to the sound of that bird, and how he'd never once really thought about that fact until right then. He'd never heard it when he was on deployment. That place had its own birds with their own calls. This was a sound from where he'd grown up, a sound he'd known all his life. It only took something that simple for the world to solidify.

Once he realized where he was, Thad's mind worked to remember how he'd gotten there. Ever since he'd come home there was always this washing around between the during and after, between here and there. He'd spent so long trying to build this separation so that he could navigate those two worlds, and suddenly he was back to where he'd started. All of it was mixed up and he couldn't make sense.

The first image that came clearly was of Loretta Lynn, though it wasn't how he and Aiden had found her. Rather it was when he watched the outline of her tiny body show through the blanket as he filled the grave and the shovelfuls of dirt weighed down the fabric around her. Something had seemed to happen at that exact moment on the hillside. Something had broken and the two worlds collided, and after that he could only make out fragments scattered about his mind like seed: the way a moth had patted its wings against his face as he stood by the porch light in front of the Dietzes' trailer and nodded for Aiden to bust the door down; the way that trailer reeked of mildew and baby powder and sex when he cracked Doug Dietz in the skull and rained down on the back of Meredith's head; the way Julie

Dietz had this bright red lipstick smeared on her mouth, like she might've been sitting in her room playing dress-up when she poked around the corner with that bag of frozen corn niblets melting against her face; or the way Doug had woken up after Aiden left and how the veins in his neck looked like roots in the ground as he screamed against the gag. After that, things were less clear.

Thad tried to remember what came next, but it was blurry. After a few minutes, he recalled swinging the shotgun over Meredith's back and centering the brass-bead sight between her shoulders, but nothing afterward. Everything was blank after that moment, just a long stretch of time that had been burned away like undeveloped film ripped into the light, all of the images, every frame, erased. What came next in his mind was the rain. He remembered being flat on his back on a giant rock in the gorge when the first drop hit his cheek. He remembered sitting up then and scanning the hillsides and realizing that he was alone. Then he remembered how he was almost to the dam when the sky opened up and a rain came that soaked him to the bone. The details were muddled, but he could remember everything after the dam, and that answered how he got to this place.

But how he came to sleep beneath the cut bank wasn't what he needed to know. He was missing the important part of the story. Thad lay shivering for a long time, wet and cold, but no matter how hard he tried, he could not remember. He crawled out from under the bank, knelt by the stream, and cupped water to his mouth and drank, wiped it across his face to try and wake what little of his mind the drugs had yet to squander. He stood and stared downstream, wondering how long he'd been there and how much rain must've fallen to make the water rise. Hiking back would be harder than going farther, but he had to know. Thad simply had to know, and there was only one way to find out. So he headed downstream to find the place from where he'd come.

The sun wasn't up, but the morning was cloudless except for a low-lying fog, and so the woods grew with light for a long time without the sun ever rising over the ridgeline and trees. The rain had made the stream high and off-color, though the lake being down left no need to open the gates at the dam and rush the gorge with overflow. Even with high water, the stream was less burdensome. There was no solid ground, just mud and rocks slick as owl shit, and Thad had already fallen three or four times to make his way back to the giant boulder he remembered lying across when the first raindrops slipped from the sky the morning before.

He knew he was almost there when he passed a creek bed that ran up a hillside, the moss-covered stones like the armored scales of some giant green reptile dormant on the slope. The place was shaky with the movement of ferns, bowed and hanging bracken lace that shuddered in the breath of early-morning fog.

When he saw the boulder angled over the river and the holes time had drilled into the stone, he knew that this was where he had been. Kneeling, he ran his hand across rough circles of lichen that seemed to have grown inseparable from granite.

As soon as he touched that place, what he had done hit him with the same horrible intensity as thoughts of killing that little girl. The line between good and evil was fine as frog hair, but at least what had happened to the girl was an act of war. Maybe what happened over there was a matter of survival, and when he thought about it for long enough after growing sweaty with guilt, he could slowly come to justify what he had done while he was deployed. When he woke up from nightmares, he could tell himself that he did what anyone would have done, and if he repeated that over and over to himself, he could eventually turn those memories into something he could live with. But the guilt he felt now was entirely different.

Thad felt like his body had been dredged in something he could not get off. That feeling was like working for days in a dust bowl with the sun cooking you alive and how your body just gets covered in dirt and sweat and how all of that seems to build into some weighted thing, a coating that hangs there and that you can't help but feel cloaking you all the time, all of your attention focused on how you're caked with it. Thad could hear what Aiden had said as he stood in the yard outside the Dietzes' trailer. "You're not going to be able to live with this," Aiden had said. Those words now held meaning. All he wanted in this world was to wash that feeling away.

(29)

THAD CROUCHED BEHIND A PILE OF RIPRAP NEAR THE edge of the woods and studied a man who was kneeling beside a small boy. He figured they were father and son, and he watched the man run a worm onto the hook at the end of the boy's fishing line.

The father led his son to the water's edge and seemed to be giving instructions that Thad couldn't make out from that distance, the words just a muffled voice in the late-morning air. The man stood behind the child and leaned down to place his arms on the boy's, and they swung at once together to cast the line into the water. The boy failed to release the button on the Zebco and the plastic bobber smacked against clay-covered rocks just a few feet in front of them. He looked up at his father, who only smiled and helped his son reel up the slack to try again.

The child was bare-chested with a pair of acid-washed jeans that were too small on him. He couldn't have been more than six or seven years old. Even from where Thad was hiding he could see that the boy's breakfast was smeared around his mouth, but Thad paid little attention to the kid. He focused on the father, and more important, on the shirt the man wore.

A red T-shirt had the word FIRE in big white letters across the back. Budgets raised by boot drives and hot-dog suppers meant that the Little Canada Volunteer Fire Department wasn't exactly handing shirts out. Of course the shirt could have been from another department in the county, maybe even from Balsam Grove, which wasn't but a few miles down the road. It wasn't like Thad could make out the tiny letters circling the Maltese cross on the breast pocket. But the chance that the shirt the man wore was from Little Canada meant there was a chance that he'd know Thad Broom. If he was from Little Canada, he certainly would, and that's why Thad hadn't moved.

From where he was hiding, he could not be certain if he knew the man or not. A ball cap pulled down on the man's head and dark hair ducktailing over his ears and neck made him difficult to discern. His face was scruffy and he had a thick mustache that seemed to completely cover his lips. He didn't look familiar, but then again Thad hadn't seen anyone in some time. Two years he'd been back, but aside from running into somebody he knew at Walmart or the ABC store when him and Aiden went to Sylva, folks in Little Canada mostly kept to themselves and they certainly never came looking for fuckups like Aiden and Thad. Thad could see the man's pickup, an old black Toyota with paint dulled by the sun, a tall antenna waving from the hood as a breeze pushed off the water. An old '80s-model Toyota with a dog box in the back could have belonged to half of Jackson County. There just wasn't any telling.

The boy still stood but his father had sat down Indian style on the rocks and smoked a cigarette. Thad watched the bobber tap at the water's surface, but he was too far away to tell if it was a fish biting or just undulations of water. All of a sudden the bobber disappeared and the boy whipped his whole body to the side to set the hook. The man jumped to his feet, dusted sand from the seat of his pants, and yelled encouragement. There was a fish on and they were paying no attention, so Thad moved quickly and was behind them before either saw a thing.

The father and son knelt with a saucer-sized bluegill flopping on the clay between them. The fish flipped its body from one side to the other and finally tired, with its navy-colored flanks speckled gray by mud and sand, a crescent of red showing briefly each time its gills opened for breath. Thad stepped closer and his shadow spread over the ground where the fish lay, his boots crunching loose rock at the same time, and the father and son turned in unison, their eyes squinted in the sunlight to try and see who was there. The man stood and the boy stayed crouched by his catch, and as the man spoke Thad realized he didn't know him at all.

"Can I help you, mister?"

"Maybe," Thad said. "I was going to see if you might give me a ride to Charleys Creek."

"Charleys Creek?" the man questioned. He looked Thad up and down, ran his eyes over the muddied clothes Thad wore, but seemed to focus most of his attention on the shotgun Thad held by his side. "We ain't headed that way."

"Well, you got a cell phone I could use to call somebody?"

The man stood there for a second thinking it over, then, "Yeah," he said. "I've got a cell phone in the truck if it'll get service out here."

"That'd be awfully kind," Thad said.

"Run up there to the truck and get my cell phone."

The boy looked down at the fish, then up to Thad and over to his father before looking back down at the fish. He seemed like he didn't quite know what to do, but then his father's words settled and he tore off in a sprint for the truck.

The man watched the boy go and when his son was inside the pickup and out of earshot he looked at Thad skeptically and asked, "Now, where was it you said you come from?"

"I ain't said, but I was down there in the gorge. There came a rain and I got all turned around and before I knew it I couldn't find my ass from my elbow."

"How long was you down in there?"

"Two days," Thad said.

"And what was it you was doing down in there to start with?" The man had his attention focused back on the gun that ran the length of Thad's leg.

"I was down in there checking on some ginseng patches," Thad said. He noticed how the man kept eyeing the shotgun and he shook the gun by his leg as if to try and snap the man out of his trance. "Snakey country down in there."

"That's federal land," the man said. He took the ball cap off and then pulled the hat onto his head with one hand clenching the bill and the other guiding the back down. "You can't dig 'seng out of there."

Before Thad could answer, the boy skittered to a stop with the phone outstretched in his hand. "Here you go."

The father took the cell phone from his son and eyed Thad like he wanted an answer, but he didn't ask for one. He just held the phone toward him, and Thad took it and thanked him.

Thad pretended to tap a number onto the screen and then held the phone up to his ear. After a good thirty seconds, he raised the phone in front of his face, looked at the screen, and pressed it once like he was ending a call. "Ain't picking up," he said. "Any chance I could text him?"

"Yeah," the man said, and nodded for Thad to go ahead.

Thad fiddled with the screen, opened the messages, and immediately found the contact he was hoping for, a feed of messages between the man and his wife. Thad tapped the cursor onto a new line, turned the phone on its side, and thumbed in two quick lines: "Truck broke down. Need you to come get us." He hit SEND and the second the word DELIVERED showed under the speech bubble, Thad reared back and threw the phone as far out into the lake as he could.

The boy turned, shocked, toward the water and the man looked completely confused for a split second, but didn't wait for an answer to come to his mind. He bent over hurriedly and fumbled with the bottom of his pants leg, his hands getting tangled in the canvas, and by the time he had his hand on the grips and was trying to draw the boot gun from his ankle holster, Thad had come forward and had the shotgun pressed straight into the top of his head.

"You just as well set that on the ground, mister," Thad said. "Now stand on up and kick that gun past me."

The man did just that.

Thad backed away and swiped the snub-nosed revolver from the ground, slid it down the back of his pants till the handle caught on the waistline of his jeans. He yanked his shirt up at the base of his back and let it fall over the wooden grips, completely concealing the revolver.

The boy stood beside his father and held tight to the man's leg. The man settled his hand on the back of his son's neck and said, "You're more than welcome to anything I've got, but there ain't no reason to have my son watching. He ain't got nothing to do with this."

"I know he don't," Thad said. "I ain't going to hurt that boy. I ain't aiming to hurt either one of you."

They all just stood there for a second or two looking at one another, the father and son staring at Thad, and Thad keeping focused on the man's eyes. The man looked confused, like he wanted to say something, but didn't know the words.

"Your wife know y'all was coming fishing? I mean did she know where y'all was headed?"

The man nodded.

"Well, that's good," Thad said. "That's good because I texted her a message telling her to come get you, and I imagine she'll be headed this way directly. Any chance I can get one of them cigarettes off you?"

The man slid the pack from his pocket and offered them toward Thad.

"You can just toss them on the ground right there will be fine," Thad said. "And I thank you."

The man tossed the pack of cigarettes onto the ground, and Thad knelt and took one from the pack. He grabbed his lighter from his pocket, lit the smoke, and left the rest of the pack lying where he'd found it. Crouched there with the shotgun across his knees, he took a long drag and blew the smoke into the sky. When he finished exhaling, he stood. "I'm going to need your keys now," he said.

The man immediately took his keys from the side pocket of his carpenter pants and tossed them onto the ground just the same as he had the cigarettes.

Thad grabbed the keys and kind of cocked his head to the side as he spoke. "I'm sorry about this," he said, seeming to speak more to the child than the man. "I really am." But neither the father nor son said a word.

. . .

THAD ROUNDED A HAIRPIN CURVE between Tanasee Lake and Wolf on tires so big that they whined as he drove. In the road, a high-shouldered buzzard ducked its featherless head and took air with three onerous flaps of its wings. The buzzard lit on a post along the guardrail and Thad craned his neck to get a better look of the bird perched there through the passenger-side window as he passed. The buzzard's red face and mottled feathers were almost turkey-like, except for its beak, the sharp white hook bloodstained and menacing. Thad glanced into the rearview as he hit the gas down a short straightaway. The buzzard hopped back into the road and continued its meal, a roast of bright red flesh center lane on the pavement, in no hurry at all.

The fireman's handheld radio lay on the passenger seat of the pickup and Thad was thankful it hadn't been clipped to the man's belt. He hadn't thought to check him for a radio and knew it was sheer luck that the man left it in the truck. Something that simple could have ruined it all. A click of a button and that man could have cued dispatch and had the law barreling up Highway 281 to cut Thad off before he was halfway back to Charleys Creek.

The truck thumped couplets as Thad drove over the sectioned concrete of Wolf Lake dam. He geared down in the middle of the dam and the sound beneath him slowed as he braked to a stop. There was an unopened pack of cigarettes on the sun-cracked dash. Thad packed the box of smokes against his hand, ripped the cellophane off, lit one, and slid the revolver from the back of his jeans. He tossed the snub-nosed .38 onto the passenger seat and pressed hard into the place where his back hurt. He took a drag from the cigarette and rested the hand that held it onto the steering wheel as he leaned forward and tried to press deeper. But it did no good at all.

The lake was calm and bluebird skies didn't cast a single thing across the surface, just the sun pushing toward noonday, flicking sparks on what little movement the water had. The reflections of mountains and trees wrapped the edges of the lake, and, turning his head back, Thad could see the cliff some sixty feet high where boys, looking to impress girls, dared each other to jump. There was no one there now, but Thad remembered a time when he and Aiden skipped high school and drove to the lake to watch the college kids climb the rock face and chuck themselves off over the water.

On the day Thad was thinking about, he and Aiden had taken a bag of weed and gone down to the water to try and get in with the girls who lay on beach towels and watched the boys. They lied and said they were older, but it was obvious they didn't fit in and the college kids just seemed to mock them as they rolled joint after joint until the bag was gone. Thad and Aiden were so stoned they could barely keep their eyes open as they watched the boys lead one of the girls onto the cliff. The older boys had been making fun of the girls for being scared all afternoon, and finally this girl figured she'd shut them up by answering the dare. Thad and Aiden didn't say a word about it, though Thad figured they both thought the same thing. She stood there for a long time bent-legged on a tiny ledge, probably second-guessing having gone that far, but there was no way to climb back down. She had to jump.

The boys shouted directions for her to jump as far out as she could to clear the rocks beneath her and finally they counted her down, and while she didn't jump on their go, she did just a few seconds after. She was into the air and her arms flailed and her hair waved from her head. She tightened her legs together into a toothpick and pinched at her nose with one hand, her head tilting back when she did, and all it took was that one movement to throw her off center.

Her body started to shift and she leaned farther and farther back and it was too late to correct the mistake. She slapped down out of the sky onto the backs of her legs and sank like a stone just as soon as she hit water.

The girls on the shore screamed. One of the boys on the cliff rushed to the ledge and hurled off after her. Thad and Aiden didn't move for a second or two, a mixture of smoke and shock holding them captive, but when they realized that none of the other boys were moving from the cliff, they dived into the water and swam to help. Thad could still remember how the water seemed so cold against his sunburned skin and how hard it had been for the three boys to tread water with her body. She wasn't dead but her legs were useless and her arms did nothing more than clutch at the boy's shoulders as she cried. By the time they got her to shore, her legs were completely black. Everyone crowded around her gasping and in awe, and after a long time they carried her out.

On the ride home that afternoon, Aiden and Thad joked that if those were the types of things learned in universities, then they weren't missing anything. Most of those college kids looked down their noses at folks like them, but every year there was one or two who jumped off that cliff and sank to the bottom. There were two types of lives, and he and Aiden had been born into one where AS-VABs made more sense than SATs. But, looking back now, Thad couldn't seem to draw that separation. Whether a man was born one way or another, he wound up doing things that haunted him the rest of his life. People made mistakes that couldn't be fixed, and in the middle of the dam staring out over Wolf Lake, Thad could see everything he'd ever done. When it all boiled down to it, the only difference between one person and another was whether there was someone to jump in and keep you from drowning.

(30)

WHEN AIDEN WOKE UP, HE WAS IN APRIL'S BED, BUT SHE
was not beside him. The sun shone a soft white glow through the
curtains. He hurt all over and his head throbbed. Aiden rolled over to
check the time on an alarm clock on the bedside table, and that's
when the stabbing pain in his ribs hit him. He figured at least a
few were broken, but he just lay there and took short breaths so the
pain was bearable. It was eleven a.m.

He found some of his clothes folded in a neat pile on the seat of
a cane-back rocking chair in the corner of April's bedroom. These
weren't the clothes he'd worn the night before. There was a fresh
pair of jeans with a camouflage Mossy Oak T-shirt on top, a pair of
plaid boxers, and some socks. He kept clothes at April's and some
down at the trailer, though she never set clothes out for him. His
boots were on the floor in front of the rocking chair and there was a
little bit of mud still caked on the soles. There was no sense lying
there any longer. Staying in bed wouldn't do anything. He'd get up

and find some Advil if April had any, maybe take a hit of her weed if there was any left. That might numb the pain a bit.

There were muddied brown and yellow bloodstains on the pillow when he stood, and he noticed the slashes scabbed over his stomach. He patted at the back of his head and traced his fingertips around the wound, winced as he tried to bend over and get his boxers. He left the rest of the clothes on the chair and limped into the living room. April was sitting at the computer and she looked over her shoulder at him as he came close, but turned back to the screen once he was behind her. He put his hands softly on her shoulders, but even right then, it felt like she was already gone.

"You got any Advil?" he asked. He felt bad asking her for anything at all.

"If I do, it'd be in there in the cabinet over the sink," April said. She double-clicked the mouse and a website opened on the screen, a slideshow of pictures—the beach, and buildings, a swimming pool and a gym—playing out over the text. "I think there might be something in there."

"You care if I make some coffee?" Aiden asked.

"There's some left from the pot I made this morning that you can heat up."

He stood there, not sure what to say and not sure how to thank her. He knew that him coming into the house like that was just another thing she hadn't needed to deal with, but like always, she didn't say anything about it. She just picked up the pieces. April deserved better than what life had given her, and Aiden knew that. Maybe he didn't deserve any better, but she did. "What are you looking at?" he asked.

She didn't answer. She scrolled through the rest of the page quickly with the mouse and closed the browser, then sat there and stared at the screen as Aiden bent down and kissed the top of her head. She stood from the desk and walked over to the couch and picked up the remote to turn on the television. She didn't turn to look at him. Aiden just stood there and watched the TV flick on.

There were a few Aleve left in a bottle in the cabinet over the sink in the kitchen, and he took one and left two. The coffeepot was still about a third full and condensation sweated on the inside of the glass. He hated old coffee about as much as anything, but he didn't want to take something else, so he just poured a cup in a Christmas mug he found in the cabinet, heated it up in the microwave, and sat down at the kitchen table. The cigarette he smoked evened out the burnt taste of old coffee, or at least made it bearable, and he just sat there sipping that coffee and smoking that cigarette, thinking of how things had fallen apart so quickly.

When life went bad it always seemed to go bad in a hurry. Nothing came gradually so that a man might have a chance to grit his teeth and swallow a little bit at a time. No, life had a way of heaping shit by the shovelful like God was up there cleaning out the horse stalls and you just happened to be standing where He threw it. Aiden had been standing in a pile most his life, but the past few days had been the worst he remembered, maybe even worse than when he was a child. That thought sent his mind racing and he wished to God that Aleve would kick in so his head would quit pounding, but they didn't, and his hands started to sweat and he hated that feeling. God, he hated that feeling.

He lit a second cigarette off the tip of his first and stubbed the one that was gone into an ashtray on the table. When he stood, he tilted his shoulders side to side, trying to test his ribs, and when he bent to the right, everything was fine but if he turned his body to the left, it felt like someone had stabbed him. There was nothing he could do to make it better aside from going to the doctor, and he wasn't going to any doctor. He'd let time heal it into something misshapen and twisted as everything else.

In the living room, April didn't even glance when he took a seat at the other end of the couch. Mittens hopped onto the cushion beside him and climbed into his lap, and Aiden reached for an ashtray on the coffee table in front of him and set it on the armrest.

"I got an offer on the house," April said. There was a rerun of *Law & Order* on TNT and the volume was loud enough to muddy her words, especially with how she didn't turn to speak them.

It took a second or two to register as he took a drag from his cigarette. "Who?"

"Some people from Atlanta," she said. "The husband said he wants to turn it into a tree farm."

"Trees?" Aiden asked confusedly. "There ain't enough land."

"I know that," April said. She leaned toward the coffee table and grabbed her pack of cigarettes and lighter. "But they made an offer and that's what they aim to do."

"How much?"

"How much what?" she asked.

"How much did they offer?"

"Not nearly what it's worth. Not even half of what it's worth." April clicked off the television and the room was suddenly silent except for Mittens purring in Aiden's lap. She turned and looked him square. "But I'm going to take it."

"What the hell are you talking about, April?"

"I'm going to cut my losses, take the offer, and get the hell out of here."

He sat there for a long time without saying a word. He stared through the window that looked out over the yard and down the hill toward the trailer, and though he couldn't see any of it from where he sat, he knew exactly what was there, because it was the same thing that had always been there, a place he knew by heart.

"And where the hell are you going to go?"

"I don't know for sure." April sat there shaking her head. "But I don't think it really matters. It doesn't matter where I go just as long as it's away from here, just as long as it's absolutely nothing like this place. I want to go somewhere where nobody knows a thing about me, where nobody knows who I am. All my life I've been right here on this mountain, and all my life I've been filling up picture books with bad memories. I've always been too chickenshit to do anything about it."

Aiden understood what April said in a way that he couldn't have explained. That's all he'd ever wanted, a fresh start. But Thad wasn't going to Asheville, or anywhere else. He knew now that he could wait an eternity for Thad, and that in the end he'd never make it off that mountain. Aiden had to get off that mountain. He had to leave, but he was scared to do it alone. "And what if I told you I'd go with you?"

"No," April said. "You're not going with me, sweet one."

"Why?"

"Because this isn't about you." She set her hand on the cushion between them. "It's like I told you before, sometimes you just have to do something entirely for yourself. There's a part of me that thinks you were right."

"About what?" Aiden asked.

"About me never having done anything for myself."

"And what the hell are me and Thad going to do? Where the hell are we going to live?" Aiden was getting angry.

"I can't keep worrying about that," April said. "I just can't."

"But I love you, April."

"I know you do, sweet one," she said, and just one time he wished to God that she would say it back.

Aiden could feel his entire world crumbling around him. Everything that he'd ever known, the only two people he'd ever been close to were burning off like fog and there wasn't a goddamn thing he could do to stop it.

"When I get the check, I want to give you some money for all the work you did."

"I don't want it," Aiden said.

"I want to give you five thousand dollars," April said. "I know that ain't much, but I owe it to you just the same." She leaned toward Aiden and put her hand on top of his. "It won't last forever, but I think you can string it out a few months if you try. I think between that and the money you've been saving, it's enough that you can go to Asheville and find something."

"I don't want your money," Aiden said, and it was true. As much as he wanted for him and Thad to head off to Asheville, he didn't want it to happen that way. He didn't want to walk away feeling like he owed somebody something.

"I don't care if you want it or not. I'm going to give it to you. I owe you that much at least."

"I ain't going to take it," Aiden said. He stood up and walked over to the window and stared down over the property. "You don't owe me anything."

April started to speak, but Aiden limped over to the front door and hobbled out of the house. He closed the door behind himself and stood on the stoop, looking out over the yard. It was hot outside, even standing in nothing but his boxers, as he watched a wake of buzzards fly circles over one another in the cloudless sky. There was no breeze, just heat, like all the air had been sucked out of this place and all that was left was that temperature that bore down on everything. All the weight of this world seemed to be on him right then and he just stood there staring out into nothing at all, unsure how much longer he could go without buckling beneath it.

(31)

THAD PARKED THE STOLEN TRUCK AT AN ABANDONED brick house with the windows broken out and the front door gone so that from the yard he could see the trash that littered the floor inside. The house was just up Sols Creek Church Road on the hill that stretched toward Dodgen Ridge. He'd seen the place many times but never stopped. In the yard, a derelict shed crumbled in on itself, its tin roof rusted and sinking on grayed boards half-rotten beneath. An oil tank stood beside the shed, and farther, two crashed cars sat side by side, with their tops smashed in, grass high over the dry-rotted tires and hubs, with no one around to tell their stories.

Down the hill, across Highway 281, on the corner of Charleys Creek sat the church. Cars filled the gravel lot, and Thad waited in the pickup for the noon bells to chime. He studied the church, just a plain white clapboard building with brick steps leading to the door, no front windows, a steeple holding its cross into the sky. From the outside it was like most churches in Jackson County, the only difference being that this was where he'd been baptized, once shortly after he was born and once years later.

That second baptism came after confirmation, and that time both he and Aiden got dunked. That was one of the few things George Trantham ever forced them to do. At home the boys were nonexistent, just eyesores that picked about his property like wharf rats. But on Sunday mornings he loaded them into the car with April and, for those few short hours, pretended they were something else entirely. Thad suspected Trantham did this because he made his living off the congregation. And Thad and Aiden played along because Trantham kept them from living solely off mayonnaise sandwiches and, otherwise, left them to do whatever they damn well pleased.

Soon after the church bells rang, the church deacon, Samuel Mathis, opened the front door and the congregation filed out. Children were the first down the steps. Little girls in cotton dresses and patent-leather shoes strung daisy chains in the grass, while boys yanked their shirttails loose and chased one another around the building. The older kids huddled into circles. Teenage girls pulled out their cell phones to text one another. They snickered as they glanced back at boys the same age who kicked the dirt with the toes of their shoes and told lies that Thad could read in their gestures. Middle-aged men helped widows down the stairs while the men's wives desperately tried to round up their kids and corral them into the cars. The older couples were always the last to leave. They stood hunched over and slowly grazed their way around the gravel on canes until all their good-byes had been said. Only then did they drive away to lonely farms that no longer had crops to grow. They'd eat their Sunday suppers and wait for Wednesday service, and when the day came that they were widowed, they'd take their meals alone.

Thad had seen this a thousand Sundays before, but never from this vantage. In the years before Trantham died, when that old cock-sucker still dragged them to church like some make-believe family, Thad had stood right there among the congregation week after week, year after year, like clockwork. But that was years ago now. He had not been back in a very long time.

When only one car was left in the lot, Thad lit a cigarette and cranked the truck. He watched Reverend Donald Messer drag his oxygen tank behind him, pick the tank up step by step until he'd climbed the stairs and disappeared into the church alone. The reverend was why Thad had come.

He drove down Sols Creek, crossed the highway, and wheeled the stolen pickup beside the reverend's Buick. There were just the two of them, and Thad left the shotgun in the passenger-side floorboard. The snub-nose lay on the passenger seat. He smoked the cigarette until there was no more tobacco to burn and stubbed the butt out into an ashtray on the dash. It took him a while to build up the nerve. Minutes passed before he was ready. But when the time came, he shoved the revolver down the back of his jeans and headed inside. The end had finally come.

THE REVEREND DONALD MESSER shuffled between the pews and centered each Bible and hymnal just so on the bench. He seemed to disregard the wheels on his oxygen carriage, opting instead to lift the tank off the floor and set it ahead of him with each step, as if it were a cane. He wore a pair of ironed black slacks, a white dress shirt, a bright-red tie, and a brown glen-check wool blazer even in the middle of August. The sanctuary was dim with scant sunlight through frosted-glass windows so Thad couldn't make out all of these details, but he knew them to be true just the same. That's what Reverend

Donald Messer wore every Sunday, and Thad was certain that once he got close enough he'd see the gold tie clip with an oblong jasper stone clamping the reverend's necktie to his shirt.

The reverend did not notice Thad standing there until the door latched. With one hand braced on the handle of his oxygen and the other reaching into the pew, he turned his head up to see who'd come into the sanctuary. One of his eyes always stayed half-closed and his mouth hung slightly open like a fish. That's how he was looking at Thad as he straightened. He lowered his upper lip to resituate the tubes in his nose and moved them about with his hand when he couldn't seem to get comfortable.

"My heavens. Is that Thad Broom standing at the back of my church?" He hadn't seen Thad in eight years or more and still he recognized him immediately. The reverend walked with his oxygen tank out of the pew before answering himself. "Why, yes. It sure is."

"I hate to show up like this," Thad said.

"Why, son, you ain't keeping me from anything. I was just closing up. About to head down to have lunch with the Gunters, but I'm not in any sort of hurry." The reverend's hair had thinned but was still raked across his head how he'd always worn it. Liver spots freckled his face, and his neck sagged like a turkey wattle under his chin. He slowly walked toward Thad, and Thad couldn't help but notice how much the reverend had aged in the time he'd been gone. "Lord, I hope that woman has us something to eat other than chicken." The reverend stopped just a few feet short of Thad, turned his head to the side, and shook it down theatrically on his next word. "I'm tired of chicken," he said. "All these years, it don't matter where I go, these people want to feed me chicken. I'm telling you I've eat so much there's pin feathers coming in on my shinbones."

Thad knew he was supposed to laugh, but he couldn't. In all honesty, he could not imagine bottling what was inside a second longer. The drugs still had him and the thoughts still had him, and just a minute more and he knew he would explode.

The reverend laughed through his nose and shook his head, then eyed Thad curiously. "I've got to get off of my feet," he said, and stepped over to the last pew in the church. He eased himself onto the bench with a grunt, and once he was situated, rested one hand on top of the other, both braced over the handle of the oxygen carriage in front of him. "Go ahead and pull you up a chair," he said. The reverend wallowed against the wooden bench and looked up at Thad. "These old pews ain't the most comfortable seats God ever made, but they'll sit."

Thad hadn't moved since he came inside. His back was against the door. "I think it'd suit me just to stand," he said.

"Then you go on and stand, but I think I'm going to sit a spell. Standing gets to be like work when you get this old," the reverend said.

Thad stood there for a long time without saying a word. He knew what he wanted to do, but he just couldn't get up the nerve to do it. He put his hand around his back and felt where the revolver was stuck in his waistline. He nudged the handle just a hair and felt the cold steel of the cylinder and barrel shift against his skin. The reverend watched with that one eye half-closed and his brow lowered like he wasn't quite sure what to make of Thad, and then he slowly began to nod his head. He'd always seemed to know the things most folks were scared to say.

"Now, I think you've got something you want to tell me," the reverend said. "Is that right?"

Still Thad did not speak.

"Now, First John tells us, '*If we confess our sins, He is faithful and just to forgive us our sins, and to cleanse us from all unrighteousness,'"* the reverend said. Pieces of Scripture were stockpiled for moments his own words escaped him.

Thad could feel himself moving closer and closer to some invisible edge that he knew was right in front of him, but he didn't know how to stop himself from going over. He stood there and did not speak. His hands were sweating and he reached around and felt the revolver again, the weight of it now adding to all of the things he carried.

"Well, let me ask you this." Reverend Messer inched to the edge of the pew and lifted the oxygen carriage and tank by the handle, jabbed it back to the floor like he was driving a post. "Have you been saved?"

"You're the one baptized me," Thad said.

"Now, I know I am. But what I'm asking you is if you've accepted Jesus Christ as your Savior. Baptism's just an outward expression of an inward act, something inside. You understand?"

Thad nodded.

"When we've got Jesus in our hearts, our repentance is our water," the reverend said. "Those times of renewal come from the Lord once we've done that. You take Jesus into your heart and the old has gone and the new has come. *'As far as the east is from the west, so far hath He removed our transgressions from us.'"*

At that moment, Thad could bear no more. He knelt to the floor and wept, his tears never even touching his face as they fell and spotted dusty slats. The reverend stood from the pew and bridged the small space between them. Thad could see the reverend's worn leather brogans in front of him, the cylinder and the wheels of the oxygen carriage beside his shoes. His hand came to rest on the crown of Thad's head, and though Thad shook beneath him, the reverend's hand never waned.

"All you have to do is ask," the reverend said. "'In Him we have redemption through His blood.' The Lord said it Himself, 'though your sins be as scarlet, they shall be as white as snow.' All we have to do is ask, Thaddeus. 'To the Lord our God belong mercies and forgivenesses.'"

"You don't understand what I've done," Thad said.

"I don't need to understand what you've done," the reverend said. "Now, if you want to tell me I'll listen. I'm more than happy to listen to anything you've got to say. But as far as forgiveness, as far as taking Jesus into your heart and asking for mercy, that's something between you and Him."

"I don't know what to say." Thad looked up and the tears washed down his face.

"Well, I can probably help you with that," the reverend said. He pressed his hand firmly against the top of Thad's head. "You just repeat what I say now, son."

Thad nodded wildly, his eyes squinted as he faltered for breath.

"I recognize that I am a sinner in need of a Savior."

Thad snorted to clear his nose, and spoke the words brokenly, barely more than a whisper.

"I believe with all of my being that God raised Jesus from the dead."

"I confess Jesus Christ as my Lord and my God."

"I receive Jesus Christ as my Savior forever."

Thad echoed these things and just like that it was done. He'd been washed without water, washed clean by the very thing for which he sought forgiveness. Blood. And the hand upon his head became that of God Almighty. Thad felt all of this. He felt a great burden lifted.

But he still needed to say it. Saying what he had done was the only way to set it aside. There had been so many things that he'd wanted to say to someone, anyone who'd listen, for so long. But no one listened anymore. No one. And perhaps it was that not listening that led to things like this. Perhaps it was that not listening that made the world so volatile. He looked up to Reverend Messer and said, "I need to tell you what I did."

"I told you, son," the reverend said, "I'll listen to anything you want to say."

Thad started with what haunted him most, the little Afghani girl that he shot in the chest, her body dropping like so much weight. He told the reverend how his finger had felt on the trigger and how he still wasn't entirely sure whether he consciously squeezed or whether he was holding right there at the break and it just happened. But that didn't make a difference because she was dead just the same. He told him about picking up pieces of Billy Thompson out of the moondust and how all of those parts went into a bag on a helicopter, a bag that was shaped for a body but whose shape no longer mattered because there was just pieces of him, pieces that Thad was partly responsible for, pieces that were shipped back to Georgia to a mother who couldn't put any of it back together. All she could do was bury what was returned. He told him about the engagements and the uncertainty of just how many bullets had found their mark. There was really no telling how many. He spoke of the men they captured and what they did to them. He said he carried those things home like a sickness.

Thad explained what Doug Dietz had done. He told the reverend about what that sergeant had said about the infantry being the hand of God, and how when he saw his dog stabbed right through the back with that screwdriver, that long metal pick pinning Loretta

Lynn there, something inside had snapped and those words meant more than they ever had before. He made no mention of Aiden. Aiden had nothing to do with how things had unraveled, but he told the reverend of the trailer up Booker Branch, how he'd stormed inside, and of the bodies of the two girls that now lay on the floor. The reverend asked why he had killed the girls, and Thad said because he wanted Doug to hurt. He told the reverend how he forced Doug Dietz to look at those bodies, then how he'd stolen the car and driven to Bonas Defeat. He unclasped the sheath on his hip when he reached the grizzliest part. Pulling the knife from his belt, he showed the reverend just what he'd used to do it. He told him about forcing Doug to walk the gorge and how the leaves and dirt had stuck to the bottoms of his feet, how Doug crawled those last few steps and went unconscious when his body could go no farther. He described that giant stone, the moss-covered hillside just upstream from there, the unseen place where Doug's body was probably wedged between rocks.

The reverend stood there with his brow low, the oxygen tubes running from under his nose and across his cheeks to behind his ears. His mouth hung slightly open and to the side the way it always did. Thad expected a look of horror, but that's not how the reverend looked at all. What Thad saw on Reverend Donald Messer's face was a look of conviction. "And you repent these things?" the reverend asked.

"I do," Thad said.

"Then it's forgiven," the reverend said. He placed his hand on Thad's shoulder and squeezed. "The Bible tells us you are a new creation. *And their sins and their iniquities will I remember no more.*'"

The reverend spoke then of what was promised. He told of twelve gates and twelve angels, the names written of the twelve tribes of the children of Israel. He took his tie clip between his fingers, rubbed at the stone, and spoke of walls of jasper. There would be no sun and no moon, a never-ending day with no night. There would be no more pain and no more sorrow, and he shook the oxygen carriage and said there would be no need for him to lug that around anymore either. But all of these were things to come after. There were things that had to be done now. There was a price paid for heaven, and one owed on earth. The reverend said he'd make the call if Thad needed him to, that he'd be right beside him every step of the way.

Thad's mind raced with the thought of what the reverend said. He was not going to turn himself in. There were only two outcomes for holding out his arms and letting the law clink handcuffs around his wrists: life in prison or a death sentence, and a death sentence would be the more merciful of the two. Thad would not spend the rest of his life in some concrete box with a bed bolted to the floor. He would not take three squares and an hour outside as the only light he saw between now and the day he died. His mind tore out of control and he suddenly felt the need to run. He shook his head and reached at the base of his back as he rose from the floor. "I'm sorry, I'm sorry, Reverend," he stuttered, "but I can't do that."

"This isn't something you can run from, son. You have to pay what you owe in this old world."

Thad stuttered and his thoughts whirled and all of a sudden the door opened behind him and hit him square in the back. He yanked the revolver from the waist of his jeans, spun into the open, and had his left arm cinched around the person's throat before he even saw it was a man. Thad dug the barrel into the man's temple so hard that his head cocked to the side before Thad saw who he was. He smelled the man then, the smell of cheap aftershave, and he felt him trembling against his chest. Thad saw the red hair and knew immediately who he was holding, Samuel Mathis, the church deacon, who reeked like a drunk even on Sundays.

"I'm sorry," the man said. "I'm so sorry." He whimpered and Thad didn't ease up at all, just kept him hemmed against his chest with that snub-nose pressed into the side of his head.

"There ain't no need for this," the reverend said. "Now, put that gun down, Thad. You just put that gun down and we'll figure this out."

Thad could hear sirens coming up the mountain outside and couldn't put his finger on a single thought, his head electric with the way the world was spinning so fast.

"I'm sorry, I'm sorry," the man kept saying, and Thad wasn't sure what he was sorry for. He'd just walked in at the wrong time and now here he was, and Thad could hear the man piss himself, he could hear the sound of it tinkle from his leg onto the floor where they stood. "I'm sorry, I'm sorry."

"Let him go, Thad." The reverend hammered the oxygen carriage against the floor so that each syllable he spoke resounded. "You let him go and me and you are going to figure all this out."

The sirens were closer and Thad did not understand how they knew, but they did, and here they came, and there would only be seconds before they were here to take him. The time to run had come and gone, and even if he kept the gun to Samuel Mathis's head and backed his way out of the church and into the parking lot just as the patrol cars came sliding in, even if he made it all the way to that pickup truck and onto the highway, how far could he go before the showdown, how far could he make it before they threw Stop Sticks across the road, everything coming to a screeching halt with only six shots to hold them off?

At the very least he'd tried, and maybe trying was enough for forgiveness. The sirens were loud now, the law just seconds away, and

Thad suddenly realized that dying wasn't dying anymore. Dying was a one-way ticket to judgment, and it made no difference whether it came now or years down the road. He would be judged. Thad pulled the gun back from Samuel Mathis's head and shoved him forward. Samuel tripped on the edge of the pew and fell sprawled in the center aisle at the reverend's feet. The time to face God had come and that made doing what he had to do so easy and thoughtless, and he angled the revolver into the roof of his mouth without a second thought because he was not going to die. He could no longer die. He was headed for eternity. He saw the reverend's eyes widen and his mouth begin to open, and the reverend was going to try to say something to stop it but Thad was bearing down on the double action and it broke before he ever heard a word. The sound was deafening in such a silent space, all of that sound held within the sanctuary. The two who remained could not escape that sound, and they did not even look up as the sirens screamed past the church. They were oblivious to that final decrescendo. They just stood there thunderstruck as the patrol cars barreled away.

(32)

GRAYS RIDGE ROAD WAS CRAWLING WITH SHERIFF DEP-
uties and the vehicles of volunteer firemen when Aiden got there at
four o'clock. The minute he saw the lights flashing and the proces-
sion of patrol cars, his heart sank. He knew they were there for one
reason. He knew it had something to do with Thad.

Two deputies leaned against the back of one of the cruisers and
faced in Aiden's direction. They didn't seem to be paying attention.
One of the deputies slapped the back of his hand against the other
one's chest as he spoke. There was a driveway halfway between Aiden
and them, and he hated to pull that close, hated to give them a chance
to see him there, but he didn't want to whip around right in the road
either. They weren't blocking anyone from passing and so turning
around might seem stranger than just pulling on up.

When Aiden got closer, the deputy who swatted the other one
took a dip of tobacco from his partner's box of snuff and handed
the can back. The deputy craned his head away from his body as he
shoved a wad of tobacco into his bottom lip, then brushed tobacco

he'd dropped off the chest of his uniform. The one he was bumming from must've said something funny right about then because he slapped his knee and went to poking and prodding at the other one's stomach and chest, and before Aiden knew it, they were wrestling around behind the Crown Vic like two middle-school boys. They never even saw Aiden pull behind a graveyard of busted trucks onto a gravel drive that led to a farmhouse.

The driveway sank down a small hill where a grayed barn rotted into ruin at the bottom. Aiden had the windows down and could smell the dried hay in the barn when he tucked in on the far side and threw the Ranchero in reverse to turn around. The two deputies noticed him when he pulled back into the road, though, from the looks of it, they just as well might've figured he owned the place. One of the deputies threw up a hand and the other spit onto the pavement. Somehow the two bulls standing there were the only two in the whole sheriff's office who didn't know Aiden's face, who didn't know that car. Aiden waved and the one who'd spit nodded as he wheeled into the road and left them in the rearview.

The thoughts swarmed him once he got back to the two-lane highway and drove north toward Charleys Creek. There were so many cops. A dozen cars. Maybe twenty. Blue lights going crazy. There was no telling what all of those cops were doing, but the sheer number alone guaranteed they weren't hanging around for coffee and donuts. There was a red Geo Tracker up ahead of those patrol cars. Aiden had seen that thing outside the Dietzes' trailer. Aiden saw it at the end of Grays Ridge Road. He'd gotten out of the car and looked inside, for Christ's sake. Thank God he hadn't touched it. Had he touched it? Could you leave fingerprints in the rain? You could guarantee those pigs would dust for prints. That Tracker probably looked like it'd been rolled in flour by now. Probably had Aiden's prints all over it. He was probably already fried. Hadn't done a thing and he was fried.

Aiden was panicked, but he tried to stay calm by convincing himself that he didn't really know anything at all. He didn't know what had happened. The last time he saw Thad he was standing on the front porch of the Dietzes' trailer and Doug and Julie and Meredith were all alive and breathing. Sure, he'd heard a couple gunshots, but for all he knew, Thad had just blown a few holes in the wall or given them a skylight in the ceiling. Maybe Thad just pulled off a couple rounds to scare them a little, and after he was done scaring them, maybe that's when he took the SUV and headed back into the woods, back to the only place that felt remotely like home to him anymore.

At the head of Charleys Creek, Aiden could see the church parking lot filled with patrol cars, deputies everywhere. There were black-and-white Crown Vics and black-and-white Expeditions and dark gray unmarked Expeditions that were newer, with tinted windows. There were silver-and-black Chargers like the state troopers drove all parked bumper to bumper in the church parking lot like the whole Jackson County Sheriff's Office was about to get baptized. Maybe they were having a funeral. Maybe some deputy from Little Canada had died, but surely he would have heard something if that had happened. April would have seen something about that on Facebook. She was always on Facebook. But she hadn't said anything about someone dying. Then again, he hadn't asked. They hadn't talked about much at all over the last few days.

He headed down Charleys Creek and tried to convince himself that there were a thousand reasonable explanations that had absolutely nothing to do with Thad. When the flashing blue lights flew up behind him at Neddie Mountain, he figured there was probably just some tweaker who'd set off a burglar alarm or maybe a domestic dispute between some drunk and his old lady, the siren screaming past as he steered off into the ditch to keep from getting hit at Parker Gap. There was no telling where that deputy was headed so fast. He grabbed his pack of cigarettes off the seat and lit a smoke to stay calm. There was no need to worry. Everything was fine.

But then there was no more denying what he already knew when Aiden pulled through the hedge of laurel that lined the drive into April's property. There was one patrol car parked at Thad's trailer and a deputy stood on the porch. Aiden didn't look at him, but he could feel the deputy's eyes watching him as he crept past and looped around the switchback to climb the drive to April's house. There was an unmarked Expedition and another black-and-white Crown Vic parked at April's, and Aiden could see her on the front stoop in a pair of boxer shorts and a T-shirt. April tapped her foot as fast as she could and had one hand gripping the bicep of her opposite arm, the other hand holding a cigarette up by her face.

Two officers stood by April on the stoop and they both turned to look at Aiden as he put the car in park and killed the engine. There was a young deputy with a high-and-tight crew cut who wore the standard black slacks, tan dress shirt, and metal badge as all the others. He was thin, and the bulletproof vest under his uniform made his torso look like it didn't belong on the rest of his body. He stood there with his hands braced on his belt as Aiden stepped out of the car. Aiden recognized him as the deputy who'd blown past on Charleys Creek, a deputy he'd had run-ins with for years. The other officer was higher in the department, probably a lieutenant or major, who wore khaki cargo pants and a light gray polo shirt, the gold star embroidered on his chest rather than pinned to him. He walked over more like an old farmer than a lawman and met Aiden halfway between the car and the house.

"How are we this afternoon, Mr. McCall?"

Aiden's cigarette had burned out between his fingers but he didn't toss it into the yard and he didn't move to light another. He just stood there with the butt held between his fingers. "I'm all right, I guess."

"That's good to hear," the officer said. "I don't know if you remember me or not, but I'm Lieutenant Shelton and I was wondering if I might have a word with you."

"Have I done something?" Aiden looked confused and flicked his eyes up to April, who looked at him now almost pitifully.

"Well, no. Not that I'm aware of. We just had some questions we needed to ask you." Lieutenant Shelton looked at Aiden with squinted eyes and tilted his head a bit to the side. "Now, you look like you've been in a fight with somebody, that bruise there on your face and the way you was limping. You been fighting?"

Aiden wasn't quite sure what to say. He wasn't in the right mind for questions. But before he could think of a lie, April came off the stoop and walked toward them.

"I already told him about you and Thad getting into that fight over wanting to go see those girls," April said.

"Mrs. Trantham, I'm going to need you to go back over there with my deputy while I have a word with Mr. McCall."

"Now, I don't know why I'd have to do that. I haven't done anything wrong," April said. "This is *my* property and I've been more than cooperative with you and your deputies, so I don't know why I need to go stand over there if I don't want to."

"You can't interrupt while I'm in the middle of talking," Lieutenant Shelton said. He didn't turn to look at her. He just cut his eyes to the side to glance her way. "When was the last time you saw or spoke with Thad Broom, Mr. McCall?"

"Now, I've already told you that too," April shouted. She spoke quickly and with anger and there was little Lieutenant Shelton could do to interrupt her, him interjecting, "Mrs. Trantham! Mrs. Trantham!" every two or three words but none of it doing anything to shut her up. "I told you the last time either one of us saw or heard from Thad was two nights ago, when him and Aiden got into that fight because Aiden didn't want to take him over there to see those girls. He knew how much trouble they were. I told you, Aiden, just—"

"Mrs. Trantham, you're about to go to jail!" Lieutenant Shelton yelled. "Do you understand what I'm telling you? Just one more word!"

"What for? You tell me what law I'm breaking!"

"Just one more word!"

"You're going to have to charge me with something to take me to jail," April said.

"Failure to obey. Obstruction. I'll charge you with anything I come up with on that ride from here to Sylva," Lieutenant Shelton said. "Now, if you've got any sense about you at all, you'll walk back over there to the house and wait with my deputy."

The lieutenant stood there with his finger pointed back to the house and the deputy came off the stoop to take April if she wouldn't go. She slid a pack of cigarettes she'd had stashed in her waistband, lit one, and stood there tapping her foot against the ground, settling her hands just how she'd had them moments earlier. Smoke rose against her face and she chewed on the inside of her cheek as she scowled at Lieutenant Shelton like she just might skin him alive. Only when the deputy came up behind her and placed his hand on her elbow did she turn.

Aiden wanted a cigarette too and realized he was still holding the one that'd burned out between his fingers. He dropped the butt into the pea gravel, but didn't move any farther than that. His smokes were still in the car on the bench seat, and he was afraid to move. He was afraid to do anything without being told. Aiden just hoped that what April had said was all she had told them. He hoped she hadn't gone into any details that he might not know. He hoped that, if he stuck with what she said, their stories would match up and everything would be all right, that everything would be over soon. He still didn't know what had happened, what Thad had done, or maybe what had happened *to* him. All Aiden knew for sure was that he was nearing the end. One way or another, he was about to find out.

(33)

SMOKE HUNG CHEST-HIGH IN THE LIVING ROOM, BUT neither Aiden nor April was standing. They sat on the couch with blank stares, every slow wave of the smoke's movement visible as if they were watching wisps of clouds roll and build in the room. Both of them lit cigarettes end to end, maybe to calm their nerves or maybe just to keep from having to talk to each other.

The television was the only sound, and a commercial of some blonde walking around a warehouse of rugs in Asheville cut to a commercial of a car dealership in Canton, where these two gap-toothed children slurred how their daddy's business was the best place to buy a new car in all of western North Carolina. April didn't need to look at the television to see what was happening. Those two commercials played over and over every day no matter if it was lunch-time and *The Young and the Restless* was on, or it was a two-in-the-morning infomercial. She'd seen them a thousand times.

Mittens slept on the top of the couch behind April's head and she felt him wake for a second to lap a few strokes down his side. The place was so still that even that slight movement startled her, the world having become so fragile all of a sudden. Neither had said a word since the deputies left, nor had they shed a tear, Aiden having never cried that April'd seen, and she was just unsure what to feel. She was numb. Nothing had sunk in.

The television flicked to the ten o'clock news, and both April and Aiden turned when they heard her voice. A short young blonde with big hips who wore a black pencil skirt and white blouse stood in the church parking lot and delivered the opening story, the headline at the bottom reading, At Least Three Dead in Jackson County.

"We have breaking news out of Jackson County tonight as a gunman confesses to killing three before taking his own life." The camera broke away and panned across the parking lot filled with patrol cars, then zoomed in on the front door of the church as her voice unfolded over the scene. "Authorities have yet to release the suspect's name but confirmed that an armed man walked into the church you see here in the Little Canada community of Jackson County this afternoon and admitted to killing three people before turning the gun on himself. Lieutenant Jimmy Shelton of the Jackson County Sheriff's Office has also confirmed that upon arriving at one of the locations given by the suspect in his confession, deputies uncovered a grisly scene."

The camera turned to a recording of Lieutenant Shelton standing in the church parking lot with his feet spread shoulder-width apart and his hands behind his back.

"Upon initial investigation into one of the locations our suspect identified, deputies found the bodies of two female individuals, both deceased," Lieutenant Shelton explained.

The camera zoomed out and showed the reporter standing next to the lieutenant, her line of questioning ensuing thereafter.

"Can you say how these two women were killed?"

"I can't give any details at this time."

"Can you identify the victims?" the reporter prodded.

"All I can say is that, upon arriving, deputies found the bodies of two female individuals. We are not releasing any names at this time."

"Do you know if there is any connection between the suspect and these women?"

"Not at this time."

"What other locations are deputies looking into?"

"I *can* say that the suspect indicated a second location and that our deputies are on scene as we speak."

"But deputies have not found the body of a third victim?"

"Not at this time. We're releasing no other information. This investigation is ongoing." With that, Lieutenant Shelton walked off camera and left the young reporter standing in the parking lot.

"While it is unclear how the suspect knew the victims and whether or not there is, in fact, a third victim involved, a witness at the church when the gunman took his own life says that the suspect indicated a third."

"I wasn't actually there when he said it, but, yes, he told the pastor there were three." He stood on-screen in black slacks and a white button-down shirt and scratched at the side of his face, the runner beneath him identifying him as Samuel Mathis, Church Deacon. All it took was seeing him, hearing his voice, for April to panic. She slapped around the couch looking for the remote before seeing it on the coffee table, and April snatched it and mashed the POWER button over and over with her hand quivering at the screen. The television stayed on and Samuel Mathis slicked his red hair back on his head and continued. "We're praying for everyone involved." He was staring directly into the camera, his green eyes holding that same hollow deadness she would always remember. "It's always horrible when something like this happens."

Rising from the couch, April threw the remote at the television as hard as she could but missed and hit the wall. The remote broke apart on impact. In two strides, she was there and she hit the power on the set, but it didn't turn off. Samuel was still on the screen and the reporter was asking him another line of questions and April jabbed the button over and over but the TV stayed on. She rained down on the top of the set with her fists, hammered as hard as she could, but none of it was doing any good, and Aiden stood to help her. Grabbing behind the set, she slid the television off its stand, and as it rolled onto its face, the cord yanked from the outlet and there was silence.

She forgot Aiden was there until he touched her arm, her scared and flinching when she felt him. Aiden wrapped his arms around her and held her so tight that she couldn't fall, and she wept against his chest.

April had cried like that only one other time in her life and there had been no one there to comfort her then. She shook with her hands clenched against her chest, her face buried into Aiden, and shuddered from somewhere deep inside. She could feel the pain and the fear and the memories physically push out of her body bit by broken bit, piece by shattered piece, until there was nothing left to give.

As the tears waned, April's thoughts cleared and she realized that she was weeks away, a month at most, from leaving behind this place and everything that haunted her. For the first time in her life, she felt in complete control. She felt all of the fear that had kept her in secrecy for so long vanish, and all that was left was an unbearable anger. She was filled with it. She could feel the words roiling inside of her. She could feel them taking form and rising from within, a fire that had smoldered for so long in the absence of air. She could taste the words in her mouth and she began to speak them, and the minute they touched air the entire world caught fire. She told Aiden everything that she'd sworn she would never say, everything that had nearly gnawed her into nothing. And as those words came, she could feel everything she'd ever known burning. She could feel herself being rebuilt, something new taking shape.

There was a memory of being young and pregnant and crying her eyes out in her car after being spit on by some woman she didn't know, some woman who held a Bible as April walked out of the abortion clinic. April had somehow missed her when she went inside and it was her own guilt that had kept her from filling out the paperwork, that kept her from doing what that woman cursed her for when she left. Sitting there in that room just minutes before, she hadn't even been able to spell her name.

She remembered having to sit her parents down and tell them when she finally started to show, her having hoped for so long that maybe she'd miscarry, praying to God she'd miscarry, but that prayer going unanswered just the same as every one before.

She thought of the day she gave birth to Thad and how she was scared and in pain and how there was no one there to tell her that things were going to be okay, that everything was going to be fine, and she didn't know if hearing those things that most people hear would've meant anything to her right then or not, because none of those things were true right then. Things weren't okay. Everything wasn't going to be all right. The world was entirely broken.

She remembered when the doctor handed over her son to her for the first time and how she couldn't bear to look at him, much less bear the thought of having to raise him and take care of him. Everyone makes sacrifices, the hospital chaplain told her, but he could never understand. This was having your innocence stolen and then being told that you're going to hold that feeling in your hands and nurture it. You're going to look into its eyes and smile. You're going to grit your teeth and love every minute.

Now that all of that fear and anger had settled onto the place it belonged, she was filled with an immense sadness. She could see so clearly what she'd done, the person she'd punished and how that punishment had led to this.

"I'm sorry I never loved him," April said with her face still buried in Aiden's chest, and though Aiden squeezed her tighter he did not say a word.

So much of April was still that scared little girl, but there was an older, wiser self now that just wanted to go back and hold that eighteen-year-old and tell her that everything *was* going to be fine, everything *would* be okay. But she couldn't go back and there was no sense in it even if she could. The only place she could go was forward.

She was headed to someplace better.

(34)

WHEN APRIL EXPLAINED WHAT SAMUEL MATHIS HAD
done to her, Aiden knew Thad was right, that some people deserved
to die. Everything he'd ever thought suddenly made sense, from the
way April would sit almost trembling on the pew with her eyes
straight forward as Samuel Mathis burned holes in her with his stare
to the way she'd never seemed capable of loving her son. Aiden
thought about that as he drove to the house. He was thinking about
how much shit had been piled onto her over the course of her life
when he parked a quarter mile from the driveway, shut off the headlights, and stepped into the night.

There was a chill in the air for late August, a reminder that it would
not be long before summer was gone. In a little over a month, the
leaves would start that slow smoldering, setting the mountains ablaze
with autumnal fire. Then a few weeks after that, the color would be
gone. There was something to be said for how quickly it ended.
There was a lesson to be learned in that short-lived breath of beauti-

ful. Good things never lasted, and when things fell apart, it happened in the blink of an eye. That was true for everything on this mountain.

Aiden took the tactical rifle Wayne Bryson had folded in half just seconds before he died out of the diamond-plated toolbox stretched across the bed of the Ranchero. He hit the release and checked the mag, the spring-fed magazine fully loaded with 9mm hollow-points, the copper jacket of that top bullet glowing in the moonlight. He slapped the magazine back into the pistol grip, folded the fore-end forward until the barrel locked in place, and racked the bolt to chamber the first round.

The moon lit the world with an electric blue that voided the need for any other source of light. Even from the car, Aiden could see the lights at the house showing through the woods. The road would've been easier, but he could not chance being seen, so he hopped the ditch into a briary thicket, where thorns tore at his pants as he walked. As soon as he reached the trees, he could see the house more clearly, the two squares of yellow light from the front windows, two more lit just the same along the side of the house. He crossed a small creek that, despite the heavy rain the night before, didn't top his boots. Some animal he couldn't see busted through the brush upstream when he approached, and Aiden was on such high alert that he shouldered the rifle at the sound and nearly fired into the darkness.

Trees stood on both sides of the creek, a mixed stand of poplar and oak, some old and so wide that Aiden couldn't have stretched his arms around the trunks, some young and thin as telephone poles. There was white birch and maples and even a few scraggly locusts growing right against the bank, but there was little undergrowth. The grove of trees seemed to have been picked clean by deer, or maybe just kept up by whoever owned the property. Whatever the case, Aiden could see clearly through the spaces between the tree trunks. He could make out the field where the trees ended, the field that stretched from where he stood to the house.

The barbed wire was into his stomach before he even knew a fence was there, and when he hung against the wire, his abs seized, and that pain in his ribs froze him for a second. But he just took a step back and untangled his camouflage shirt from the barb. He grabbed hold of a thin birch and put his boot onto the wire, hopped the fence, and crept into the field. There were no horses or cows that he could see in the pasture, but they might've been there. The field was waist-high with oat grass, and Aiden kept to the edge of the woods until he'd reached the far side.

The locust post tying the fence together shook in his hand as he stepped up onto the barbed wire, the line swaying beneath him, and crossed onto the property. He was almost to the house now. He could see the lowboy trailer in the yard with an old mustard-colored CAT trackhoe chained down to the wooden bed. He could see the aboveground pool on the other side of the trailer, the busted-up shed just across the yard near the cars in the driveway. The night was nearly still aside from a slight breeze, but despite the coolness of the air, Aiden sweated all over. He skulked to the side of the house and stood with his back against the clapboards, the porch just around the corner. The television was loud and he could hear the words muffled through the walls. He knew who he was looking for was just on the other side.

Turning the corner, Aiden slunk onto the edge of the porch and spun his legs onto the planks. He crawled from there until he was beside the window, his cheek almost flush against the shutter as he lifted his head past the sill and peered inside. The man he was looking for was right there in front of him. Leland Bumgarner was on the far end of the couch with his eyes focused on something Aiden couldn't see. The television must have been against the front wall, just past the window and past the door, somewhere on the other side from where Aiden was prowling. Leland wore a pair of blue jeans plastered with dried concrete. His shirt was off, and Aiden could see some dark tattoo on the left side of his chest, some shape he couldn't make out. There was a cross inked from his shoulder down his arm, and he was spinning a gold can of Miller High Life on his knee, his bare feet kicked onto the table in front of him.

The youngest boy was in pajamas with blue pants and long blue sleeves on a white shirt that had a picture of Spider Man swinging through a city on the front. The boy had his feet toward his father and was lying down on the couch with his head in his mother's lap. Karen was at the other end of the couch and she was running her fingers through the boy's hair. A pair of shorts rode high on her legs, the boy's head against her bare skin, and she wore a tank top that hugged tight to her chest. Behind her at the dining room table, the older boy had his head braced in one hand and scribbled with a pencil on a loose sheet of paper, a textbook open and spread in front of him.

Aiden's first thought was how perfect they all looked. It was as if he were peering through a window into everything he'd ever wanted. What if he'd been the one to date Karen in high school? What if this was his family, if she'd been his wife and those had been his boys, or even if he'd just grown up in a family like that? Some folks just didn't realize how good they had it. Some people had every fucking thing in the world and took it all for granted. Leland was one of those people. He'd always had it all and it filled Aiden with anger. Leland Bumgarner was the reason everything had gone so badly. Leland Bumgarner was the reason the world fell apart.

Aiden clenched the rifle so tightly that his hands felt numb. Leland turned up his beer and sucked back the last drops of Miller before he crunched the can in his fist and stood from the couch. He hovered there for a second and rubbed circles around his stomach with his empty hand, watching the television, waiting for the break to commercial. The sound of some woman selling a facial scrub on the television was clear as day through the wall. Aiden watched as Leland headed into the dining room and then the kitchen, all of his movements visible across the open floor plan of the house.

Leland tossed the empty can into the trash by the cabinets and swung open the door of the refrigerator to grab another beer. When he came back and sat down and popped the top and threw back that can for another swig, Aiden would bust through the front door and fire the first shot before Leland had time to lower his head. After that, he would swing the gun and fire the second shot into Karen. He would have to. She would recognize him. He couldn't stand the thought of seeing her as he pulled the trigger so he'd close his eyes and squeeze. The boys would be running by then and they'd tear off into the back of the house into their rooms. There'd be so much happening and they'd be so filled with terror that there would be no way they'd get a good luck at him, no way they'd be able to give an accurate description.

Leland stepped off the tile into the dining room and walked up behind his oldest son. He stared down at what the boy was doing and said something that Aiden couldn't make out, and the boy looked up at his father and scrunched a funny face. Leland said something else, then tousled the boy's hair and jumped away. The boy reared back and threw the pencil at his father, and Leland braced like he was about to be hit by a train. When the pencil bounced off Leland's stomach, the two of them laughed and Leland headed back toward the couch while the older boy scuttled across the floor to pick up his pencil.

Leland was still laughing and smiling when he got back to the couch. He set his beer down on the coffee table and hovered over the smaller boy, who still lay across the cushions with his head in his mother's lap. Karen looked up at her husband and the boy started to grin as Leland lifted his hands over his head with his fingers gnarled like claws. All of a sudden he sprang down on his son and dug his hands into the child's ribs. The boy immediately tightened into a ball and writhed with laughter, his head rolling in his mother's lap, his legs pedaling against the air. Aiden rose to his feet.

Something Aiden had never remembered until right then flooded his mind and consumed him. He could not have been more than five or six years old. His father had come home early from work and Aiden was out in the yard rolling a Tonka dump truck across the bumpy ground. When he was little, he played with that truck every day, no telling how much dirt he moved, the yellow all but gone from rain and snow and sun. His father came barreling across the grass, and before Aiden even had time to look up he was in the air. His father scooped him from the ground and swung him up into the sky, letting go of his body. All of his weight seemed to rush into his chest as he flew upward, Aiden just floating there for a moment before falling back into his father's hands. When he came down, his father laid Aiden onto his back in the grass and tickled him until he couldn't breathe. Aiden thought in that moment that a boy could die of laughter. He believed that a child could literally suffocate from happiness. These were things he had never thought of since. These were feelings he had forgotten until right then.

He was startled by where he was and what he was doing. He knew then that he could not go through with it. For all his faults, Leland Bumgarner seemed to be a good father. Despite what he'd done to Aiden and Thad, Leland loved his sons. If Aiden pulled the trigger, he would fulfill the nightmare that had haunted him his entire life. He'd be setting those two boys up to be just like him. He would become his father. Aiden couldn't imagine anyone else having to see what he'd seen, having to see what he couldn't stop seeing. He could hear that voice just like in his dream, that voice declaring that, "In the end, blood always tells," but for the first time he knew that it didn't have to be that way. These things weren't set in stone. A man had choices. Aiden had a choice and he needed to leave. He needed to turn around and leave. And as all those thoughts rushed over him, Aiden was standing directly in front of the window. The boy was still laughing and Leland was still giving him fits and Aiden looked over at Karen, that simple turn of his head being some visible thing that she must've seen, because right then their eyes met and her eyes widened and her mouth opened slowly. She started pushing herself off the couch.

"Leland," she said, her husband paying her no attention. "Leland! There's someone on the porch!"

Leland Bumgarner let go of his son and turned toward his wife almost confusedly before he looked over his shoulder. Aiden met his eyes, and while he knew that Leland could see him standing there, he didn't know whether or not Leland could make out his face in such darkness. The minute their eyes met, Aiden took off running across the porch. He jumped into the yard and that pain surged into his ribs and he almost fell from how bad it hurt, but only stumbled and cut around the back of the house because that was the nearest place to find trees, the nearest place he could hide. The field that stretched to the side of the house seemed so empty and so vast that he knew he didn't stand a chance of making it out the way he'd come. He needed to find some new way out, so he shot up the hillside where the root cellar was buried and broke through the brush and the trees until he was in something so thick that everything was snapping around him, limbs and vines and bushes beating against him, and still, farther he ran. He didn't stop until he had crested the slope and had found some ledge of flat ground, where he hit the dirt. He looked down and saw the lights flick on at the corners of the house. Leland's yard was illuminated as he made his way into the backyard with a shotgun in his hands.

Aiden lay out of breath where he could see but not be seen, trying his best not to breathe, to keep entirely still. He watched as Leland stood at the base of the hill and scanned the trees to make sense of shadows and darkness. Aiden waited there a long time, scared to move. Leland seemed to be listening for a sound, some small crack of a twig snapping beneath a footstep, to give him a sign of where the person had gone, to give him some place at which to draw his aim. But Aiden did not move. He stayed put until his breathing slowed and only the sounds of the night remained. There was no time too great. Aiden crouched there waiting. He had no place to go and had already seen forever.

EPILOGUE

HEAVY RAINS ALL SEASON STOPPED THE MOUNTAINS from ever seeing much color that fall, just a dull yellow fading to brown, then gone. The trees were empty now and had been for weeks. It was early November and the world as Aiden McCall had always known it was no more.

He'd driven to Sylva to pick up some things he needed: some lamp oil, stove matches, and a tarpaulin to fix the hole rusted in the roof, a carton of cigarettes, and a fifth of Travelers Club that was marked down. Dented cans of Dinty Moore beef stew were on sale, so Aiden stocked up with about twenty cans of that and some potted meat and a sack of potatoes and onions. He grabbed a pack of salt-cured ham, then a loaf of bread, and some Duke's to make mayonnaise sandwiches for lunch. The bread was the only thing that wouldn't keep, but the mice had been getting into stuff anyways, so he'd have to eat it quickly whether the mold got to it or not. Aiden didn't mind sharing with the field mice. They were almost like pets. But he did wish they'd stick to a single slice or two rather than nibbling the corners off every piece in the bag. If they kept that up, he'd probably have to set traps.

There were only a few hundred dollars left from the cash they'd found at Wayne Bryson's, but he'd yet to spend any of the money April gave him. She wouldn't take no for an answer, and when everything was packed and she was just about to drive away, she shoved a wad of money into his hand. They stared at each other for a long time and didn't say anything. Looking at her, he could tell she had just as many thoughts running through her mind as he had in his, but there wasn't time to say what needed said, and maybe there weren't even words. They both knew it was the last time they'd ever see each other. Aiden was the one who finally broke the silence. He told her he loved her. She smiled and told him good-bye. Then she was gone.

There were five thousand dollars in hundreds. He'd counted the money at least once a day. It was enough to get out of Jackson County and put him up for three or four months until he found a job or the money ran out, whatever happened first. He was going to go to Asheville like he'd planned and make a go of it. He didn't know how things would pan out, but he knew he had to leave. There were still just a few things he had to do first.

He drove past the logging road that wound up the mountain to Sugar Creek Gap and headed farther up Charleys Creek like he'd done a thousand times before. He could almost see the property from the road, but pulled in and drove up like he still lived there. This time he stopped short and just sat and looked at what was left. The trailer had been smashed into a pile of warped metal and dirtied pink insulation, jagged scraps of two-by-fours and heaps of trash. Whoever had bought the place had hired someone with a dozer to tear the single-wide to pieces. It was probably cheaper to haul scrap than move the trailer in one piece, and that appeared to be what they were going to do, but for now it was just a mound of crumpled metal and wood.

Up the hill, only a few sections of framed walls remained standing, the posts and beams black and crumbling into coals. The rest of the house had burned into cinders that still smoldered in places, little trails of smoke wavering out of ashen rubble. The people who bought the place had donated the home to the fire department for a training exercise for the firemen and a tax write-off for themselves. A bunch of young boys in turnout gear with shit-eating grins had lit the fire and watched everything Aiden ever knew burn to the ground.

April had said the people who bought the place were going to plant Christmas trees. There wasn't any money in Christmas tree farming, especially not on a place this size and especially not when the people growing the trees didn't know poplar from piss oak. There was no chance in hell they'd ever succeed. Aiden figured they'd never be able to grow anything at all on that ground. From everything he'd ever witnessed, the place bore hardship. But the more he sat there and thought, the more he came to realize that maybe a place couldn't be cursed, maybe only people could, and maybe that's why there'd never been a goddamn thing worked out for him, Thad, or April. Perhaps God just had it out for certain folks and he'd been born one of the unlucky ones. So maybe those people would be able to grow those trees after all. Maybe they'd be just fine.

The locust rail fence he'd laid around April's property was still there and the radio tower stood with its metal frame piercing the sky. He and Thad had spent entire summers listening to country out of Nashville or the rock-and-roll sets students at the university in Cullowhee spun some nights when they had the air. He and Thad used to sit on the porch and drink cold beer and smoke cigarettes and stare off into nothing with the only sound between them that crystal-clear music humming down from above and coursing through the speakers without even a tick of static.

Aiden wondered what April would have thought about the place now, the place she'd spent some twenty years of her life, demolished into ruin. He wondered where she had gone when she packed the few things she wanted and drove away. He hadn't asked her and she hadn't told, and he wondered if she'd gone to Tybee Island like she'd always talked about or maybe someplace different entirely. There was no way to know now, and he wasn't sure if he wanted to know. He liked to think that there would have been some sort of sorrow in her heart to see the place like this, that maybe, despite all of what had happened, there was a tiny piece of sentimentality she held for this place, if nothing else a single good memory that made her smile when she thought about it.

But when he was honest, he knew how stupid it was to think anything like that. That's the thing about growing older in a place, is that eventually all the things remembered are torn down and replaced with something new. Most people get nostalgic, but to miss something that was gone was to have loved something that had been there in the first place. There'd been nothing here for her to love. The fact that the house was gone would make it easier to forget, and, in time, maybe it would be as if the place had never existed at all.

He lit a cigarette and backed down the drive onto Charleys Creek. He headed back the way he'd come, and this time, when he reached the old logging road that twisted up the mountain to Sugar Creek Gap, he hung a right and headed up the gravel. About halfway up the mountain, the trail to Bee Rock cut through the trees to the right and he thought about Thad camping there when he was little. He thought about how Thad had always sworn up and down that he was

Cherokee and how he'd caked himself in mud and run around carving spears and arrows and bows, and setting booby traps. One time Thad got a head full of lice from sticking feathers he plucked off a dead crow he found on the side of the road into his hair, and he had to slather his head with turpentine and petroleum jelly to kill the bugs. A redheaded Indian. That son of a bitch was a sight.

When the road peaked out at Sugar Creek Gap, Aiden parked and walked over to the clearing where a view stretched until the farthest mountains were nothing but hazy blue curves on the edge of the horizon. There were only a few hours left of daylight, but the overcast skies kept the mountains in a dim gloom even with the sun having yet to sink. A crow cawed from somewhere behind him and Aiden turned just in time to see three of them burst out of the black balsams and sail down into the valley in search of a new place to light. That stand of balsams was where it all began.

Under the trees, he kicked at the roots with the toe of his boot and knelt just as he had so many years before. He could remember not knowing Thad was there until he spoke. He could remember Thad pulling that crumpled centerfold from his Velcro wallet and spreading it right there on the ground and that moment of them joking back and forth being the happiest he ever felt in his life. That was the day that Thad Broom went from being a friend to something closer than blood kin. It wasn't like having a brother or a father. What Thad became was something new entirely, something that the world had yet to name.

Now that Thad was gone, it wasn't so much sorrow that Aiden felt as disbelief. Every single day, he found himself looking around and waiting, listening for the sound of Thad's voice, wondering what Thad was doing, thinking Thad had just run off into the woods for a while. Then he'd remember and there was this confusion that accompanied that first second of remembering. It would take him a second or two to recognize that Thad was gone. There would be no coming back.

He drove into the valley where Sugar Creek Gap meandered its way down the backside of Rich Mountain into Caney Fork. The road wasn't kept up like it was when he was younger. Back then a man could've driven a Cadillac from Charleys Creek to Caney Fork, but nowadays the road was washed out and rutted. Curves were washboarded into rippled gravel. The state had come in and dug boulders off the hillside and dropped them into the road so that people couldn't even pass all the way from one side to the other by vehicle anymore. Nothing was like it had been. Everything was suddenly changing.

The bottle of whiskey sloshed around on the other side of the bench seat and he leaned over to grab it, almost running off the high side of the road when he did. He opened the bottle and took a slug, wiped his chin with the back of his hand, and screwed the cap back down. He was thinking about all of the things he'd never know about Thad, what had happened while Thad was deployed, and how what he'd seen and the things he'd done had become something physical that he had to carry through this world. Aiden wondered what it must have felt like to grow up in a place where you saw your mother every single day of your life, and you always knew that no matter what you did or how hard you tried she would never love you. It was no wonder Thad had hated her, and though Aiden had lost both of his parents so early, he almost imagined it would be worse to live with that constant reminder.

At the same time, Thad had never known the reason for April being the way that she was, and now Aiden did. Knowing what had happened to April and how her son was a living, breathing reminder of that memory wasn't something that justified how she'd treated him, but it did explain it. There were so many horrible things they had buried inside themselves, all of the memories that had come to govern their lives. He found himself wishing that he could have been the one to bear it all. He wished that he could have taken all of the bad in this world and piled it onto himself so that he would have been the only one to ever know that kind of suffering.

Just up ahead, the boulders blocked him from driving any farther. A four-wheel trail cut off to the right, where a small creek ran under the road through a culvert, the black stone streambed stretching from there and stacking a cobbled streak of rock up the mountain. Aiden steered onto the trail and pulled up a few hundred feet to where the cut dead-ended into a thick stand of rhododendron, its green leaves rolled up like cigarettes in the cold. He parked and climbed out of the car, grabbed the carbine from the toolbox in the back, then spread the tarpaulin onto the ground. He kept the tarp folded into a square and loaded all of his supplies onto it. When everything was there, he pulled the four corners of the tarp into his hand and slung the load over his shoulder with one hand, the rifle by his side in the other. From there, a game trail led a little over a mile to the camp.

There must've come a time when people gave up on those shanties at the hunting camp, because it was obvious no one had been there for years when he first went back. None of the buildings were worth living in anymore, but he took scraps from here and there and fixed up the shack farthest from the road as best he could. He stepped onto the rotten porch planks of the place he'd been living. A busted screen door with chicken wire at the bottom and a torn piece of mesh screen hanging down from the top opened to a heavier door with nine windowpanes, only two rectangles of glass unbroken. He set the rifle standing on the porch with the barrel balanced against the door frame, kept the tarp over his shoulder, and entered. The man inside was just how Aiden left him.

Samuel Mathis was tied to a metal folding chair with his feet tucked behind the crossbar running between the front legs. His ankles were bound with rope that continued behind to where his wrists hung from the empty space between the chair back and seat. His wrists were wound tightly with the same rope, and from there the cord spun around his chest so that the metal folding chair had become a part of his body, something inseparable from him. If he moved at all, he would fall, and he had, many times those first few days, though now he seemed to have given up and just sat there hunched over, huffing through his nose, his mouth duct-taped shut. The left side of Samuel's face was so swollen that his eye seemed nothing more than a black slit cut across a plum. He was covered with blood that had dried almost black in his hair, down his face and neck.

Aiden set the tarp down by the door and started to unload the supplies. He took the cans of stew beef and the loaf of bread, the mayonnaise, the salt-cured ham, the potatoes, and onions and he put all of those things on a counter that stretched from the door along the front wall. He grabbed the carton of cigarettes and whiskey, the lamp oil and the kitchen matches, and put them on a small card table beside Samuel in the center of the room. It had looked like it might rain, or maybe even snow outside, but it was starting to get dark now and he figured it was too late to climb onto the roof and try to secure the tarp over the hole that had rusted through the tin. He bought one of the largest tarps the store had, and was planning to just stretch it all the way over the eave so that water couldn't run beneath and seep inside. The chinking on the board shack was rotted through so that the walls did little to stop the wind. It was cold outside and getting colder. He could feel the air blowing through and he wished that there was a stove to burn wood and keep warm, but there wasn't. The first snow had come a few days before and it would not be long until more.

A glass lamp was on the table and he removed the globe to fill the base with oil. When the lamp was filled, Aiden struck one of the kitchen matches and lit the tattered wick into a tall flame that licked at the air before he dialed the fire down into a low, steady glow. He lit a cigarette as the match burned into his fingers, drew a few swigs of whiskey from the bottle of Travelers Club, and blew a trail of smoke into Samuel's face. A wind howled through the valley and straight through the shack, and Aiden shivered with how cold the world had become. Winter was almost upon him, and he no longer wished to stay. He would keep Samuel alive a bit longer, maybe a day or two, maybe a week. He still wasn't sure, but what he did know was that killing Samuel Mathis would prick a pinhole in the darkness. When it was over, he would bury him and there'd be a glint of light in this wicked world because of something he'd done.

Nightfall came on and the last bit of daylight filtered through the windows. In a few minutes, the only light to be had would be that which he made. Aiden turned up the bottle and drank until the whiskey washed over him. He studied the way Samuel Mathis looked, the way he breathed, the way his eyes seemed to be begging Aiden to end it. Everyone was begging for the end. But not yet, Aiden thought. Hold off just a little bit longer. He was not quite ready to be alone.

ACKNOWLEDGMENTS

To Ace and George for pouring me a drink when I was lying in the mud. To Terry McCall for riding and smiling and laughing. To A. J. for holding off on the eviction. To the North Carolina Arts Council for believing I was something other than a bumbling drunkard. And, most important, to my agent, Julia Kenny; editor, Sara Minnich; and the entire team at Putnam, without whom my work would be illegible.

THE WEIGHT OF THIS WORLD

DAVID JOY

———

Discussion Guide

———

Essay by David Joy,
Digging in the Trash

———

Excerpt from David Joy's
next novel,
The Line That Held Us

———

BOOK
ENDS

DISCUSSION GUIDE

1. Discuss the longtime friendship between Aiden and Thad. What is the source of their deep connection? In what ways does this relationship both benefit and disadvantage each man?

2. Each of the main protagonists is shadowed by a past trauma. How does this play out in the novel? How is each able to cope, or not?

3. Consider the relationship between April and Aiden. How would you characterize it? Why do you think it developed the way it did? What does it mean to each of them?

4. In this novel, author David Joy sometimes injects humor into even the darkest situations. Which were your favorite such moments?

5. The relationship between April and Thad is fraught for reasons that are revealed to the reader only late in the novel, and which are never known to Thad. What did you think of their relationship? Is April a bad mother? Did the revelation of her past change your perspective? What do parents owe their children?

6. Much of the conflict is concerned with the characters' ambitions versus their ability to achieve those dreams. What most holds these characters back? What changed for April that allowed her to move forward? What prevents Thad and Aiden from doing the same?

7. What is the significance of the Appalachian setting? How does it uniquely shape the experiences of these characters?

8. The novel contains numerous acts of violence, acts that both propel the plot and shape the characters. Discuss the importance and impact of these incidents. How did you respond to each? Which shocked you the most?

9. How did you feel about each of the three main protagonists? Did any resonate with you more than the others? Which was the most sympathetic?

10. What did you think of the ending? Did the fates of the protagonists surprise you, or not?

THEY SAY WE NEED TO LEARN TO TALK TO EACH OTHER. They say we need to bridge the rural-urban divide. But that's hard when folks see trailers and immediately think "trash." David Joy, one of the most celebrated young Southern novelists, today brings us some nonfiction—some genuine truth about his people, who are among the most misunderstood in the South.

DIGGING IN THE TRASH
STORY BY DAVID JOY

WE DROVE THERE ON BIRTHDAYS AND HOLIDAYS. PAST farm ponds colored chocolate milk. Past yellow fields of oat grass that waved and flickered in sunlight like heads of windblown hair. Gravel crunched under tires as we eased along a dirt road just a few minutes from where we lived to the trailer where my grandfather survived.

My grandfather, or what was left of him, was worn down and wiry. Hair slicked back, his eyes were the same pale blue color of his work shirts. He wore a pair of Dickies dirtied at the knees. His veins rose from his arms like tree roots, tattoos aged almost green in his skin. For lack of a better way of putting it, the old man had a look like he could strangle the life out of you. The fact of the matter was there was more to that look than just words.

When I was growing up, my grandfather was married to a crazy-haired woman named Dez who named all her daughters after flowers—Rose, Lily, Daisy, a whole garden of kids. Dez might've been as close to wicked as I've ever known in this world, but for reasons that escaped most folks, my grandfather always found his way back to her. One time they were fighting about God-knows-what and she loaded the shotgun, walked him out into the front yard, pulled the trigger, and peppered his back with bird shot. My uncle went to see him while the doctor was still picking the pellets out of his spine. When the law walked in and asked the old man if he wanted to press charges he just shook his head. The officer asked what he was going to do when he got out of the hospital, where he'd go, and my grandfather said simply, "I'm gonna go home."

He paused and added, "And I'm gonna kill the bitch."

In the end, he didn't kill her, and deep down it's because in some incomprehensible way he loved her. One of his deepest truths was that he was a horrible alcoholic and he knew how bad he was without her. Ultimately, my grandfather knew she was the only one who could keep a bottle out of his hand and so despite what she did to him, he always came back because in that single way she was what kept him from drowning.

To say my grandfather was tough as nails would be to sell him short. As a kid, he slit his femoral artery on a rusted pipe diving into a river, should've bled out, but didn't. He fought on the front lines in World War II, smoked and drank all his life, walked away from countless car wrecks, survived cancer time and time again, even when doctors cut out his tongue.

I remember when I was little riding with my father to the VA in Salisbury, North Carolina, every couple days while my grandfather lay in bed dying. That's what the doctors said: dying. They gave a short timeline and we visited often. Every time we came, we stood there in the room and he lay there in bed, eyes closed, machines keeping him breathing. We'd sit there a while waiting on the end and eventually turn around and drive home because the end never came. One day my grandfather decided he'd slept long enough and he opened his eyes and climbed out of there like he was waking from a catnap. Turns out we could've waited on the end forever and it still wouldn't have come because once again the old man wasn't ready.

The thing about it is, I'm not talking about men being like cats, having nine lives. The way my grandfather did it wasn't like that at all. What I'm talking about are people being too mad at this world to lie down and die. That was him in a nutshell. His survival was a matter of stubbornness and anger. His survival was a matter of looking bitterly at the hand he'd been dealt and saying, "Sorry, boys, but I ain't done playing."

TO LOVE THE HELPLESS

My father didn't have it easy growing up. Some of his earliest memories are in a one-bedroom shack he called the rat house where he was afraid to go to sleep because he was terrified the rats would gnaw his feet off while he dreamed. He remembers scrounging around for cans of vienna sausages to fight off stomach pangs, killing squirrels to keep from starving. He was only five or six, but life was a matter of survival.

Eventually my dad was raised by his aunt, his father's sister, who took him in as her own the way it happens so often where I come from. Still, if you were to ask my father to this day to recall his dad, he wouldn't tell you stories about his old man kicking him out on the side of the road or giving him presents only to horse-trade them away soon as he was drunk at the bar. What my father would say is that his daddy was a fine carpenter and was hell with a twenty-gauge come rabbit season. He'd tell you stories like how his old man could talk to animals. He'd tell you how one time he sat by a campfire along the river while his father and his friends drank their minds into oblivion jug-fishing for catfish, how he heard a screech owl in the woods, and how his father drunkenly fought his way through briars and brush into the dark and brought that owl out to his son like he was fetching a dog.

When I think about the relationship between my dad and his father, there's a line from a Maurice Manning poem that always eats me up. Even conjuring the words to my mind, I find my eyes filling with tears. The line reads, "I loved the helpless people I loved." That's the truth of it. That's why my dad will never say a cross word about his father, because despite all his faults, it was his daddy. It was his daddy we went to see every time we rode back into that trailer park, the rest of us dreading being dragged there. It was his daddy he laid in the ground when the old man finally decided to die, and that's exactly what my father said as he stood there with his eyes glassed over at the grave, Dez not even bothering to get out of the car.

"He was my daddy," my father said. Just those four words. Nothing else.

Nowadays, I make my living as a full-time novelist. I write about fathers and sons. I write about friendship. I write about poverty and hopelessness, addiction and violence. I had a novel come out a few weeks back, *The Weight of This World*, a book *The New York Times* called "bleakly beautiful" and "[a] pitiless novel about a region blessed by nature but reduced to desolation and despair." The Associated Press praised the pacing and prose, and noted how trailers and churches dot my landscape. A part of me couldn't understand why that was noteworthy, but I guess it seems strange to people on the outside. What I hope they see too, though, is that this is a place sopping wet with raw emotion, a landscape drenched with humanity. It is all I know and it is beautiful.

So often people hear that word "trailer" and their minds follow with "trash." Maybe it was growing up going to my grandfather's or maybe it was growing up with a trailer park just across the road, but as a child I don't remember ever thinking that I was better than the kids I played with because I lived in a house and they lived in trailers. It wasn't that I was oblivious to class. I recognized some folks had more than others, that I had a little more than them, and the rest of the world had a lot more than any of us. I recognized class. It's just that I don't remember ever equating class to a person's worth, and I count myself lucky for that. We all rode the same bus and went to the same school. We bickered and fought, made up secret handshakes and loved each other like brothers and that's just the way it was, kids being kids.

Any one of them could find their way into a novel of mine.

There was a big, black boy named Darrell who was one of my best friends at Tuckaseegee Elementary. Both of us were about a foot too tall for our age, but I was a vine and he was built like a tank. I remember he had one of the best laughs I've ever heard, a smile that could warm you up like you were standing by a woodstove. I remember one time he cut the eyeball out of a fish and brought it to school in a little Ziploc bag he stuffed in his pocket because he thought I'd like to have it, and I did. I did like it. So the next day I brought him a pocketful of .22-caliber bullets as a thank you.

There was a little, stubby moon-faced boy named Smokey who was a few years younger than me. We all smoked cigarettes. He was about eight or nine years old and he'd steal soft packs of Doral 100s from his mother's carton she kept in the freezer. One time, a buddy and me pushed Smokey out into the middle of a farm pond in a leaky johnboat without a paddle and pelted him with rotten goose eggs till he threw up over the side. One time I remember a kid making fun of Smokey for living in a trailer. Smokey hauled off and hit him right in his mouth and exclaimed, "I don't live in a goddamn trailer! I live in a double-wide!" The bottom line was Smokey understood class just like I did, that where you live doesn't have a thing in the world to do with what a man deserves.

I remember these two brothers named Bubba and Lyndon. Bubba was my age and had greasy hair and a pair of cloudy, coke-bottle glasses that he couldn't see through. We played machine-pitch baseball together and he never hit a thing. His brother Lyndon had pale eyes and bright orange hair. When he was about sixteen or so, he and his old man got into a fight and Lyndon tore off out of the trailer, hopped in his car, and made it a quarter mile out of the park when a truck T-boned him and severed his head clean off.

The kids I grew up with came to know truths that don't reach most people until they're adults if they ever reach them at all. There's a poem by one of my favorite writers, the Kentucky poet Rebecca Gayle Howell, titled "My Mother Told Us Not to Have Children," and in that poem she has a line where she asks, "Is gentleness a resource of the privileged?" She answers, "In this respect, my people were poor. / We fought to eat and fought each other because // we were tired from fighting. We had no time / to share. Instead our estate was honesty, // which is not tenderness." And maybe that's all I've ever really known: honesty. Maybe that's all any of us knew.

A SECOND TO BREATHE

The other day I was watching a BBC interview about poverty in Baltimore. One of the people being interviewed said something that really struck me. He looked into the camera deadpan and beaten and he said, "Desperation is a way of living." When he said that, I couldn't help but think, maybe it's not just gentleness that's a resource of the privileged. Maybe hope is a resource of the privileged, and maybe that's what people don't get about the kids I grew up with, about the characters I write about in my novels.

I get asked all the time why my characters aren't hopeful. What I say again and again is this: It's hard to be hopeful when you're worried about your next meal, when the only thought to ever cross your mind is how you're going to make it through the day. I grew up in a place where we drank red Kool-Aid out of old pickle jars and mayonnaise jars used for pitchers. When they took me inside their trailers and invited me to eat, we cherry-picked slices of white bread off the loaf to miss the slices mice had nibbled the corners off. The mice always ate the corners. Just the corners and wasted the rest. Even then it seemed so cruel to me, a world where that happened. I'll never forget that. And the thing is, the kids I grew up with had it relatively easy compared to some.

I get the same kind of questions about addiction. People don't understand what would push someone to drugs like methamphetamine or heroin. They don't understand what would make a man drink like my grandfather. The reason they can't understand it is because they've never been that low. When all you've got is a twenty-dollar bill, twenty dollars doesn't ward off eviction notices. Twenty dollars doesn't get you health insurance. Twenty dollars doesn't make a car payment. Twenty dollars doesn't even keep the lights on. But twenty dollars can take you right out of this world for just a little while. Just a minute. Just long enough to breathe. That's what every single addict I've ever known really wanted: just a second to breathe.

I've known addicts all my life. I walked along that edge a long time myself and stumbled time and time again, but luckily never fell over. I've had friends die from heroin overdoses. I helped look after a little boy born addicted to crack and watched him struggle to learn the simplest words, all of us doubting he'd ever be able to talk. The boy's father was a friend of mine's uncle, a man named Donny. Years ago, Donny wrecked his car and a telephone pole swung down from lines like a wrecking ball, crashed through the windshield, and smashed his fiancée's brains out right there in the seat beside him. When the law pulled up, Donny was picking pieces of her out of the floorboard and trying to stick them back on her face. He was talking to her like she was still alive. I might've wondered a lot of things about him over the course of my life, but I never once wondered why he used. I never once wondered why all he wanted was to leave this world for a little while.

A few weeks ago, I was reading at a bookstore in Raleigh, North Carolina and three of the people in the audience worked in mental health. One of them was an addiction counselor. At the end of the reading, she asked me what was the one thing I thought could help people most. My answer was the same as it's always been: listen. Just listen. The truth is we live in a world where we don't listen to people anymore. So often we're just waiting for the next opening to respond. What we need to realize is that sometimes people don't need advice. Sometimes people just need to be heard. Sometimes the greatest gift we can give someone is just to keep our mouths shut and let them empty themselves into our hands. When they're finished, we don't need to do anything with what they've given us. We just need to show them that we're holding it for them till they can catch their breath.

There's a moment in my latest novel when the only thing one of the characters has ever wanted was exactly that: "But no one listened anymore. No one. And perhaps it was that not listening that led to things like this. Perhaps it was that not listening that made the world so volatile." Just as I'm asked about hope and drug use, I'm always asked about violence—why is there so much violence in my work— and for me violence is tied directly to this idea of being heard.

Over and over again I watched the kids I grew up with explode because no one would take the time to hear them. Sometimes when no one will listen all you can do to be heard is to make them feel you, a sort of now-do-you-hear-me plea when you just can't take anymore. I lost my first friend to suicide when I was eighteen years old. I lost the next one almost a year later to the day. I've lost six friends to suicide altogether and I'm only thirty-three years old. When I think about why, I think about listening. I wonder what would've happened if I'd just been there to open my hands, if I'd just been there to say, "Pour yourself onto me. I'm here."

WHO TO BET ON

I dedicated this last book to a friend I grew up with named Paco. He had strawberry-blond hair, a face that glowed like sunrise, and could absolutely skin an electric guitar. Paco worked on fishing boats in Alaska for a while and at the end of those four-month trips he'd step off the boat and they'd hand him a check for twenty, sometimes $30,000. One night he showed up in front of my dorm when I was in college and he'd bought an old '80s model stretch limousine and we rode all around the mountains blasting the theme song from *Cheers* through busted speakers laughing like tickled children.

After 9/11, Paco joined the Marine Corps and served multiple deployments to Iraq. There are pictures of him standing in the moon dust over there, cigarette dangling in his teeth, holding up an M-249

SAW machine gun like he's Kerry King playing a B.C. Rich guitar for Slayer. There's another photo of prisoners they'd taken, on their knees, hands bound at their backs, black sacks over their faces, Paco standing between them with his thumbs up like The Fonz. I don't know what all Paco saw on the front lines of combat or how it affected him. But what I do know is that when he came home, one day he walked into his house, shot his brother, shot his father, and killed himself. What I do know is that when the news told the story, I watched how they stripped my friend of his humanity like he was trash. I watched helplessly and all I could think was that if I listened hard enough I could still hear the echo of his laughter as we rode through the mountains in that beat-up limousine.

Maybe that's why what I read in a trade review recently struck me so hard. The reviewer didn't like my book, and that's all right. A whole lot of people don't like my books, and that's perfectly OK. My books aren't for everyone. This reviewer didn't like what he called my "Southern Poverty Law Center photorealism." This is what got me, though. He wrote that I should "leave the peeling trailers, come down out of the hollers, and try writing about people for a change." He actually italicized that word, people, to be sure and say that what lives in those trailers, what finds itself in a world consumed by hopelessness, addiction, and violence, those aren't people at all. I'm not sure what he thinks men like my grandfather, boys like Darrell, Smokey, Bubba and Lyndon, men like Donny, like Paco are, other than to use his own words, "trailer trash."

But what he misses is this. These are people who just like everyone else experience happiness, sadness, fear, anger, surprise, and disgust. These are people who love and hate, people who cry their eyes out when they lose someone close, people who cry their eyes out when they laugh so hard they keel over, people who'd sell the last thing they had to put food on the table, people who work eighty hours a week to break even. These are people who'd strangle the life out of a man who dared stand in front of their children and say a word like trash like he had any idea what their life was worth. When I think about my family, my father and grandfather, when I think about all the boys I grew up with, all the ones who ended it, when I think about the hopeless, the addicts, the violence, I again remember that line from Maurice Manning. I loved the helpless people I loved, and maybe that's why I can't sit back while someone spits in their faces.

As I write this essay, I find that I'm tired. I'm tired of standing by silently while privileged people in privileged places strip those less fortunate of their humanity. I'm tired of living in a place where men like my grandfather and Paco are shipped off to front lines to die for profit margins. I'm tired of an America where all the folks I've ever loved are dismissed as trash, where people are reduced to something subhuman simply because of where they live. I'm tired of having to explain it. I'm just goddamn tired.

One of my favorite writers, Larry Brown, was once called the "King of White Trash," and he had enough of a sense of humor to joke about it, to laugh and tell his daughter that if he was the king that effectively crowned her princess. Ultimately, I think the reason Larry was able to shake it off and laugh is because he'd grown used to it, just as we all have. We know we're something that outsiders will never understand, that it's noteworthy to see a landscape dotted with trailers and churches. We know we're something perplexing to those who have never been here. We know that they'll never be able to see that there is a tremendous beauty in day-to-day survival, that there is sufficient grace in refusing to buckle beneath the weight of this world.

A friend of mine sent me an article recently from *The New Yorker* titled, "Doomsday Prep for the Super-Rich." It was basically an essay about how some of the richest people in America have been preparing for some sort of societal breakdown. I guffawed at the thought when I read it, not at the idea of America collapsing, but at the idea they think they'll be the ones to survive. I laughed at the boldness, at the arrogance.

I've never been a betting man and the truth is I don't have much money to lay down, but what I'll leave you with is this. While all the privileged have been coasting through life so often on the backs of my people, we've been surviving. Survival is not new to us. As the man from Baltimore said, Desperation is a way of life. So if the time comes and there are bets to be made, I'd think long and hard about where you slide your chips. If I were you, I'd try to imagine my grandfather waking up off that bed, staring God right dead in His eyes as he'd done a dozen times before, and saying with a sly grin spread across his lonely face, "Sorry, boys, but I ain't done playing." I'd think about all of us in trailers, the lot of us, the trash, and if all I had were a dollar to my name, that's the bed I'd make.

KEEP READING FOR AN EXCERPT
FROM DAVID JOY'S NEW NOVEL,
THE LINE THAT HELD US.

(**1**)

DARL MOODY DIDN'T GIVE A WET SACK OF SHIT WHAT the state considered poaching. Way he figured, anybody who'd whittle a rifle season down to two weeks and not allot for a single doe day didn't care whether a man starved to death. Meat in the freezer was meat that didn't have to be bought and paid for, and that came to mean a lot when the work petered off each winter. So even though it was almost two months early, he was going hunting.

The buck Darl'd seen crossing from the Buchanan farm into Coon Coward's woods for the past two years had a rocking chair on his head and a neck thick as a tree trunk. Coon wouldn't let a man set foot on his land on account of the ginseng hidden there, but Coon was out of town. The old man had gone to the flatland to bury his sister and wouldn't be back for a week.

The cove was full of sign: rubs that stripped bark off maples and birch, scrapes all over the ground where button bucks scratched soil with something instinctual telling them to do so but lacking any rhyme or reason. A mature buck knew exactly what he was doing when he ripped at the ground like he was hoeing a line with his hooves, but the young ones ran around wild. They'd scrape all over the place, trying to add to a conversation they were too inexperienced to understand.

Darl locked his stand around a blackjack oak that grew twenty feet high before the first limbs sprung off. He climbed to a strong vantage and surveyed a saddle of land where early autumn cast patches of the mountains gold in afternoon light. An unseasonable cold snap following one of the driest summers the county had ever seen brought on fall a month ahead of schedule. It was the last week of September, but the ridgelines were already bare. Down in the valley, the trees were in full color with reds and oranges afire like embers, the acorns falling like raindrops. The nights were starting to frost and within a few weeks the first few breaths of winter would strip the mountains to their gray bones.

Darl sipped a pint of whiskey he had stashed in the cargo pocket of his camouflage pants, took off his ball cap and slicked the sweat from his forehead back through a widow's peak of thinning hair shaved close. He scratched at the thick beard on his chin and listened closely for any sign of movement, though just like the past two evenings, he'd yet to see or hear a thing but squirrels. Soon as the sun sank behind the western face, the woods dropped into shadow and it wouldn't be long for nightfall. Still, he would stay because there was no telling when that buck might show, and in full dark, he would find his way out by headlamp.

Somewhere up the hillside, a stick cracked beneath a footstep, and that sound came through his body like current. His heart raced and his palms grew sweaty, his eyes wide and white. Dried leaves rustled underfoot, and behind the scraggly limbs of a dead hemlock he could see a slight shift of movement, but from such distance and in such little light, what moved was impossible to discern. Through the riflescope, he spotted something on four legs, something gray-bodied and low to the ground. The 3-9x50mm CenterPoint was useless in low light, but it was all Darl could afford and so that was what he had.

Sighting the scope out as far as it would extend, he played the shot out in his mind. At two hundred yards, the animal filled a little less than a quarter of the sight picture. He rolled the bolt and pulled back only enough to check that a round was chambered, then locked the bolt back and thumbed away the safety.

A boar hog rooting around the hillside for a meal. Each year those pigs moved farther and farther north out of South Carolina, first coming up from Walhalla ten years back and now overrunning farms all across Jackson County. There was open season on hogs statewide due to the damage they caused. A father and son out of Caswell County were hunting private land between Brevard and Toxaway earlier that year when the son spooked a whole passel of hogs out of a laurel thicket, and the father drew down on a seven-hundred-pound boar. That was right over the ridgeline into Transylvania County. That pig weighed 580 pounds gutted, and they took home more than 150 pounds of sausage alone. Do the math on that at the grocery store.

All his life there'd been a thoughtlessness that came on before the kill. It was something hard to explain to anyone else, but that feeling was on him now as he braced the rifle against the trunk of the oak and tried to steady his aim, a mind whittled back to instinct. A tangle of brush obstructed his view, but he knew the Core-Lokt would tear through that just fine. He tried to get the picture to open by sliding his cheek along the buttstock, but the cheap scope offered little play. When the view was wide, he toyed with the power ring to get the picture as clear as possible, nothing ever coming fully into focus as he drew the crosshairs over the front shoulders. He centered on his pulse then. *Breathe slowly. Count the breaths. Squeeze between heartbeats. On five, pull the trigger.* The sight wavered as he counted down. *Three. Two. Squeeze.*

The rifle punched against his shoulder and the report hammered back in waves touching everything between here and there and returning in fragments as it bounced around the mountains. He checked downrange and the animal was felled.

"I got him," Darl said. His body tingled and his head was swimming. Adrenaline coursed through him and left him breathless. He was in disbelief. "I fucking got him."

Darl sucked down the last of the whiskey in one slug, slung his rifle over his shoulder, and climbed his way down with his treestand. In less than an hour, the light would be gone. He knew he had to hurry. There'd barely be enough time to field dress the pig and get it out of the woods before dark. Maybe Calvin Hooper would help him dress out the hog. Cal had a nice hoist for dressing deer, and that sure beat the hell out of the makeshift gambreling stick Darl had at the house. Whether you were scraping hair or skinning him out, a pig was a whole lot easier with two sets of hands working than one. Cal wouldn't want anything for the trouble. Never had. As soon as Darl got that pig back to the truck, he'd head to Calvin's. "I fucking got him," he said.

A small branch of water ran at the bottom of the draw, and through a thicket of laurel, the hillside steepened. Darl staggered through the copse of trees and slowly climbed until he was near the ledge where the pig had fallen. He tripped on a fishing line strung between two dogwoods, a pair of tin cans with rocks inside clanking loud in the limbs above him. Darl froze and looked around. As his eyes focused, he saw rusted fishhooks hung eye level from the trees, trotlines meant for poachers, and he brushed them back one by one as if he were clawing his way through spiderwebs. That's when he saw him. Not a pig but a man, flat on his stomach. A brush-patterned shirt was darkened almost black with blood, his pants the same grayish camouflage as his shirt.

Darl stepped closer, knelt by the man's legs, and placed his hand on the man's left calf. His body was warm, but there was no movement, no sound of breath. In absolute shock, Darl crawled forward and saw where the bullet had entered the man's rib cage. He'd been quartered away, the hollowpoint opening as it cut through him and exited behind his right shoulder, blowing the top of his arm ragged. The man's left arm hung by his side, his hand open, palm up, and Darl could see a few shriveled red berries balanced at the tip of his fingers. He realized then that he was kneeling in a thick patch of ginseng, mostly young, two-prong plants, but some much, much older. The man had an open book bag on the ground beside him with a tangle of thick, banded roots stuffed inside, the thin runners off the main ginseng shoots snarled like a muss of hair.

Darl knew the man shouldn't have been there the same as him. This was Coward land, and they were both trespassing; two poachers who shouldn't have been there, but right there they were. There they were, one of them gone from this world, and the other facing it in its enormity. While he crouched there on hands and knees, dumbstruck as a child, his mind washed between astonishment and terror.

The man's face was turned and angled into the ground. His neck was sunburned red and dotted with dark orange freckles, the back of his hair thick and curled, a yellow blond the color of hay. Darl stepped across the body, being careful not to get his boots in the blood around him. The man wore a camouflage hat with hunter orange lining the edge of the bill, the words CANEY FORK GENERAL STORE stitched across the front. The hat was knocked crooked on his head and Darl grabbed the bill to try and turn the man's face out of the dirt.

As soon as he saw the dark purple birthmark covering the right side of the man's face, Darl knew him. Carol Brewer, who everyone called Sissy, lay stone-cold dead on the bracken-laced ground. Darl had known Carol all his miserable life, a half-wit born to a family that Jesus Christ couldn't have saved. Some people believed Carol's daddy, Red, might've been the devil himself. There was a meanness that coursed through him, a meanness that was as close to pure evil as any God-fearing man had ever known. Carol was the runt of the family and, by most accounts, the only one who ever had a chance. Some thought if he'd been able to get out from under the wings of his father and older brother, Dwayne, he might've been all right, but things didn't work out that way, and Carol wound up being as much trouble as the lot of them.

Darl let go of the cap bill and Carol's head came to rest on the ground. His eyes were closed with his mouth slightly opened. A yellow jacket buzzed by Darl's ear and landed on Carol's lips. The wasp started to crawl into his mouth but Darl swatted the bug away, his fingers brushing Carol's face. He stomped the bee where it hovered above the ground, then looked to the west to gauge what light remained. Darl knew it wouldn't be long, though nightfall didn't matter like it had minutes before. His thoughts were wild with what would come, but he knew the darkness was a gift now and he welcomed it. His mind raced as the night slowly closed around him like cupped hands. He had until dawn to dig a grave.

(2)

DWAYNE BREWER GOOSE-STEPPED DOWN THE BEER aisle of the Franklin Walmart wearing a latex chimp mask he'd found on the floor by the Halloween decorations. The mask was hot and his breathing was loud. The inside smelled of cheap molded rubber and he slicked the nylon hair back through his fingers while he chuckled at a woman who sneered.

She wore pastel-colored scrubs and white tennis shoes, her highlighted hair pulled back in a ponytail. Through the eye slits of the mask, he saw a little girl, maybe six years old, with one of her fingers hooked in the corner of her mouth standing beside the woman. Dwayne scratched under his armpit with one hand and clawed at the back of his head with the other, hopping around bowlegged like a monkey, and the child laughed. He pulled the mask off and tossed it into the open cooler, his skin cold with sweat as he ran his hand over his face and reached for a case of Bud heavy. Tearing a ragged hole in the cardboard, he fished out a beer and cracked the top.

"Have a blessed day," he said with a wide smile, tilting the open can toward the woman and nodding. She eyed him like the fiend he was, her little girl hiding behind her leg, spellbound with curiosity as the giant man before her swallowed half the can in one tremendous gulp.

The thing about Walmart was that even a man like Dwayne Brewer could go unnoticed. People pushed their buggies with dead-eyed stares, everything sliding by in the periphery. Consumerism scaled this large had a way of camouflaging class.

At the end of the aisle, he squeezed past a beefy gal in tiny shorts who had a baby on each hip and three children running circles around her. One of the kids reached out as he made his next lap and knocked an endcap of Cool Ranch Doritos onto the floor. The woman was in the middle of a conversation with someone she knew, an older woman who had a toddler with her finger up her nose riding in the buggy. The beefy gal kept saying over and over, "Lord no this ain't mine," shaking the child on her left hip, "Me and Clyde stopped after this one," shaking the one on her right, "This here's Sara's. You remember Sara, don't you? This is Sara's little girl, Tammy. She's my niece."

Buggies were banging and lights were flashing and cash registers were beeping and kids were wrestling a Halloween blow-up ghost decoration that was meant to stand in a front yard and the sheer madness of it was enough to send any sane person into a seizure, but Dwayne didn't have a care in this world. He strutted right through the middle of the chaos, smiling because it was Friday and he had a wad of cash in his pocket from pawning five stolen chainsaws and a flat-screen TV.

Black teddies and bloodred lingerie were rolled back to $9.87. He finished that first beer standing by the floor rack running satin through his fingers with his eyes closed, daydreaming about the last woman he'd slept with. When he was finished, he crumpled the can in his fist, balanced it in the cup of a beige-colored bra, and opened another.

From where he stood, he could see straight down the shoe aisle where a kid sat on a bench. The boy reminded Dwayne of his brother. Shaggy, strawberry-blond hair covered his ears, and his red skin was dotted with freckles. Aside from a thick pair of Coke-bottle glasses, black military frames, he could've been a spitting image of Sissy at thirteen or fourteen years old. Shabby shirt and grass-stained jeans that were muddied at the knees. He was trying on a pair of gray-colored tennis shoes, some off-brand jobs with Velcro straps. Out of nowhere two boys came around the corner and loomed over him. A boy in tight jeans, with hair that sliced at an angle across his eyes, snatched one of the shoes out of the boy's hands, looked it over, shook his head, and crowed.

At that distance, Dwayne couldn't hear what was said, but he understood. He could read it on that poor boy's beaten face. He'd heard it all his life, about the house he grew up in and the car his daddy drove, that his shoes weren't any good and neither were his clothes. He heard it about his drunk grandfather who stood on the bridge in town and cussed at the river when he was old and lost his mind. He heard it about having a funny haircut and for smelling musty after gym class, heard it for getting free lunches, heard it because someone saw him standing outside the laundromat, heard it because his mama worked the register at Roses. He'd heard that word *trash* all his life and, over the course of thirty-six years, he'd heard about enough.

There were two ways to cope, but Dwayne had only ever known the one. He'd haul off and open a boy's head to the white meat in the blink of an eye and that'd be that. *They don't talk so much with blood in their mouth,* he thought, and it was true. But he'd seen the other way of coping in his brother, the way bitterness and anger, sadness and sorrow meld into a vacant stoicism.

Bury it inside. Keep your eyes forward.

The boy stared straight ahead, expressionless and empty.

The kid with tight jeans jerked his head to the side to flip his hair out of his eyes. He fit his hand inside the shoe and pressed the sole against the boy's face. The boy didn't move or say a word. He kept his eyes on the boxes of shoes in front of him while they taunted him. The longhaired boy shoved him hard in the side of the head then and Dwayne's blood rose up into his eyes. He could feel his fists clenching tight and he took a long slug of cool Budweiser to try and ease that feeling. The bully hesitated for a second, testing the water. When he saw the kid wasn't going to react, he shoved him again, harder this time, so that he fell onto the floor. They stood there chuckling and the kid climbed back onto the bench and gazed straight ahead until they walked away with wide-set smiles, their eyes aglow with arrogance and pride.

Dwayne watched the boy on the bench for a long time. The boy didn't cry. He didn't lash out in anger. He went right back to what he was doing, trying on a pair of kicks, like nothing had happened at all. Dwayne wanted to go over to him and tell him that things didn't have to be that way, tell him he needed to stand up for himself and bash that little motherfucker's head in next time, that then they'd learn, but he didn't. He wandered on back toward the sporting goods, hoping they might have a brick or two of Winchester white box.

He finished his third beer at self-checkout while the attendant verified his ID and plugged his birth date into the computer. At first she seemed like she wanted to say something about him drinking in the store, but in the end she shook her head and stamped away because it's hard to give a shit for $7.25 an hour. He fed a twenty-dollar bill into the machine and waited for it to spit out his change.

There was a commotion by the entrance, and when Dwayne looked up he saw those same two boys strutting along, the one with long hair hobbling pigeon-toed with his hand limp at his chest making a face like he had some sort of mental defect. Dwayne looked behind him and that's when he saw the woman the boy was mocking, a handicapped greeter with a bowl cut and tinted glasses staring on like she was witnessing a miracle. The longhaired boy tossed a set of keys to his buddy and turned into the bathroom as his buddy headed for the far exit.

Dwayne set the suitcase of beer by the opened men's room and stuck his head inside long enough to make sure the kid was alone. The boy was facing the ceiling with his eyes closed at the urinal, and Dwayne knelt down to make sure there weren't any feet in the stalls. There was no one in the bathroom but the two of them. A CLEANING IN PROGRESS sign was stashed behind the door and Dwayne barred it across the jamb to stop anyone from interrupting. He walked inside and stood directly behind him, the boy not having a clue he was there until he turned.

Dwayne Brewer was a giant of a man, six-foot-five and 260 if he weighed an ounce. When the boy turned around, there he stood, and the boy jumped back like he'd walked onto a snake. "Shit, mister, you scared the hell out of me."

Dwayne didn't say anything. He stood there for a moment, silently studying him.

The boy had on a black T-shirt that read YOUNG & RECKLESS. A pair of mint-green jeans painted his legs. He had long hair that cut down his face and he kept flipping it out of his eyes like some sort of nervous tick.

"How old are you, boy?"

He looked at Dwayne funny. "Sixteen," he said.

Dwayne scrubbed at the back of his head with his knuckles, squinted his eyes like he was weighing a tremendous decision. "That's old enough," he said. He pulled a 1911 pistol from the back of his waistline and aimed it square at the boy's forehead.

The boy's face immediately fell and his arms came up instinctively, hands raised as if by strings.

"You scream and I'll blow your little pea-headed brains out. You understand?"

The boy's mouth sagged open and he nodded.

"What's your name?"

"Brett," he said.

"Brett what?"

"Starkey."

"Starkey? I don't believe I know anybody named Starkey."

"I live up Clarks Chapel."

"Where up Clarks Chapel?"

"Sunset Mountain Estates."

"Your family from around here?"

"What?"

"I said is your family from around here?"

"My mom and dad are from Saint Pete."

Dwayne pinched the bridge of his nose between his fingers and closed his eyes for a second, then nodded his head. He looked down at the boy's clean pair of high-tops. He wore the shoes loosely with the laces untied and stuffed inside, the tongues pulled over the bottoms of his jeans. "How much them shoes cost?"

"I don't know," he said.

"What do you mean you don't know?"

"I mean, I don't, I don't know," the boy stuttered. He had one of those faces that turned beet red when he was about to cry. His eyes were almost crossed as he stared down the gun.

"You mean you don't know because you don't remember, or you don't know because your mama and daddy paid for them?"

The boy gaped dumb and speechless.

"Which is it?"

"My mom bought them."

Dwayne grunted and nodded his head. "Well, I'm going to need you to go ahead and take them shoes off."

The boy didn't move.

"This is the last time I'm going to say it, boy. Take them shoes off your feet."

Toe to heel, the boy slid his shoes off and stood on the wet floor in bleach-white socks.

"Now, pick them up," Dwayne said.

The boy did as he was told.

Dwayne nodded toward the beige metal partition sectioning off the stalls. "I want you to go over there to that first stall and open the door."

The boy walked over and pushed the door open with his elbow.

Dwayne followed and stood with his back against the tile wall by the sinks, the gun still raised and steady. He peered around the boy and saw what he expected: a commode backed up with toilet paper and tinged water. "Go ahead and put your shoes on in there."

The boy looked at him in disbelief. Tears glassed his eyes. He hovered over the commode and set his shoes down gently.

"Don't just float them on top. I want you to put them down in there."

The boy pushed them slightly so that water lapped at the soles.

"I said push them down in there!" Dwayne growled through clenched teeth. He lurched forward until the gun was less than a foot from the boy's face, and the boy dunked his shoes underwater, his arms wet above his wrists.

He cried hard now. His cheeks were slicked with tears and his breath sputtered from his lips.

"Don't go getting soft now," Dwayne said. "You were a tough guy a few minutes ago with that boy, wasn't you? I saw how you were shoving him around. You was tough with him, so be tough now."

The boy's eyes were squeezed shut and he looked like he was going to be sick. He had his head turned away from the toilet and his face shone like a moon lit by the yellow light above the stall.

"That's good," Dwayne said. "Now put them on."

"What?"

"I said put them on."

Setting his shoes on the floor, he slid his feet inside like he was putting on a pair of bed slippers. A puddle widened around him and his feet squished inside.

"Go on and tie them now," Dwayne said. "We wouldn't want them falling off your feet, or you tripping over the laces. That's no way to walk."

Again, the boy did exactly as he was told. Dwayne found himself thinking that the kid might've been all right if it had been a gun to his head every second of his life. The boy hovered there like he was trying not to put all his weight down. He looked like it was the first time in his life he'd ever been put in his place, and that made Dwayne proud. *Everyone needs to be broken,* he thought. Empathy's not standing over a hole looking down and saying you understand. Empathy is having been in that hole yourself.

"I want you to remember this," Dwayne said. "All your life, I want you to remember this day. What could've been and what was."

The boy stared at him, confused.

"The two of us, we crossed paths for a reason. It was fate that brought me here. You understand?" He tucked his pistol in his waistband at the small of his back and flipped his white T-shirt over the grip to conceal what he carried. Checking himself in the mirror, he strolled toward the door and took down the sign, heading out the way he'd come and picking up his beer as he passed. Outside, things were the same as they were a few minutes before, but inside, inside felt different.

One man could not even the hands of Justice, but he could tip the scales for a moment, pin down the privileged at least long enough to smile. The sun was going down and Sissy had said he'd be home by seven.

Dwayne couldn't wait to tell his brother the story.